Assurity

by

Anthony Barbera

Space & Science Advisor

Jim Bickford

Other Books by Anthony Barbera

Catching Baby Moses

The First Rains of October

Jonah In the Time of the Kings

Full Grace Publishing

Sonoma, CA

Dedication

This book is dedicated to my wife, Cynthia, who has helped me unwavering love and devotion. Thank you so much for your steadfastness.

Author's Acknowledgment

I wish to take a moment to thank those who assisted me on my journey to complete *Assurity.*

First and foremost, *Assurity* was written as a screenplay, and the novel was completed second. Typically, I would accomplish this in the opposite order. However, I felt that the story's vastness, both on Earth and in space, required the screenplay structure's tighter constraints to begin my journey. That finally, it would assist me in the overall quality. Only you can be the judge of that.

From the beginning, I wished to write a space drama, not just a space action-adventure or thriller. The crew of *Assurity*, thrown together out of necessity, is not your every-day space crew. Young and unseasoned, they are . . . well—you'll see.

Eric Bork was instrumental in helping me tighten the world of *Assurity.* Pacing and timing, and making sure that each idea in the plot was fulfilled by "buying into" the otherworldly events confounding the characters.

Jennifer Grisanti assisted me with what she does so well, *Character.* She made sure that I set my love and affection on the right characters(s).

Jim Bickford was the best possible Space and Science Advisor imaginable. Always there to read, correct, and provide inspirational ideas, he assisted in my understanding of the realities of space flight. Not to forget some of the "special ideas" he contributed to the story. I am deeply indebted to his insight.

Tammy Gross is a patient and helpful editor. She took my dinosaur of a first draft and helped me trim, trim, trim.

And finally, my wife Cindy, who listened, suggested, edited, and ultimately is a fabulous part of *Assurity*.

Also, my beta-readers: Susan Edwards, Tammera Pewick, Rick Baggett, Dean Hamilton & Jeffrey Moore. They took from their valuable time and kept me focused on my reader's experience in a very different world.

Thank you all for your support.

Anthony Barbera

Reno, NV

Nov 3, 2020

MAIN CHARACTERS

VERONIKA TAYLOR MORGAN . . . Exec. Officer

AZAZEL . . . Leader of the Nephilim.

HUMAN CREW

ZEKE ALEXANDER . . . Navigator/Officer

TATIANA KOROLEV . . . Chief Engineering
Officer

POLDI STOSS . . . Science Officer

JADA COLE . . . Medical Officer

XIAO XING . . . Linguist, Language Expert

SABINA TESLA . . . Engineering & Propulsion

ENHANCED LIFE FORMS

ISAAC NEWTON . . . AI: Ship's Intelligence

PHILEX-B . . . Android: 2nd Officer, E.L.F.

RIGEL . . . Android: Commander, E.L.F.

HYBRID ORGANICS

CHIFFON-F4 . . . Hybrid Organic, E.L.F.

RUBY-903 . . . Hybrid Organic, E.L.F.

PLUM-8E4 . . . Hybrid Organic, E.L.F

CHARACTERS ON EARTH

Dr. NILES MORGAN . . . Dir. Disease Control, W.H.C.

CASSIA MORGAN . . . Daughter of Niles & Veronika

I'JAZ NEJEM . . . Professor of Ancient Studies

EARTH & SPACE THE YEAR 2107

The League of American States L.A.S. (Former
United States.) Now Included: South & Central
America, Mexico & Canada

Africanis

European Islamic Caliphate

Commonwealth of Britannia (Great Britain)

Italia

Chindia (China and India)

Russian Federation

Israel

Asian Pacific Empire

OUR SOLAR SYSTEM

Deep Space Tracking Station, Pico de Neblina,
Brazillia

Moon Bases: A.P.U., E.S.U, L.A.S.

Commencement Bay, Mars Settlement

Cassini Sol Station

Saturn's Moon Mimas

Chindian Station Tiapong, Orbiting Ganymede

Alexey Leonov Federation Space Station

Planet Rhema (Antimatter Mining Sector)

Final Realm Military Depot

(Chindian/Russian Depository & Emergency
Supply near Rhema)

Interstellar Geological Survey and Astrogeology

Science Ctr. on Triton (Neptune's moon)

Nemesis - The 9th Planet

ASSURITY

Ship Class: Deep Space Mining Transport

Propulsion System: Nautilus Antimatter Stardrive

Taylor Interstellar Mining & Manufacturing Inc.
(TIMMI)

Final Inspection Completion: April 12, 2089, Cassini
Sol Shipyards (Contract # 2304 C.S.S.)

Prologue

London Ministry of Health

— May 8, 1945, VE Day —

IT WAS VE Day, May 8, 1945. Exuberance filled the air as thousands of celebrants flooded the streets, hurrying to the London Ministry of Health. Mothers scurried their children along. Fathers carried the little ones, and the grandparents were not far behind—if either was still alive.

Pressing in from every side, British and American victory flags swayed in jubilation.

All eyes were transfixed on the London Ministry of Health's balcony as cigar-smoking Winston Churchill, surrounded by cabinet officials, stepped forward and waved his two-fingered signature of determination—the "V" for victory.

The throng squeezed in tighter from every corner, alleyway, and street, erupting into thunderous cheering.

Churchill took the last puff, dropped his cigar to the floor, and stepped forward to the microphone. With his booming voice, he began, "My dear friends, this is your hour . . . a victory of the great British nation as a whole."

He thrust his finger, shaking it. "We were the first in this ancient island to draw the sword against tyranny. Left alone against the most tremendous military power that has ever been seen. Did we give in?"

His voice echoed throughout the streets, and the flags waved enthusiastically.

The crowd yelled, "*No!*"

Churchill continued, "Were we downhearted?"

The crowd boisterously repeated, "*No!*"

Winston extended his arms in a grand gesture of relief. "The lights went out, and the bombs came down—"

These Brits knew what hell looked like; they'd passed through it with all of its anguishing fire and torment. Winston would never forget; over 2,300 rockets struck London. Well over five thousand deaths. Not to mention the injuries. He cringed at the devastation, the misery his country had endured. The thousands of pilots and soldiers who had died.

"We came back after long months from the jaws of death," he continued. "Out of the mouth of hell!"

Winston smiled broadly as the crowd hollered in exultation: "Hip hip hooray! Hip hip hooray!"

If they only knew how close I came to surrender, he remembered. Churchill's lips touched the microphone as he thrust his arms into the air. "When shall the reputation and faith of this generation fail?"

"*Never . . . never!*" They cheered with exhilaration pent up through years of suppressed fear and anguish.

***

At the same time that London was in the throes of unbridled celebration, a German U-boat escaped from the Port of Vigo, Spain. She clandestinely marked 17.7 knots atop the churning waters of the Atlantic. Twenty-five minutes later, she disappeared beneath the wind-swept seas.

Chapter 1

Ross Sea, Antarctica

— May 28, 1945 —

ON MAY 28, 1945, the hatch of U-865 twisted and screeched open. It had been a grueling twenty-seven days from the Port of Vigo, Spain, to Antarctica's Ross Sea. Over 9,400 miles. They'd passed through at least two torrential storms that kept them submerged for thirty-two hours.

The lanky commander climbed up the ladder and stepped out onto the conning tower. Unusually tall for a U-boat commander, he took a moment to stretch and then looked about at the dimly lit sky. Lifting his binoculars to his eyes, his view of the glassy cobalt sea met an endless, icy-white coastline. He settled his focus on a strategic passageway into the wall of white. He'd been here before. Overhead, a Nazi escort plane dipped its wings and flew off.

The commander raised his arm in Nazi salute, "*Heil, Hitler!*" Stepping to the voice pipe, he bellowed, "*Vorbereiten zum tauchen.*"

Underwater, the U-boat navigated iceberg tails through the crystalline water. Activating sonar, she entered a perfectly etched tunnel, broad enough for two U-boats to pass one another.

Bubbles rose as U-865 surfaced within the high ceilings of one of three Nazi Antarctic submarine bases. A crackling echo shattered the quiet as the ocean cascaded off her deck.

One by one, seven scientists climbed up the ladder and onto the gun deck. Before them stood an alien citadel, unlike anything they had ever seen before. An icy world. The scientists pointed and whispered at the otherworldly sight, both wondrous and terrifying. There was fear. Along the frozen shore stood timeless statues. Lofty, muscular men—ancient-looking, weapons in hand, with elongated skulls. Men of war.

The U-boat crew scrambled to heave the seven matching suitcases ashore. Two powerfully built German soldiers stepped forward, awaiting the passengers. One of the soldiers restrained a young black-and-silver German Shepherd. At the end of a taut leash, the Shepherd barked harshly as the scientists disembarked—five males and two females.

Ashore, the two women stopped and looked back as the commander descended back into his U-boat. Already they were leaving, not staying an hour—not for even a moment. The male scientists, heads down, maneuvered around the women, following one of the waiting soldiers up the path, where they disappeared into the citadel.

The U-boat's hatch slammed shut with a loud clang, followed by a screeching twist. U-865 submerged. Bubbles rippled as the women, downcast, turned away and followed the path up and into the citadel, escorted by the remaining soldier and his restive German Shepherd.

Chapter 2

On Approach to the Planet Rhema—
Sol System

— April 10, 2107 —

IN THE VASTNESS OF DEEP SPACE gleams an immensity of stars—beyond that, endless, almost fathomless oceans of lonely darkness between destinations.

As they neared mining claim #3708-AHG-0201, the transport completed her fourth rotational adjustment. They were en route to the mottled planet Rhema. Along the ship's bow were the words: "*Assurity,* a Taylor Interstellar Mining and Manufacturing Transport." The heavily armored bow, the illuminated bridge, and the radio array atop were followed by the gently spinning Artificial Gravity Ring (AGR). Rolling on her axis, *Assurity* began a scheduled decrease in velocity. Even though the planet Rhema was still days away, most of the crew was still in cryosleep.

Second Lieutenant Philex-B (pronounced *fy-lex* B) stood before a tactical grid screen in the communication room. She was twenty-five-ish, with spiky blonde hair and the body of a sprinter. Her eyes glimmered, riveted to the luminescent glow. Swiping her hand before her face, she updated the feed. A blip of light raced across her screen, accentuated by a rhythmic bell, and followed by:

IMMEDIATE ATTENTION REQUIRED

To Captain: Assurity . . . Classified

From: NORTH AMERICAN DEEP SPACE TRACKING STATION, NEBLINA, BRAZIL—[accelerate] to Cassini Space Station, orbiting Saturn's Moon Mimas—[accelerate] relay buoy #6 confirmed received by Assurity.

CLASSIFICATION: SECRET. Subject: Anomaly with CryoLife Sure-State Hibernation System. Time Stamp FSS: 04-11-2107: 02:12:34. Transpired Time since Initial Transmission: 12 hours 54 minutes 275 seconds. [NADSTS.]

***

Philex-B stood transfixed. "Mr. Newton," she announced over ship's com, "your assessment, please?"

Isaac Newton, the ship's AI, answered over com with his namesake's British accent, "I suggest, Lieutenant, that you hightail it to the bridge and assist the commander."

The blip increased speed, confirmed by the beeping run of numbers on the sidebar.

Philex-B scowled. Striding quickly from the room, she took a shortcut and dashed through the dimly lit galley, darting between the comfortable chairs and tables, and entered the lift. *"Bridge,"* she instructed.

It would take at least twenty-five seconds for the lift to complete its circular path to the bridge.

Her crystal-blue eyes stared ahead, fixated. Thinking. Stunning as she was, she wouldn't have been mistaken for a human, not with the small security stamp engraved on the right side of her forehead, indicating that she was an E.L.F. (Enhanced Life Form). Within those twenty-five seconds, she would accomplish several tasks that didn't require her presence. Aligning the recycling filters and checking temperatures in cold storage were all daily responsibilities.

From the lift, Philex-B rushed onto *Assurity's* dimly lit bridge where Lieutenant Commander Rigel stood. His attention was fixed on the bridge's viewscreen. If you didn't know any better, you'd think he was human. Precisely six feet tall and appearing perfectly fit, he was unquestionably pleasing to look at. He, too, was an E.L.F.

This was her first tour of duty with him, and, so far, it wasn't going at all well. She didn't trust that he'd satisfactorily assessed their situation. Her experience with human commanders had been much more agreeable. They listened when she spoke and seemed to value her analysis. Then again, she was a Philex-B, and he a Multan AI prototype—self-actualizing. When the captain and the crew were in cryo-sleep, he was in command; doubtless, he looked disparagingly on her model.

There were eight workstations on the bridge of *Assurity*. Seven were vacant. Only the captain's station was active.

Philex-B took a position standing beside Rigel. Both were silent. Both watched the bridge screen, now set on aft view. They waited. Millions of luminous solar particles were closing in on *Assurity* from behind.

Rigel's lips tightened. "It's imminent!"

She glanced at him, his expression an anxious grimace. Alarms pierced the bridge as a deafening roar built inside the ship.

Before her face, Philex-B brought up an updating grid view. It revealed millions of solar flare particles encircling *Assurity*. It was so loud she had to shout. "Commander, the magnetic pressure is now deforming the field lines!"

Rigel raised his voice as the roar intensified. "Mr. Newton, expedite an updated time of envelopment."

Philex-B, insistent, grasped Rigel's arm. "We must awaken the captain!"

Isaac Newton responded over ship's com, "Commander, I'm reading emissions at three thousand kilometers per second . . . in 10.725 seconds, we will experience complete envelopment. Outside, the antimatter fuel will be stripped from the magnetic containment holder by the energetic particles of the solar flare. Moments later, the stream of flashing particles will overtake and engulf us."

Before the screen, Rigel and Philex-B remained riveted. From the radio array camera above, they watched the view of *Assurity*'s. The roar increased for fifteen seconds, then diminished evenly over the next thirty.

Like a dandelion blowing in the wind, feathery multi-colored ion particles fluttered past them in a stream of glittering light. The particles from the sun were faster than *Assurity* herself and disappeared into the infinity of space. Finally, it quieted, leaving the gentle throbbing of the ship's systems.

"Mr. Newton, cease alarms," Rigel ordered.

Philex-B, insistent, turned to leave. "This is much worse than anticipated." She pointed to the run of declining fuel numbers on her sidebar. "I'm awakening the captain *now*."

"*Remain, Philex-B*! We are not authorized to awaken

crew in advance of time watch unless first approved by L.S.E. —or if a severe cataclysmic event occurs."

He focused his eyes on Philex-B's fuel bar. "Mr. Newton, provide an aggregate of fuel dissipated."

"Must I remind you, Rigel," Newton responded, "*timely* approval from Earth is no longer an option. Transmission from Earth—not allowing for the time to problem-solve this critical situation—is a minimum of 16.25 hours. We've passed Laser Buoy 78; we're on our own, Commander. Certainly, you've calculated that?"

"Provide the requested estimate, Mr. Newton! Don't disquiet me."

Philex-B, unable to stand still, said harshly, "*This is a severe cataclysmic event, Commander!*"

Rigel looked down at her. "That is not confirmed. If we awaken the captain now, life support systems will not sustain eating, breathing humans for the remainder of the voyage. I am acting commander on this ship—"

A new klaxon alarm *blared* over ship's com.

"Bloody hell," Isaac insisted. "We are experiencing a system malfunction. The cryolife system is failing. Get them out . . . all of them. *Now!*"

***

Dimmed royal-blue light illuminated *Assurity's* cryolife chamber. Down here, you could feel the deep throbbing of the ship. Six horizontal cryolife sleep pods, each labeled with a crewmember's name and rank, displayed their continuously updated health status.

Two additional pods stood in vertical automated exercise mode. A male crewmember (asleep in suspended animation) pedaled a stationary bicycle. Beside him, a female (also in suspended animation) walked briskly on a miniature treadmill. The blinking red emergency shutdown light indicated that the exercise protocol for the two crewmembers had been terminated. This began the incremental shift of the two exercise pods to a horizontal sleeping position.

Three Enhanced Life Forms, laboratory conceived and called Hybrid Organics, stood together. Their job was to perform maintenance throughout the ship. They also oversaw the crew's exercise and learning protocols while the humans were in cryosleep. The three five-foot-five faceless hybrid-organic creatures were named Chiffon, Plum, and Ruby. Translucent, each was named for their skin color. They looked very much like what the ancients referred to as ghosts.

Nervous, their mouths faintly appeared from their now

blank faces as they huddled together, jabbering quietly in their Asian-sounding language.

Under the emergency protocol, the chamber lids were designed to snap open. One by one, each lifted with the expulsion of escaping gas. As the blue cryofluid drained to a level below each crewmember's face, Plum hurried to remove their breathing apparatuses and unhook their monitors. Ruby and Chiffon followed her in order. With three arms each, they lifted the half-sleeping crewmembers out of their hibernation pods. They placed each of them, dripping, on the floor—hurrying on to the next cryo-chamber. The process that usually required over an hour needed to be completed in less than four minutes.

The two exercise pods reached their horizontal position but remained closed.

Rigel and Philex-B arrived. Running through the cryo-chamber, they scanned the situation. Six crewmembers, all in their twenties, writhed on the drenched floor, coughing up blue cryofluid. Noticing that the malfunction alarm was still beeping and that the still closed exercise pods were not opening, Philex-B dashed into a tool locker. She grabbed two jack bars from the rack. Tossing a bar to Rigel, the two of them feverishly pried open the exercise pods.

Commander Zeke, twenty-eight and trying to recover focus, dripped fluid from his military-trained body as he painfully stood up. He called out to Chiffon, "Did you get the captain out?"

Chiffon didn't answer. The ghost-like E.L.F. kept her stare fixed at the still closed pod below, her eyes shifting from side to side. Finally, a pop and a swish. She let out a sigh. The cover of the captain's pod opened. The blue cryofluid began draining. Chiffon leaned down and reminded the captain, "You are awakening from cryosleep, Captain. Please do not attempt movement."

The captain attempted to speak.

"Speaking not recommended," Chiffon repeated.

A dreadful *yell* resounded throughout the cryo-chamber.

As the remaining crew lifted themselves from the adjacent room floor, Zeke stood over what was left of two of the crewmembers—Raul Núñez and Lela Chalice. Both had been in their exercise protocol.

"Ah! God, no!" Zeke yanked off his hairnet, throwing it to the ground.

Raul and Lela were still lying in their sleep chambers, the blue fluid boiling, both of their bodies shriveled like prunes.

Zeke kneeled in despair. "Look at them. They were boiled alive!"

Like zombies rising from the dead, the six remaining crewmembers shuffled into the other room in their underwear, still dripping blue cryofluid. They huddled together and peered down in horror.

Philex-B and Rigel stepped away as the captain squeezed between the crew.

Chapter 3

The Morgan's' Home, Chicago

— Five Months Before —

DR. NILES MORGAN SAT AT HIS KITCHEN TABLE, scrutinizing the double helix DNA hologram projected before his face. Dark-haired and with a neatly trimmed beard, Niles, forty-eight, didn't look his age. At first glance, he could have passed for a grad student working on a science project. His surroundings, however, hinted at his actual age. A substantial kitchen window within the elegant home revealed a lush illuminated garden bordered by a densely wooded forest. The Morgans lived in the prestigious Meadowood district of Chicago.

Twisting the double helix with his fingers, Niles chose one strand from the spiral of deoxyribonucleic acid. He drew it out, examining it closely.

His wife, Veronika, walked into the kitchen, smiled, and shook her head. Her dimples gave her a playful look when she smiled, which wasn't often these days. Veronika Taylor Morgan sat down at the table across from her husband, unfolded her napkin, and laid it across her lap. Sharply dressed, her auburn hair spun neatly atop her head, she gently reminded her husband, "Niles, can you put that away, please? I haven't seen you in almost three months."

Nanette, a slight, utilitarian android, placed two piping-hot dinners before them.

"Sorry, V." Niles tapped his right temple, turning off Temple-Talk, his holographic data-retrieval system.

Nanette poured them each a glass of wine.

"Thank you, Nanette," Niles said.

"You're most welcome, sir. I will check on Ori now." Nanette glided into the next room.

Veronika took a sip of her wine. "When are you speaking before the Continuum, Niles?"

"Tomorrow. I leave for London on Thursday."

"What are you going to say? Would you like me to come with you?"

Niles chewed his broccoli as he gazed at his wife, then mixed his peas with his rice.

"Niles, I haven't seen you . . . you haven't updated me. It's not like you. Are you making progress?

He put his fork down and dropped his head. "They never took this seriously. They're claiming, now, that Delirium is a new disease. Even back in 2055, a half-billion people had some form of dementia . . ."

Veronika took a deep breath. He was already getting upset, and he'd just gotten home this morning.

He threw his hands up. "So, for decades, they've been sloughing the whole thing off—as though it were a normal part of the human cycle of life."

Niles stopped, placed his hands along his face, and put his elbows on the table. "I'm sorry, V . . . I know you don't want to hear this—it's just—they've dumped this insidious disease, which they kicked around for God knows how long, on *me* . . . on my team. It's much worse than anyone realizes."

She dared not say what she really felt. Niles had never shown this kind of attitude. At least, he'd never revealed it to her. Exuding confidence, Niles Morgan was the most intelligent person she'd ever known. Brilliant, in fact. When they'd first met, he came off aloof. Then later, she realized that it wasn't because he was arrogant—he was shy.

His parents had arranged their first meeting when they were teenagers. The Morgans were English—old money. Her family, the Taylors, were new money and Americans. A year after graduating from the Massachusetts Institute of Space Mining and Technology, she was recruited into the League of Space Exploration. That part of her life didn't last as long as she expected.

When she did marry Niles Morgan, she married into one of the wealthiest families within the Commonwealth of Britannia. Amongst many of their businesses, PharmaLife Sciences, founded by Niles' father, Frederick Morgan, quickly grew Life Sciences into the most significant drug developer within Britannia.

Veronika's father, James S. Taylor—they called him "Smitty"—began his rise to success at seventeen. Within a year of working as a laborer for a mining colony deep in Colorado's mountains, he became their quality-control supervisor. A driven individual, Smitty utilized all of the knowledge he'd acquired along the way. By the age of twenty-eight, he had founded Taylor Interstellar Mining and Manufacturing Inc., which later became TIMMI.

Veronika had no brothers or sisters. When her father died, her mother, who had been happy to serve her husband as a dutiful housewife, assumed control of TIMMI. But Mother was anything but qualified or capable. At thirty-two years of age, and with her mother's blessing, Veronika Taylor Morgan became CEO of Taylor Interstellar Mining and Manufacturing—the most significant ore mining and fuel collection concern within the inner solar system.

Veronika was quick to realize that a substantial presence on the moon Mimas would be crucial for interstellar mining. In a few short years, Cassini Sol Station, under construction and orbiting Mimas, would be the primary hub for mining and manufacturing. Mars could not continue to serve in the same capacity as it had. Simultaneously, as they pushed deeper into the solar system, antimatter became TIMMI's main mining concern.

Mimas could house hundreds of workers and function as their manufacturing center. She was convinced that Saturn's rings would serve as a rich antimatter mine for years to come. So, she took a bold step. She purchased significant holdings on Mimas and invested in a long-term lease on Cassini Sol Station. It wasn't a popular move with the board of directors. Nonetheless, within a few years, and with Niles's help, she purchased all of Taylor Interstellar Mining and Manufacturing's outstanding shares.

Niles cared deeply about his family and about their children, Cassia and Ori. He called them every night from London, where his research team was stationed. This last year he'd been gone for extended amounts of time. Veronika missed him terribly. Tenacious, he'd lock into a problem, probe it, and wrestle it until he found his answer. That's why they'd made him head of PharmaLife Sciences and now head of Disease Control for the World Health Continuum.

But my god, this man she was listening to, this man she respected—he'd lost his confidence. Something was off.

"It's been a generation of genetic tampering," Niles

continued complaining. "A poisoned food supply, super drugs, and untold foreign implants—honestly, the human body wasn't designed for this onslaught—"

"Is that what you're going to tell them, Niles?" Veronika threw her napkin on the table. "Sorry, doctors, humanity's genetic blueprint is compromised forever, and humankind is doomed to go insane from Delirium, a disease we can't cure? Oops, did the best we could. Good luck with the billions on Earth. Our citizens in space? Carry on, because we don't know *what in the cosmos we're doing!*"

Niles took a deep breath.

"Darn straight. That will lead the team!" Veronika rose from the table. "I've lost my appetite!"

Bursting into the kitchen, Cassia Morgan, the Morgan's serious, plain-faced daughter, announced, "I've gotta go, parentals—meeting the study group at the library. Ori needs to be tucked in."

Veronika moved to hug her daughter goodbye and asked, "When will you be home, Cass?" *They weren't close, not like they'd once been. Maybe her daughter resented having to look after her brother Ori while her mother worked so much.*

Cassia grabbed an apple from a bowl and pretended that she didn't get that her mother was waiting to hug her goodbye.

"Med final tomorrow . . . I don't know . . . as long as we can stay focused. I'll tele you, Mom, okay? Bye, guys."

Darting out the door, Cassia left her mother standing there.

Veronika clasped her arms and sat back down. Her husband appeared as if he was off in an alternate universe, again.

"Ori's getting worse, Niles. Nanette can't adequately care for him, and I can't depend on Cassia to be here."

"You remember what finals are like? She has three more. If she passes, which she will, your daughter will be a doctor . . . Not easy, V."

Niles took a sip of his wine. "Let's buy a MedCare model—"

"I'm not letting a med bot take care of my sick son. Not an option. Besides, your son needs his father. You're gone. You don't see him—"

"What do you want, Veronika? This may be unsolvable. You do realize that?" Niles shook his head, got up, and walked to the window, looking out on his well-lit gardens. "I've never faced a disease like this."

Veronika got to her feet, walked to her husband, and

turned him around. Slender and a little taller than he was, she looked him in the eyes. "If anyone can do this—if any human being on the face of this Earth is capable of unraveling this evil disease—it's you, Niles. You can do this—you *must* do this."

She hugged him tightly. "Cassia, Ori, and I will move to London and be with you."

There was a loud crash from the other room.

Veronika and Niles rushed into the bedroom to see their son, Ori, who was only twelve, lying on the floor under his wheelchair. Trapped beneath the wheelchair, Nanette had her hand on Ori's shoulder.

Veronika dropped to her knees in front of Ori as Niles carefully lifted the wheelchair off his son and Nanette.

"I applied comfort," Nanette said.

"It's, it's not your fault," Niles assured her.

Veronika pulled Ori, so light and thin now, into her arms.

"Mom," Ori stammered, "I . . . *didn't know* . . . where you were—"

"I'm here, Ori." Veronika squeezed her son. "I'm here."

She looked up at Niles. "I'm putting TIMMI up for sale, Niles. I'll take care of Ori myself."

"Wait a minute," he said, "have you considered the ramifications—"

"Damn straight. Are we a family or not? The kids and I will move to London so we can be together. Look around you, Niles . . . this world is imploding."

Chapter 4

TIMMI Headquarters

Chicago, IL, L.A.S.

VERONIKA SAT IN HER PRIVATE OFFICE at Taylor Interstellar Mining & Manufacturing. She was completing calculations for orbital fuel consumption at their new amat collection point near Rhema. Within the last decade, antimatter, now simply called amat, had become TIMMI'S primary mining product. As missions expanded deeper into the solar system and safety measures were perfected, amat had taken the upper hand for interstellar hauling.

This was tedious work she was doing and was usually handled by a specialized mining director. Their most capable claim director had left TIMMI and within two weeks had succumbed to Delirium. Some, when inflicted, exhibited desperate paranoia; others quietly accepted their diagnosis. He'd been the latter, a first-rate claims director, and he would be sorely missed. Her HR department hadn't found a replacement, so his specialized work fell into Veronika's lap. Like she didn't have enough to deal with.

Smartly dressed, she liked the feel of her new quilted faux leather skirt. She loved the smell of new leather. At

TIMMI, associates were expected to dress smartly. A stylishly dressed staff reflected the attention to quality control and personal care that TIMMI'S customers expected. As a reward for all of the extra hours she'd put in, she'd bought herself matching low-calf boots and a brilliant blue blouse to go with her skirt. That was her one distraction these days—shopping. Soon she'd begin making inquiries about possible buyers for TIMMI.

Her view provided oversight of her entire office staff. Within the spacious, glass-divided main floor of TIMMI, employees—human and android—bustled, working together. That was the bright spot. The dark cloud overlooking TIMMI was that it was growing near impossible to hire qualified human staff. She was working more hours than ever. —Ori was at home sick, watched mostly by their robot, with help from Cassia, but she was trying to complete her medical degree.

It was daunting. Antimatter was a finite source, and so for the first time in years, they were running in the red. Saturn's mines were drying up sooner than she had projected. So they'd expanded mining out to Rhema but only with bot pilots and on a limited basis.

On the other hand, it cheered her that most of these young people accepted the androids she hired as if they were equals. Her generation hadn't. Unhappily, she'd had no choice but to hire E.L.F.s' if she wished to keep TIMMI running.

As of March 2105, androids had been legally classified as Enhanced Life Forms. Immediately, the Collective Party jumped on the opportunity to vote in a set of employment rights for E.L.F.s, which was a pain in the ass to implement, although less rigid than she anticipated. Soon, these E.L.F.s would be voting and running for government office. Veronika could never rid her mind of what her father had maintained. "The day that robots handle everything, there won't be a human within a parsec to pick up the pieces, and there's going to be an awful mess."

Some of her younger workers had made close friendships with their E.L.F. workmates. Truth be told, sometimes she couldn't recognize a human employee from a fancy robot. She didn't know any of her E.L.F.s' names except her personal assistant, Eldon. Beyond that, the E.L.F.s' could outwork her humans—but they still didn't adequately internalize feelings in the way a human person does. After all, emotion was a necessary component of rational thought. She noticed it was one thing if a worker had an E.L.F. as a workmate, but the situation was totally different if they were a boss. It depended, though, and damn straight—the E.l.F.'s didn't have the *attitude*.

Suppose an E.L.F. was a supervisor (which she tried desperately to avoid). In that case, an E.L.F. could piss off a human employee with one misspoken word. Her few teen workers would bolt at a moment's irritation. Purposefully, the E.L.F.s were programmed to blend in. They were designed to enhance output within the workforce without adding the competitive component that caused so many clashes between humans. E.L.F.s' employment hours were strictly governed by law. Mostly to protect the human workforce's well-being, she was sure. Even so, sometimes, the androids and the humans just didn't mix well. So, Veronika became the referee.

With the loss of so many of her seasoned workers, there'd been no letup in her workload. Even if she took a day off, it was a risk. Forget a vacation. To add to that, this younger generation lacked the labor ethics of their elders. When the clock hit quitting time, regardless of the job needing to be completed—they were gone. At least among the E.L.F.s, there were no shirkers! Yet, humans were better thinkers and more creative when it was all said and done.

If she could negotiate a reasonable price for TIMMI, she'd sell.

Her personal assistant, Eldon, waving both hands like dueling pinwheels, burst into her immaculate office. Eldon was stylishly dressed, gawky, and tall. She wondered why a programmer would add tasteful fashion sensibilities to a robot—at the same time—they couldn't program an E.L.F. to pilot one of her antimatter ships. (Come on.)

"Good morning, Ms. Veronika." Eldon enthusiastically pointed. "Your appointment has arrived."

Veronika rose and walked out of her office.

She greeted Simon with a handshake. Short and already balding and only in his early thirties, Simon looked like it was the end of the day rather than the beginning. He was the one rep from Allied Robotics that she trusted to give her realistic cost analysis and not try to stick it to her on pricing. His pixie-faced assistant smiled and handed a wrapped gift to Eldon.

"Ms. Morgan," Simon gestured. "Let me introduce the newest addition to our family—this is Delta."

Veronika, indifferent, eyed the security stamp on Delta's otherwise porcelain-perfect doll face.

"Nice to see you, Simon. Follow me, please," she said.

Simon, Delta, and Eldon scurried to keep up with Veronika. At five-nine and with toned legs, she moved quickly. Still an avid runner, she was agile, as well.

They entered a spacious glass conference room. Standing at a polished black wall, Veronika touched her temple. "Activate security," she ordered. The glass entrance door closed as the surrounding glass faded to black. An animation on the wall illuminated TIMMI's assets throughout the solar system.

Veronika stated, "Computer, display Mars approach, Commencement Bay."

A live feed revealed two of TIMMI's heavy ore haulers approaching Commencement Bay, Mars' orbiting space station.

Veronika pointed to the long haulers. "Simon, your robot pilots already operate our ore deliveries. No hiccups there . . . computer, show me our Saturn mining claim."

Five antimatter collection ships appeared. Veronika used a finger to draw a circle around them, all situated within the rings of Saturn.

"Here's my problem, Simon—we're losing our pilots, especially in the rings. I can't hire replacements with this disease, knocking out seasoned pilots . . . we're not delivering on our contracts in a timely fashion."

With her finger, she enlarged one of her antimatter mining ships: *Huygens*.

"Androids are too dangerous at this point, ma'am," Simon insisted. "One misstep on an amat collector and it threatens the entire system—"

"You guys should have amat pilots available for contact by now. At least we could test them out at Rhema . . . our tractors out there are all controlled from Cassini. The relay is too far. It's not efficient, and it's unreliable. Use a damn bond company if you're that worried—"

"Ma'am, I understand. We are beta testing bot pilots right now, but we're behind schedule with so many employees' loss. Just like everyone else—"

Eldon stepped forward. "Excuse me, Ms. Morgan, you have a teleview from *Huygens* marked urgent. It needs a response."

"Put it on the main office screen," she said. "Everyone needs to see this."

Veronika and all fifty TIMMI employees gathered in the main office before a full-screen teleview displaying the Rings of Saturn. Some of her staff had never been privy to this. Like an oversized beetle in space, *Huygens* ascended from within the rings of Saturn. Four lime-green, illuminated mining hoops extended out in circles from the ship.

Veronika pointed up to the screen. "Those hoops collect the antimatter from the sector we're mining in. The running time-bar along the edge of our screen there shows the delay in transmission from *Huygens* to Earth."

The camera view now showed the inside of the *Huygens'* bridge. Tightly confined, with two pilot accommodations, it was nothing fancy.

Texas-born pilot Bilt, in his fifties, snapped switches above his head and kept a watchful eye out of the port view. The now purplish-lime antimatter swirled into the hoops as he spoke into the camera.

"Good mainday, Ms. Morgan. Just finishing collection today. Not good news, boss—we're slow-go, even with four short haulers helping out. That's all I can hire right now . . ."

Static. Then the picture went black. It quickly returned.

"We should have relocated out to Rhema two years ago," Bilt continued. He called down to his copilot, "Hey, Nug, get your ass up here. We gotta make time back to Cassini."

The office staff, practically feeling as if they were on the bridge with Bilt, moved forward, chuckling together.

"Almost done!" Nug hollered back.

"E.T.A. back to Cassini Station is twenty-eight hours, ma'am. I sent you a sustainability update months ago. This mine is dried up . . ."

The picture froze and went fritz.

Moments later, the computer relayed, "Your transmission has been completed. Thank you for using Direct Send."

"Stars ablaze, I wonder what happened there." Veronika shrugged.

Behind Veronika, the staff of fifty all turned. Eldon held up a birthday cake lit with sparkling candles. With a big grin, he lifted the cake with its twinkling candles. "Happy birthday, Ms. Morgan."

Veronika's face turned white. Then a half-smile as they sang "Happy Birthday" to her.

They have no idea, she thought. *I hate my birthday.*

"Thank you, all," Veronika said. "Very much appreciated."

Eldon, with the help of Delta, passed out cider. A moment later, the video feed resumed from *Huygens'* Bridge.

Bilt's copilot Nug, who was wearing a black-and-gold "Saturn Stars" ball cap, popped his head up through the opening of the lower deck. "Hey, Bilt," he asked, "does anyone like that woman? I mean shit—"

"She's a bitch!" Bilt answered. "She doesn't listen. I

told her two years ago we needed to move out to Rhema."

Veronika froze in place. Her workers all saw and heard this.

Bilt looked at his camera. The recording had never been shut off.

"Oh, crap . . . Ms. Morgan, I didn't mean . . . I was talking about my ex-wife." He put his hand to his head. There was nothing he could do. What they were seeing on Earth now had been transmitted minutes ago. "Oh, jeez!" Bilt slammed the transmission off button, and the hot feed ended.

Veronika turned. Everyone was looking at her. She touched her temple and recorded a dispatch back to *Huygens* so that her staff could all hear.

"Hey, Bilt, when you get this, you guys stay put. Keep mining. I'm sending *Assurity* to pick up your loadout . . . and, hey, Captain, you might want to turn off com before saying such sweet things about your boss." She smiled and winked. "*Bitch out!*"

The office staff laughed in relief.

***

Still fuming, Veronika stood in her office, arms folded, staring out the window. It wasn't funny. It was embarrassing, and it hurt. She'd grown used to people not liking her. It was part of running a big company, and it bothered her more than ever. Even spilling over into her mom's relatives—those that were left—and some of Nile's family, too. Mostly those she worked with, though.

—It made her think back: *I only had a few girlfriends when I was in grade school. And college? What would my life have been like if I'd stayed in the Space Corp twenty-three years ago? By now, I would have a command of my own. Then again, the military doesn't allow for thinking out of the box. Just do your job.*

She'd never forget that day; it was stitched across her memory like a pinprick, that morning after she'd finally landed the rescue ship on Mars Station. Emergency personnel with stretchers scrambled to board as the crew disembarked. She'd climbed out from the pilot's cockpit and removed her helmet—moving to station three to file her report.

Her male copilot strode quickly to catch up. "You're reckless, Lieutenant," he yelled after her. "You don't have the temperament to be a pilot— Hey, Veronika, *stop!*"

With her back to him, she came to a halt and swung around.

He was walking fast. Still coming. Too close.

"You endangered the entire crew!" he shouted, saliva flying in her face.

"I pulled those belters off that rock by being resourceful," she jabbed at him. "If I'd listened to you, they'd all be dead, you imbecile!"

He trembled, his creased forehead and sweaty face incensed.

Was he going to punch her?

Instead, he noticed the colonel standing off to the side—

He didn't say another word, just stomped off.

Colonel Thomas Massey, arms folded, was watching the exchange. He was a patient man and had been a friend of her father. He'd kept an eye on Lt. Veronika Taylor since she'd joined his squadron. Sure as stars, she was more capable than any of his cadets. And she knew it. But Veronika had a real problem with regulations. If she thought her assessment of a situation was right—regs be damned, she'd go for it.

"Lieutenant, we have procedures that must be followed. I've told you that before." The colonel spoke calmly but sternly. "You pulled it off this time—doesn't mean you will the next. Your father would have been disappointed by this—"

"Sir, if I hadn't taken that risk, seven miners would be zipped, their bodies strewn across that frozen asteroid." She straightened and faced him. "I know you were friends—I respect that, but my father was no hero. Taking his own life on my birthday—that's not something you do to someone you love!"

"Look, Lieutenant, by the end, your father wasn't the man I'd known. Smitty lost every bit of himself." The colonel pointed to her copilot . . . "And if he files another grievance—"

"Due respect, Colonel—he can file whatever the blistering comet he wants." Veronika pulled her gloves off. "It's been almost a year since he died. My mother can't run TIMMI on her own. I'm done here, sir!"

She marched off in a fury, flinging her gloves, and leaving Colonel Massey shaking his head.

Chapter 5

World Health Continuum, Chicago

— May 13, 2107 —

SITTING NERVOUSLY IN THE MILITARY transport's back seat, Niles rode with two heavily armed soldiers, one across from him and the other beside him. The sirens of his escort, ringing in his ears, made it hard for him to think clearly.

Staring out the window, he felt aching despair in his stomach. Red Cross tents dotted the landscape as the convoy sped past suffering humanity. Block after block, it was no different—men and women, many in their prime. Children sat or squatted, clutching their dying parents—all of them with blank, hopeless stares. So many elderly lying unconscious on the sidewalk. Alone and dying.

He couldn't calm himself. They were counting on him, this team of world-renowned doctors and scientists. In the meantime, they'd lost so many. Many of the mature, educated, trained, and proficient researchers had already succumbed. At his age, thank goodness he wasn't ill.

Honestly, they were no closer to a cure than when they'd started. Every angle of research, every possibility, had twisted into a dead end. Tragically, people didn't believe human life could end on Earth—even with so many deaths already. The idea was implausible, especially to the young. Human life eradicated from the Earth? Please. There was no reference to draw from, especially for those living outside of the big cities. And yet, humanity's demise had almost come about more than once during Earth's history. The worldwide flood of Noah. Still, that was a pre-history myth to most.

During the Black Plague, as much as sixty percent of Europe had perished, though, that was ancient. There had been other close calls—major pandemics during the previous century. Even periods when millions were unable to work, institutions and businesses shuttered for years at a time. Some of the more fragile governments and smaller countries had collapsed. Vulnerable regions, out of necessity, had to unite for survival. Somehow, time and again, world governments overcame the plagues and pandemics. Life always continued. Always reemerging, a sense of innate security. Humanity was too intelligent and resourceful to be overwhelmed by a disease. As far as Niles and his team were concerned, Delirium acted very differently from any disease before it.

The convoy screeched to a halt before the World Health Continuum Conference Center. Escorted by his heavily armed soldiers, Niles hurried inside.

On stage, the deputy director of the World Health Continuum stepped to the podium. He paused momentarily as late-arriving doctors and scientists of the continuum scurried to their seats in the half-empty auditorium. Projected above them on a large teleview screen, it read: "Welcome to World Health Continuum's Delirium Control Conference."

The deputy director began, "Doctors and scientists of World Health Continuum, let me introduce the head of the Center for Disease Control, our own Dr. Niles Morgan."

The half-hearted clapping was discouraging as Niles approached the holographic microphone.

The WHC logo faded as a video began playing above him. It showed crowded streets and sidewalks within a seething Chindian city. In time-lapse photography, thousands of workers walked briskly along an avenue crammed with people, bikes, and cars. Most on their way to their jobs. They disappeared in number until there were only about two hundred left. The few uninfected stepped around or over the sick as they hurried to work.

Next up on the video—a twentieth-century porch. On it, a rocking chair where an old woman was being fed by her adult daughter.

Dr. Morgan pointed to the screen above him. "As you

all know, during its infancy, Delirium, like Alzheimer's, dementia, and senility, primarily targeted the elderly."

The video switched to the main entrance of a twentieth-century hospital. The camera moved through double doors labeled "Memory Ward." Inside, a modest number of elderly patients gathered in a living room-like setting. Sitting on couches, many were watching television. Or pretending to. A few wandered aimlessly, talking to themselves.

Sitting beside an ancient white-haired woman, a pretty nurse with cat eyeglasses looked up at the camera and smiled. She handed a cup of pills to her patient.

Niles continued. "Over the centuries, we have managed these neurological diseases and considered them a normal part of aging." He gestured again to the video above, showing a twentieth-first-century grade school filled with young students. A pleasant porcelain-faced android was teaching the class.

"Naturally," Niles continued, "we took pride in producing the smartest children with the brightest and fastest intellects." The children in the video speedily flipped holographic screens between one another. "What parent could possibly leave their child at a disadvantage in our competitive world? We had to assist them. And, assist, we did."

In the video, a robot doctor was implanting a microprocessor into the temple of a five-year-old girl. After all, it was the first quarter of the twenty-first century. She was sitting on what might resemble an old barber chair. The doctors and scientists, all watching, knew what this implant was; most everyone believed in the benefits of Temple-Talk. A person could instantly view almost any imaginable bit of science, education, or entertainment within a microsecond.

"Our quest for knowledge," Niles said, "at unimaginable speeds has altered our neurological synaptic transmitters which are advancing this—"

A female Muslim doctor, wearing a hijab, leaped from her seat, waving at him, "That is speculation—pardon, Monsieur." With a heavy French accent, she spoke passionately. "Across our European Caliphate, we find ourselves overwhelmed—these are younger and younger patients. We are losing our doctors, nurses. What do you suggest we do with this?"

"It's difficult." Niles pointed up at the chart above him. "The median age of cognitive impairment worldwide—in areas where our testing has a high degree of accuracy—has dropped into the thirties."

That caused great anguish and groaning throughout the auditorium. A wide-shouldered British doctor struggled to stand with a cane. Unsteady on his feet, it didn't hinder his boisterous voice. "Dr. Morgan, we're not here for a goddamn history lesson. Why in bloody hell hasn't your team found a cure? You damn well have enough resources under your direction."

The French female doctor stood again, waving her arm wildly. "Monsieur Morgan, we feel a vote of confidence is desirable among the leadership. I speak on behalf of most of us here. We are concerned that a new direction is urgently called for." Reaching down, she grabbed her coat and scurried up the aisle to the exit, ignoring his angry response.

Niles was becoming angry. "Do any of you even realize that Delirium didn't immerge out of a vacuum? It may have been with us for thousands of years!" Their decision to judge his progress so quickly startled him. It hadn't even been a year since he'd been chosen to lead this team.

Other doctors and scientists in the crowd rose angrily. He was sure they'd been colluding about replacing him before this conference ever convened.

The damn thing is an inquisition, he thought, *not an update. They're not even going to listen to me. Good luck—there is no one else remotely qualified in synaptic disease containment to lead this search.*

The British doctor waved his cane furiously at Niles.

"You people don't know what you're doing. That's the truth of it, isn't it? We hear you haven't even consolidated a clear line of research within your team." He hammered his cane against the floor. "You can't stop this thing, can you, Doctor?"

Niles responded, "We have eroded the core value of what makes us human—how we embrace our lives together! We are becoming machines . . .

As the remainder of the audience hustled out of the auditorium, Niles stared down at one remaining doctor. Disheveled and scrunched down in his seat, he was shaking his head.

Another know-it-all who doesn't know what I'm dealing with here.

"Do you have a question?" Niles demanded.

The little doctor rose, faced Niles, and pulled his jacket down tight. "You best revise your line of research, Morgan," he said. "This profane monster you're chasing is not going to disclose its true nature without a fight." He turned and walked off. "I'd be looking for its creator."

"Wait!" Niles called to him. "What? Who are you?"

The little doctor stopped in the aisle and turned to Niles. "I will tell you this. You've lost all hope, your humanity— that's what's really killing you. Your children have no direction, no reason to live. This disease destroys from the inside, a reflection of your fear. And fear, Dr. Niles Morgan, is a product of uncertainty. For without God, there is no certainty and no hope. For you, for me, or for anyone." With that, the little doctor shuffled up the aisle.

Who is this guy? he thought as his tele rang. Niles touched his temple and brought up a live feed of his friend Station Chief Gudrun Olsson. He was calling from Antarctica. On Niles' teleview, huddled in a fur-hooded coat, and surrounded by a wall of ice, was fifty-year-old, bearded Gudrun.

Niles was distracted as the disheveled doctor reached an exit.

"Gudrun? Hey, hang on a minute . . . I'm . . ."

Niles had to speak to the little man.

"Hey, wait!" he called out. "What do you mean? What's your name? I need to talk to you!"

The doctor exited.

"Niles—Niles, you have to see this," Gudrun interjected. "I'm below the Transantarctic Mountain Range. We've uncovered this—these beings. I sent you data samples. Giants. Not like anything I've ever seen. There are five of them."

On the live feed, Niles could see a pale humanoid

skeleton laid out on a table.

Gruden continued, "From my samples, it looks like their DNA is comprised of an expanded set of six nucleotides . . . This could be your answer!"

"That's unlikely, Gudrun," Niles said. "Six nucleotides? You better double-check—"

"I have," Gudrun insisted. "Think of the possibilities . . . it gives you 172 amino acids to utilize for your cure, not twenty."

Niles didn't hear the last words Gudrun had to say as he hurried off the stage and ran up the aisle in pursuit of the disheveled doctor.

Chapter 6

McMurdo Station, Antarctica

— June 10, 2107 —

BEYOND THE WINDSHIELD, MULTI-COLORED holographic flags lined the icy runway guiding the Falcon Transport during its buffeted descent. Niles Morgan, across from Chindian Professor Xiao Xing, sat amidst ten empty seats.

Xiao Xing was cute, in her early thirties. With layered jet-black hair and brilliant emerald eyes, she looked intelligent, and she was. Niles had chosen the professor from among the world's top linguists. Xiao Xing was a professor of ancient languages at Chindian Legacy University. During the flight, when she wasn't napping, she'd remained quiet. Otherwise, she was always at work, flipping charts and using her temple-talk in privacy mode. Meanwhile, she hadn't forgotten to remind Niles that her name was pronounced "Shou Shing—*Professor Shou Shing.*"

Niles was excited that he'd be able to see Gudrun, his graduate-school colleague. It had been a long time. To be sure, he was still trying to reason whether this trip to the remote outpost of the world would advance his work on Delirium. Every hour of research was critical. It was infuriating the way this disease had evaded a cure.

He could feel the ultramodern falcon plane whooshing to a gradual stop on its skis.

The pilot announced over the com: "To our guests—Dr. Niles Morgan, Professor Xiao Xing—welcome to McMurdo Station, Antarctica. Today is June 10, 2107. The weather is a hot and pleasant minus thirty-two degrees."

Deboarding, the cold instantly stung Niles. He looked around for Gudrun near the admin building, but it was dim and dark at this time of year in Antarctica. Still friends, Gudrun had kept Niles up to date about his work here. They'd both signed on at PharmaLife Sciences right out of graduate school. Gudrun was a brilliant tactician, and PharmaLife had been lucky to hire him. Niles stayed on to become Director of Research, and Gudrun—always an adventurous soul—became Station Chief here at McMurdo Station after three years.

"National Science Foundation, South Pole" marked the bus. They entered and headed toward the main administration building. Inside the warm bus, looking at Niles, Xiao Xing's eyebrows rose with the hint of a smile.

Perhaps she'd been afraid to fly.

In front of the well-lit facility, Station Chief Gudrun waved as the bus with Niles, and Xiao Xing arrived. As they deboarded the bus, Gudrun, a hefty Norwegian, greeted Niles with a hearty hug. Then he turned to embrace Xiao Xing. She took a step backward and wrapped her hands around her arms. Gudrun smiled and extended his gloved hand, guiding them both up the front entrance of the facility.

***

Before noon the next day, a snowcat transport, containing Chief Gudrun, Dr. Niles, and Professor Xiao Xing reached the base of the towering Transantarctic Mountains, a notched section of the range where the mountains divided eastern Antarctica from the west. The snowcat rumbled to a stop.

Exiting the warm cat, the three twisted and stretched to get the kinks out. It had been a long and jarring ride. Almost instantly, Xiao Xing's face creased-up, looking like she might just crawl back inside. —It was so cold.

Before them, at the base of the mountains, protected by copious military personnel, was a clearly illuminated tunnel opening. Towering floodlights formed a semi-circle around the base. Even in the morning hours, this time of year, it was dim out here. Two heavy tractors, engines running, waited to enter. Four dump trucks sat idling off to the side.

Something big was going on.

Two soldiers exited heated guard posts, saluted Gudrun, and motioned the snowcat forward into the high-security, frozen underworld. Nearing the opening and passing the sign, Niles read: "National Science Foundation, Subglacial Lake Project #16, Transantarctic Mountains."

He didn't believe for a second what the sign read. At the same time, he was thinking about how he had to piss like crazy. As the snowcat entered the ice tunnel, a hefty earthmover thundered past them toward a billowing white light farther down the passageway.

Exiting the snowcat at an ancillary opening, the three proceeded on foot. Fortunately, there were several porta-toilets as they arrived in a cavernous, high-ceilinged icy chamber. Niles disappeared into one of the toilets.

Xiao Xing shrugged. Taking it in, her eyes surveyed this strange, timeworn equipment. Not what she had expected.

Mill stamping and steel presses lined the room. The Nazi swastika was dye-stamped prominently upon most of the machinery.

Gudrun sensed her disquiet. "It's a machine shop,

Professor, but from another time."

Returning, Niles asked, "What was this place used for, Gudrun?"

Niles hadn't revealed to Xiao Xing what was down here in this tunnel because he didn't know himself. He was only told that there were substantial skeletal remains that Gudrun couldn't identify. They needed to study and analyze the remains in person. There were ancient panels with languages that no one at McMurdo could read. All top-secret. All classified. They needed a linguist.

As they walked into the next grand ice room, Niles pounded his arms for warmth. All three of them spewed condensation—it was even colder down here than outside. At least the porta-toilets were heated. Xiao Xing pulled her fur-lined hood tight against her face.

In the middle of the next room sat a massive, tank-like monstrosity. It had enormous, treaded steel wheels. The turret, if it was a turret, was angled at forty-five degrees and tapered to a tightly pointed tip.

Gudrun put his gloved hand on one of the wheels. "We think this was all a Nazi strategic weapons base. They could only get here by U-boat. We think it was utilized late in the Second Great War."

"And that?" Niles surveyed the monstrosity. "Did they construct it here?"

"It is a sonic cannon," Gudrun explained. "When implemented, the sound waves can kill a man fifty meters away in half a minute. Or a platoon for that matter. They tested it here on penguins and seals first . . . then on people."

"Holy God," Niles said, "what a horrid generation they were."

Xiao Xing stiffened. Turning, she leaned in, fastening her eyes to a conspicuous photograph on the wall. It was old and faded: Three German soldiers posed alongside a Nazi flag stuck in the ice, claiming a sector of Antarctica for Germany.

"And when was this?" Xiao Xing asked.

Gudrun moved beside her, pointing out the flag. "We know that secret missions to Antarctica began well before the Second World War. Several countries claimed a stake in areas of this desolate land of ice. Of course, we believe at one time that it was not a frozen world. That it was forested and teeming with diverse life. In the south, rainforests inhabited by dinosaurs thrived."

Gudrun stepped to a solid steel cabinet. "And this, Professor, will interest you—" He easily pulled open the two handles. The doors slid open, effortlessly revealing shelves of ancient books and scientific papers.

"Everything in here has something to do with the

occult," Gudrun assured her. "From Egypt, India, Babylon—the Nazis were fascinated with space visitors and flying saucers. Look at whatever you wish, Professor."

Xiao Xing leaned down and ran her finger along the titles of the neatly stacked books in the cabinet.

Gudrun put his big hand on Niles' back and indicated another work area with drawing boards and tables. Standing before a collection of architectural drawing boards, Gudrun said, "We know the Nazis were perfecting some of the world's deadliest weapons. Winston Churchill called them the secret weapons of wonder . . . but this is the least of it. Follow me, please, my friends."

Following Gudrun to another lower level, they heard the rattle of impact hammers, heating equipment, and chattering workers. Gudrun pushed a button. A thick, dense drapery opened from the middle.

Niles and Xiao Xing stopped. Shock and condensation spewed from their mouths.

Niles clapped his gloves together for warmth. "What in the cosmos . . .? You didn't tell me about this, Gudrun." They were now looking at a vast, gleaming black vessel, most of it still encased in the ice.

"I know. I'm sorry, I couldn't. Not until you arrived. Science Foundation regulations are in place over this entire project."

Workers were utilizing heat drills to melt the ice that enclosed most of the ship until their foreman blew a whistle, signaling them to take a break.

The three stepped forward, mesmerized by the smooth, flowing lines reflected below the ice wall. Cleared of ice, the forward section appeared almost prehistoric.

"Is it a boat?" Xiao Xing whispered, wavering.

"We think not, Professor. There is no apparent propeller. We also don't believe it's something the Nazis could have built—and to be sure, it's sealed tight."

"How'd you discover it?" Niles asked.

Walking closer, Gudrun said, "McMurdo Station picked up intermittent radio signals from down here. Once we located this cavern, it took us a few weeks to tunnel in. We've had listening devices attached to this ship since we cleared off the mid-section. And yet, not a signal since—"

Niles noticed the scaffolding erected at what appeared to be a large, inscribed section along the craft's forward side. Gudrun stopped and pointed. "It's about nine feet tall by six feet wide. That's where we believe there may be a way in. An access point."

"Interior structure?" Niles asked.

"We can't determine interior dimensions. Thermography, gravimetric analysis, resistivity mapping .

. . we've tried it all. We're blocked from entering—except for that." He pointed.

About midway down the indented scribed rectangle were several symbols. Gudrun turned to Xiao Xing, his thick eyebrows lifting as he motioned.

Xiao Xing walked cautiously to the end of the metal scaffolding. The two men followed.

Before her were nine colorfully etched hieroglyphs—or glyphs, as they were known. Three rows of three each. Each colorful glyph was contained in a perfect square. Each was the artistically drawn picture of an animal, a person, or a place—and all of them appeared as if they'd originated from ancient times.

"We're hoping you can get us in, Professor."

She scowled. "We will see," she said without hesitation.

Gudrun watched Xiao Xing as she examined the glyphs, admiring them, touching them with her fingertips, feeling the inscribed outlines. "They're beautiful," she said.

Niles whispered to Gudrun, "She's a master of ancient languages."

"I would think as much, my friend."

As Xiao Xing worked on the glyphs, Gudrun motioned for Niles to follow him to a long table beneath the ship.

Gudrun, approaching, waved his big glove. Before them lay a nine-foot skeleton with an elongated skull. It rested on a newly constructed table. "We found this handsome guy right here on the ice. The samples I sent you came right from him."

Niles looked oddly at the lengthy creature. "I've seen that elongated skull before . . . in Peru, I believe it was. Paracas . . . other places, maybe, when I was a graduate student. I just don't remember exactly. It was a long time ago."

"I'm sorry about your wife, Gudrun."

"Thank you. It's no coincidence that I was following your research. If she hadn't contracted that horrid disease, rest her soul, I never would have—

"I've never seen this language before!" Xiao Xing burst out. She pointed at one of the glyphs.

The two men drew near, looking up from below as she continued with her upset on the scaffold. "The Chinese language is an isolate language." She stomped her foot, glaring down at them. "In Maya, they use relational nouns instead of prepositions to indicate spatial relationships."

"Why's she getting angry?" Gudrun whispered to Niles.

Niles's eyebrows lifted, "Have no idea."

Glaring at the glyphs, Xiao Xing spoke rapidly, as if

teaching a class of students. "English is analytic. Isolating languages are morphologically un-analyzable. Sentence structure is expressed by word order, word grouping, and use of specific grammatical words . . ."

She tilted her head, expecting they were getting this. "Very few languages fit perfectly into any one of these categories. A glyph is a graphic symbol, or symbols, that provide the appearance or form for a character, but this *one* . . ." She poked her finger at that same one and glared down at the dumbfounded men. ". . . this one right here does not fit with any of the rest of them!"

The two men, concerned, simply stood motionless.

She tapped her temple and brought up a collection of glyphs before her face. She flipped them with her fingers, moved them around, and spoke each ancient word, matching one after another. Next, she placed her own glyphs atop the glyphs embedded in the side of the ship — like she was solving a puzzle.

She swiped them all away with the flick of her hand. Frustrated, one glyph stymied her.

Niles and Gudrun remained riveted as she squinted, pouted, and rattled off a parade of what were obviously Chindian curse words.

Niles smiled at Gudrun. "Not your typical cerebral professor, huh?"

Xiao Xing stepped back, annoyed, staring down at them again. "I will make a knowledgeable supposition. This last glyph is not present in any known Earth language. . ."

She touched each of the nine pictures on the side of the ship in a specific order. Nothing happened.

Angered, she did it again, using a different pattern.

Still no response. She cursed under her breath.

A third time.

Placing her ear against the side of the ship, she heard a low mechanical groaning for five seconds. "Ah-ha!" Xiao Xing shouted. As if it was all expected. Nothing to be concerned about.

There was a swish and then a blunt bang.

A popping pressure release of putrid air emerged. She stumbled backward and waved her hand in front of her nose.

"Ooooh . . ."

Smiling, with her cheeks puffed out and holding her breath, she eyed the two men and gestured as a large opening materialized. "We will go in, I think?"

***

Outside the tunnel, one of the waiting dump truck drivers heard a booming crackle. Looking through his windshield, peering at the darkening mountaintop, he thought he could see the beginnings of an avalanche. A hefty amount of snow was tumbling down the mountainside. Always a danger, he jumped down from the cab and moved away to get a closer view.

From the ridge top, a glowing ray of blue light pulsated. What was that? Squinting, he was unsure of what he was seeing. As he climbed back into his truck to grab some binocs, an isolated edge of the mountaintop exploded, spewing white ice.

With a mighty thud, an intense beam of blue light broke the ice and streamed vertically toward the upper hemisphere. The driver yanked the wheel of his fully chained dump truck and headed toward the long road leading back to McMurdo Bay. At least he had the courtesy to call the station and inform them that there was no way he would be going back into that tunnel. Ever.

Chapter 7

Alien Vessel

IN FULL GEAR AND WITH HIS HELMET light on, the hazmat tech stepped into the entrance opening. Moments later, over com, he announced, "It's all clear, Doctors. Keep helmets on, please."

The three suited scientists entered through an archway, up an almost stone walkway, and onto what appeared to be a bridge or operations center of the vessel, their headlamps lighting the dank, dark way.

At first glance, Gudrun thought that the interior walls' metal alloys appeared foreign: a stone and metal hybrid combination, perhaps.

The three stopped, astounded by what they were seeing. The air appeared cloudy, and there was a greyish-green hue to everything. Who knew how long this vessel had been sealed up and hidden in the ice? It could have been for centuries.

"Hey, Gudrun," Niles asked over com, touching the side of the ship, or whatever this vehicle was. "What is this material, do you suppose?"

"Not the slightest idea," he answered. "Nothing I've

ever seen."

Continuing, they passed beneath three elevated seats. Gudrun stopped and looked up. "Obviously, only very tall beings could sit in these seats."

"The world is going to be unnerved when they see this." Niles pointed beyond the seats and asked the hazmat tech, "Can you point your flood up there?"

The hazmat tech switched on his floodlight and directed the light beyond the seating. Laid out in a symmetrical design were a series of levers and rocky-metal alloy panels appearing to be some type of navigational screens suffused with an almost milky substance.

"Gudrun," Niles asked, "did the Nazis possess this kind of technology in the twentieth century?"

Gudrun shook his head. "That's always been a question, now, hasn't it? Still, this is not man-made, that's evident."

"Agreed. It's not of human design," Niles declared, stating the obvious. "This will change everything. Shock an already spooked world, I fear. The first real proof that we are not alone."

"Yeah, well, there's always been a question as to how the Third Reich became so technologically advanced before the rest of the world. I mean, Niles, remember, they had jet aircraft, rockets and were well on their way to planning a trip to the moon. Who knows? Where did they get all of that knowledge?"

Xiao Xing was rocking back and forth, her gloved hands clenched, staring at Niles. "You did not tell me that I would be entering into an alien ship, Dr. Niles."

"I'm sorry, I didn't— I didn't know, either."

Cautiously moving on, they entered a fluted archway and emerged into an expansive hypersleep chamber.

The tech illuminated the dark chamber with his flood lamp revealing one hundred large hypersleep pods, all open, all long and empty.

Niles raised his hands. "My God, who were these beings? Where have they gone? What are these hibernation pods—ten feet long, each?"

They were still standing near five pods—segregated from the hundred. Marked in an unknown written language, four contained skeletal remains. The fifth was empty, as were the other hundred. Each of the first four pods, with tall, conical-headed skeletons inside, had distinctive holes punched across their covers.

Gudrun stooped down close. "These four appear as though they were intentionally punctured with some kind of a device. That's why there is hardly any flesh here. I see some remnants of hair."

Niles examined the fifth pod. It was closed, empty, and had no puncture holes.

"Strange," Niles said. "No ruptures here." He motioned to the skeleton he'd seen outside the ship. "I wonder if this pod was his? The one outside. . .? What happened here, do you suppose?"

Xiao Xing said, "Bigger question might be: What happened to the one hundred or so who were in the empty pods in there?"

Stepping over to one of the inhabited sleep pods, Niles pushed a polished button.

A delay. A pop and a whoosh as it opened . . . slowly.

Niles scanned the grey skeleton using a handheld molecular sequencing device that produced a life-size scrolling DNA signature. He looked closely at his scanner. "This is too old. Not enough here for me to tell much of anything definitively. Gudrun, please, I'll need one of these beings transported to London."

"I thought you would," Gudrun answered. "I'll get transport up here. It'll take a few hours."

Xiao Xing was standing beneath a wall relief, gazing at it, and called to them, "Hey, you better see this. I think it is something."

Niles and Gudrun moved to the wall relief showing an

ancient ephemeris (a planetary map).

Radius, inclination, and azimuth—the star map clearly showed the planets of our solar system. Beyond that, a clear line leading to a recently discovered planet inside the Kuiper Belt.

Xiao Xing said, "I must use the toilet. I will be back."

They weren't paying attention as she left and retraced her steps out of the alien craft. She had no idea where the hazmat guy had gone, but she knew where she was going.

Pointing to the planet in line, Gudrun said, "The planet is called Nemesis. For so long, it was believed to be there, but we had no way to see it."

"I'm going to film this," Niles said. "From this map, I'd suggest that they were either going to Nemesis or they came from Nemesis. Would you agree?"

"I suppose. Seems like guesswork at this point. Where's Xiao Xing?"

Passing the toilets, Xiao Xing followed the main ice tunnel. Brilliant white light spilled out of a chamber farther down. She'd noticed it when they had first entered. Something was going on down there, and she wanted to know what it was. A tractor slowed and then passed her as she squeezed against the freezing wall.

As she drew closer, she could hear drilling and jackhammering. They were uncovering something. As she made her way down the ancillary tunnel, a hand grabbed her shoulder. It startled her for a moment.

The soldier said pleasantly, "Ma'am, you don't belong down here. You'll have to go back."

"I was just—"

"Please, head back the way you came. I will call ahead and let them know that you're returning."

"No, it's okay," she said. "I got lost . . . I'm going . . ."

With that, she turned and scurried down the tunnel.

***

The helicopter rose from near the tunnel entrance. As it whirled off along the Transantarctic Mountain Range, Niles could see his requested hibernation pod dangling from a long cable.

As the aircraft disappeared into the distance, the turquoise light pulsated intermittently from the mountaintop.

Chapter 8

Century Hospital, Chicago, Il

NILES HOPED THAT HE COULD TAKE a few days rest before flying back to London. He was fatigued from his journey to Antarctica. Certainly, the skeleton from Gudrun was already en route to the W.H.C. laboratory in London. But he desired to spend some time with Veronika, Cassia, and Ori. He'd missed them horribly during the last stint in London. The next one would be even longer. Who knew how much time they all had left together? He and Veronika could fall ill at any time—even Cassi, although unlikely. And Ori? He wasn't improving.

He'd made an appointment for Ori with a premier specialist at Century Hospital. He was already nervous; his transport from the airport home had picked him up late. The transport pulled up the drive, and he jumped out.

Veronika and Cassia were waiting. Ori was in his wheelchair, and all three of them looked anxious. The bot driver helped him load Ori in, and they zipped off toward Century Hospital.

***

Veronika, Cassia, and Niles followed closely behind the soldier pushing twelve-year-old Ori in a wheelchair. It was pandemonium. The corridors of the hospital were crammed full of Delirium-afflicted patients of all ages.

Niles turned in every direction. He was looking anxiously for someone. In the wheelchair, Ori's head was tipped to the side and resting on a pillow.

Veronika spotted a young doctor making his way toward them. He didn't appear to be over twenty-five.

Jostled by those packing the corridor, the young doctor put his hand on Niles' shoulder for support. "I'm sorry, Dr. Morgan. I tried to contact you through W.H.C.— I'm Dr. Milner."

To Veronika, he appeared as if he should still be in high school.

With all of this noise in the crowded hallway, the young doctor had to speak loudly. "We are not administering any trial vaccines at this hospital any longer. I'm sorry, Dr. Morgan. They have proven ineffective."

Veronika didn't like the sound of that. "Cass, stay with Ori." She pressed her way closer to her husband. "What's wrong, Niles?"

The young doctor looked around at the patients everywhere. The crowded hallways.

Niles, taking a deep breath, turned to his wife. "I arranged for Ori to be cared for by a specialist here—weeks ago. They can't take him now—"

"Let me speak to your administrator," Veronika demanded.

"Really? Ma'am, even if a specialist could see him, there is nothing we can do for your son—for any of them. You must know that." He gestured to the mindless Delirium patients crowding every space. Some were being attended to by family, but most stumbled around aimlessly, talking to themselves, imaginary friends, or ghosts.

"What are we supposed to do now?" Niles asked the young doctor.

"How would I know, *Doctor Morgan*? You're the expert. We're closing this hospital tomorrow!" He scowled at both of them, abruptly turned, and stomped off, shaking his head and squeezing his way through the melee.

Squeezing their way to an exit, the soldier, Ori now in his arms, kicked open the side door to the courtyard. Niles, Veronika, and Cassia followed close behind. Even the courtyard was jammed. Overflowing with people, some were on blankets, but most patients were strapped in wheelchairs—helpless. There were only a few nurses and one white-coated doctor to take care of so many.

Veronika stopped and grabbed her husband's arm. "Niles, my God. Look at this. I'll take care of Ori myself . . . I received a tentative offer to buy TIMMI yesterday!"

Niles regarded her with disbelief. "Why are you going to do that? Your father built that business from a small collection of mining claims into . . ."

The soldier holding Ori was struggling, wavering, waiting for the two to stop arguing. Seeing two decorated officers, hurrying up the path toward them, he stood fast.

"He's our son," Veronika insisted. "Cassia and I can move Ori to London so we can all be together. I will care for him myself. Cass will help. We can do this, Niles!"

"Mom, I *can't* move now," Cassia interrupted. "I'm graduating in a month—do you recall that? *Remember?* I'm going to be a doctor!"

Disregarding her, Veronika pointed to the lawn full of human beings in confusion and despair. "Look around you, Niles. *The world is coming apart! For real.''*

Cassia stalked off in anger, hissing, "You don't listen to me, parental."

The two decorated officers, arrived and stood politely before Niles and Veronika, waiting.

Niles stopped and looked at the shorter of the two soldiers. He was a fit, good-looking young man.

"Sir, ma'am, I am Major Collins." He gestured to his partner. "This is Lieutenant Estes. The President of the League of American States, the duly elected Sebastian Molina, has asked that you meet with him."

"*Now?*" Niles asked. "I can't leave here now. Why?" Niles stepped back and put his hand to his head.

"I can't answer that, sir."

"When must he leave, Major?" Veronika asked.

"Mrs. Morgan, the president, has requested that you both appear."

"How so?" Veronika argued. "I'm not a doctor."

The soldier looked at her but had no answer. Lt. Estes, a big guy, reached out and took Ori from the other soldier, who immediately saluted and left.

The officer insisted, "We have a plane waiting for you at Hanna Air Force Base, ma'am. I'm to provide you passage there. Perhaps your daughter can watch your son. I'll have them both escorted home; they'll be safe. If you'll please come with us."

Cassia had made her way back to her parents and stood there, scowling.

"I suppose we have no choice, then, do we?" Niles responded to the soldier.

The soldier half-smiled and motioned for them to proceed down the path where two heavily armored military transport vehicles were waiting. As the four walked toward the waiting vehicles, there was a thunderous boom.

On the lawn, a male nurse stopped and looked up to the heavens. The heavy rain showered down instantly as the lightning flashed, and the nurse lifted his arms to the sky and called out, "Why, God? How could you let this happen?"

Chapter 9

McMurdo Station, Antarctica

STATION CHIEF GUDRUN TROTTED awkwardly across the light snow; his figure dwarfed beneath the vast white dish telescope positioned behind him. He burst out of the frigid wind, into the ice room, and immediately into the control room. Two young air force operators, Devon and Leonard, manned the radio telescope.

"What's so urgent, Devon?" Gudrun questioned.

Devon was a freckle-faced twenty-year-old. Gangly, his red hair was sheared tight along the sides and flat across the top. "Sir, we have pinpointed a transmission from deep within our solar system."

"Already got that—how deep?" Gudrun asked.

"The planet is Nemesis." Devon pointed to the audio file in plain view.

Gudrun took a deep breath. "Nemesis? Impossible . . . let's hear it."

Devon nodded. He punched the audio play button. Hearing nothing but a scratchy hiss, he twisted two knobs.

The second young operator, Leonard, glared at the

screen, waiting. A moment later, there occurred a low, sonorous tone. Abruptly, an ungodly, animal-like sound wailed through the speaker. Devon moved to turn it down, but Gudrun pulled his arm back. "Wait a minute, Devon."

Six disturbing seconds later, the profane sound stopped.

Gudrun's forehead wrinkled. "There can't be a vessel out there. What was that?" Gudrun took out a handkerchief and wiped his mouth. "We've not had so much as a probe make it back from that planet."

Leonard, shrinking in his chair, pointed directly to a puzzling display of hieroglyphic pictures clearly revealed within the audio waveform. He blurted, "Do you see that, sir? Look!"

Devon and Leonard turned to him.

"It's some kind of message!" Devon shouted. "It's something!"

Gudrun peered closer, for just a moment, grimaced, and headed for the door. He yelled. "Forward the file to my office, and then delete that recording, Devon. Are we clear? *Delete it!*"

"Yes, sir. Understood, sir," Devon affirmed.

Chapter 10

President's Residence

League of American States, Costa Rica

A LIGHT BREEZE RUFFLED THE WHITE TERRACE awnings as officials from the League of American States gathered in conversation on the patio of the president's palatial residence in San Jose, Costa Rica. Waiters scurried, picking up breakfast dishes.

Seated together, Station Chief Gudrun and Professor Xiao Xing were talking together in a whisper. Meanwhile, Niles and Veronika arrived, and the two were escorted to their seats.

Sitting, Veronika noticed Colonel Massey. Surprised, she nodded. Massey smiled back as he sat down. He looked older.

Yeah, well, we all do, Veronika reminded herself. She wondered if he was still on active duty.

The president's assistant, a slim, welcoming, and charming man in his forties, entered. "Ladies and gentlemen," he spoke with a thick Spanish accent, "the President of the League of American States, Señor

Sebastian Molina."

Everyone rose as Sebastian Molina, looking to be about thirty-five, strode decisively to his position at the big oval table and stood smiling. The way he carried himself impressed Veronika. She'd seen pictures of him but had never seen him in person. Shorter than he looked from his photos, he was a powerfully built man. Sporting a neatly trimmed black goatee, he wore a dark blue suit, perfectly tailored.

"Bienvenido," he smiled. "Thank you all for coming— some of you from quite a distance. I trust your accommodations are to your liking. Please, let us be seated."

As they took their seats, President Molina smiled. "You may not know this, but I received my doctorate from your outstanding Yale University. Of course, that was some time ago." Sebastian waited until everyone else was seated before sitting down. "Air Force One will be provided for your return to the northern states this evening. So that you may all continue your work without undue delay." He glanced at his watch and looked to his assistant for confirmation.

His assistant, with a grin, confirmed, "Yes, leaving at 6:30 PM, Mr. President."

Veronika looked around the table. Gathered was quite a

collection of cabinet leadership from among the League of American States: The National Science Foundation, the League of Space Exploration, and the World Health Continuum.

"Let's get right to it, shall we?" Molina gestured. "Please, our esteemed Dr. Morgan, will you begin?"

Her husband stood and scooted a miniature black box to the middle of the table.

Veronika had a brief sense of delight. At forty-eight, her husband was still a handsome and distinguished-looking man. She smiled as he tapped his temple, and a large, multi-sided teleview screen appeared so that everyone, no matter where they were seated, had a clear view.

The NSF logo and time stamp faded. Upon each screen appeared a running video of what seemed to be a sizable shiny, black spacecraft half-immersed in ice. In the video, Station Chief Gudrun was giving a tour of sorts. There was no sound.

Some of the guests murmured between themselves.

"What are we looking at here, please?" President Molina interrupted.

Veronika gave Niles a perturbed "what is this?" look.

Niles began, "Sir, N.S.F., under the direction of Station Chief Gudrun, has unearthed the remains of five alien beings below the ice in Antarctica. By all indications—they arrived in that spacecraft." He pointed to it. "We do not, as of yet, know how it operates, but it is undoubtedly a space vessel."

The shot changed. The video panned. It started at the feet and ended at the elongated skull of a very tall, chalky-white skeleton lying on a table below the ship.

"Intriguing," Molina said. "*Doctor*, what does this have to do with today's order of business? I expected that you would present us with an update on your progress with a cure for Delirium."

Niles touched his temple again. "I am, sir. Please bear with me." A three-foot-tall holographic DNA signature now rotated before all of them.

"Mr. President, the skeletal remains of that very tall being indicate that it is not human. Further, it does not match the skeletal structure of modern *Homo sapien*, nor any of its subspecies. The relevant point is this: within this being's DNA are an additional 152 amino acids which humans don't possess." Like a rubber band, Niles pulled a holographic strand of DNA out from the signature. He continued with growing excitement. "At the same time, there is an astounding connection between our two species." Holding the strand and twisting it, he continued. "We found that the alien carries a particular Delirium marker within his expanded DNA—the same disease marker we humans carry. We believe that their expanded amino acids may serve as a base from which a gene can be utilized to produce a cure for Delirium."

Niles let the strand snap back into the revolving DNA spiral.

Veronika watched Sebastian Molina; he appeared disturbed. After a moment, the president cupped his hands under his chin. "How many hospitals have we closed in the League, just in the last month alone?" He directed his gaze around the table. "Do any of you know? Have any idea? Essential services? Police, fire?"

He wagged his finger at Niles. "Dr. Morgan, you have over fifty of the most qualified scientists from around the world working under your direction—and you're researching aliens?"

Veronika closed her eyes and put her hand to her forehead.

"We're losing our farmers!" Molina raised his voice. "I'm already airlifting emergency food rations from the Central South League into Mexico City. Soon, our northern cities will require aid, as well. How long do you think the Southern League can keep this up?" The president's face tightened. His frown lines deepened. "I'm focused today on one successful outcome, doctor—your cure for Delirium!"

Niles took a deep breath and extended his hands, "Mr. President. I'm sure that you realize scientists have been searching for a cure for this family of diseases for well over 200 years."

Veronika closed her eyes in embarrassment. "Oh, God," she whispered to herself.

"They've used different names, of course. Senility, Alzheimer's, dementia—" He scanned the room for support but received only vacant stares. "Delirium's been hiding, mutating, and evolving over the centuries, and we scientists have acted like painters restricted to a palette of black and white—"

"It's irrelevant, Doctor!" Molina interrupted, sitting forward, looking angry. "This disease, no matter how old it is, is now inflicting our people in their prime. If it drops below forty—"

"It has, Mr. President! It has dropped into the high thirties worldwide."

Molina sat back, incredulous. The entire table gasped and took a collective breath, looking one to another.

Veronika was dismayed with her husband. Niles had always been a precise, analytical researcher . . .

Niles pushed on. "The samples we have from Antarctica are ancient and degraded. If we can capture a viable sample of their expanded DNA, we can pull from the entire color spectrum, figuratively. Six nucleotides provide us 152 additional amino acids from which to construct a cure for Delirium! That's it. I see no other possible means of procuring a cure at this time." Niles threw his hands up.

President Molino leaned forward, laid his hands on the table, and spoke quickly. "So, your theory supposes that their 'enhanced' base pairs equal more DNA, which equals considerably more coding within an extra 152 amino acids?"

Molina glanced sharply at his science cabinet director and back at Niles. "Would you like to explain where the raw material for these 152 amino acids came from? Were they synthesized in a lab? Did they occur naturally—or because of some cataclysmic event that took place when the aliens, or celestials, or whatever in heaven's name they are, arrived here who knows when?"

Niles dropped his head and grinned. He was getting somewhere now.

Veronika looked more closely at the president's handsome but pockmarked face. He was not only well educated, but he was also intelligent.

She sat straight up, her stomach in knots. Niles hadn't revealed even a hint of what he'd planned for this monumental gathering. There was no reason for her to be here. This was embarrassing—

Niles touched his temple again. Millions of colored mathematical computations scrolled onto the screens before them all.

Veronika rose from her chair. "I don't mean to be impolite, ladies, gentlemen, and Mr. President, but I must excuse myself. I have a very sick son at home. I must tele him. Niles, I wish you'd have told me about this, *first*." She turned to leave.

"He couldn't, ma'am!" The director of the League of Space Exploration stood and adjusted her skirt. With a husky voice, she said, "He couldn't tell anyone. And neither can you!"

The director was a short, plump, frizzy-haired woman from the state of Brazil. Veronika eyed the woman's nametag: "Silvia Oliveira, Senior Director, L.S.E."

"Please, let me explain, Ms. Morgan, Mr. President," Silvia Oliveira continued. "There is substantial evidence to believe that these beings are, in fact, alive on a planet deep in our solar system."

Instantly, the room became a morass of chattering confusion. The space director's two eager young assistants, sitting behind her, took the moment to babble into her ear.

Veronika realized that most of these governmental

department heads knew nothing about this last discovery. Niles knew, his college friend Gudrun and Silvia Oliveira knew, and maybe her staff at L.S.E. But who else?

Everyone was talking now.

"So, you are telling me . . ." Molina interrupted loudly, ". . . you're telling all of us present that you have *proof* that these are, in fact—aliens. At one time alive in Antarctica and maybe now alive on Nemesis? Good, God!" He looked around, unconvinced.

With a stern face, Silvia Oliveira touched her temple: A picture from the interior of the alien ship showed an ephemeris. A planetary map to Nemesis. "Mr. President, we don't know how long that alien ship has been in the ice, but our own Station Chief Gudrun and Dr. Morgan gained entry to the vessel. We have confirmed Dr. Morgan's assessment that their DNA is 99.85 percent the same as modern human DNA. It's undeniable. There is a connection between their DNA and that of *Homo sapiens*. The likelihood is that they do hold the key to a cure for Delirium. Here is why both N.S.F. and the L.S.E. believe this to be our most viable approach. A message arrived at our South Pole radio telescope three days ago, Mr. President. It originated from the planet Nemesis."

Veronika sat down as the director motioned for Xiao

Xing to rise. Xiao Xing stood and brought up a hieroglyphic message written in four languages, one panel after another.

"Professor Xiao Xing," Silvia Oliveira said, "has examined this message, having visited the site in Antarctica as well, and is one of the world's foremost ancient language experts. Please, Professor."

Xiao Xing rotated the message so that everyone could see it clearly.

She began, "Mr. President Molina, this message is written in three ancient languages: Sumerian, Egyptian, and Mayan. All three languages convey a very similar meaning: "We Are Here. We Can Help You." She stopped, tilted her head, and took a deep breath. "I must add, it is also written in a fourth language—which I cannot read—

there are not enough symbols for me to decipher it yet."

Silvia Oliveira added, "Transmission origination, sir, without question—is the ninth planet, Nemesis." She then brought up a rotating hologram of Nemesis.

Xiao Xing, realizing she was done, sat back down.

Veronika whispered to Niles, "Now I know why I'm here!"

President Molina asked, "Does L.S.E. have a ship capable of making this journey?"

Blank looks all around.

Veronika slapped Niles' leg under the table and whispered to him, "Of course, they don't have a—"

Silvia Oliveira gestured toward Veronika. "Ms. Morgan, we are hoping that you will allow us to utilize your deep-space transport, *Assurity*."

Veronika said nothing.

"We will provide Colonel Tom Massey, as well as a young, well-trained crew."

Tom nodded at Veronika.

Veronika didn't say a word for five seconds . . . "I know the colonel," Veronika affirmed. "He is very qualified . . . *Assurity* is not."

Silvia responded quickly, "Ms. Morgan, we believe that with some minor modifications, *Assurity* can perform this mission."

Veronika stood and pointed toward the planet. "It's too far. The shield will never hold up."

"Ma'am," Silvia encouraged, "an improved forward shield, and an advanced thruster, are both being constructed on Mimas as we speak . . . if you agree, of course."

Veronika's eyes opened wide— "So, what were you

going to do if I said no? The Chindian government has made me a very lucrative offer to buy my company, TIMMI." Veronika gazed around the table, collecting her thoughts. "Beyond that, no human-crewed mission has ever attempted to reach Nemesis."

Veronika sat, leaned back, and crossed her arms. Biting her lip, she closed her eyes—then rose again quickly. "I will personally supervise any and all fittings to my ship. Are we agreed on that?"

Everyone at the table, except the President, smiled.

"We are agreed," Silvia said. "Absolutely." One of her assistants leaned over her shoulder and whispered rapidly into her ear.

"This is a hail Mary, at best," the president interrupted.

"Mr. President," Niles said, "we can continue our research here as they make their way to Nemesis. If that is agreeable."

"L.S.E. will be required to provide insurance for the trip, Ms. Director," Veronika added.

"Of course," Silvia agreed.

The president waved his hand in the air. "I guess you have my tentative blessing." He rose from his chair and stepped away from the table. Tightening his mouth, he looked discouraged. "I hope that you people are right—we are running out of time."

Standing, Veronika looked at Tom Massey, "We're looking at ninety-five days for TIMMI to mine enough fuel for the first leg of your journey, Colonel."

They all rose, pleased with the outcome, shaking hands all around.

Silvia stepped close to Veronika and extended her hand. "We're agreed, of course, Ms. Morgan—except— *Assurity* will need to leave within sixty-seven days." She smiled. "We'd better get you to Saturn."

Antimatter Mining Operations-*TIMMI report*
#1213_Fuel_Nautilus Stardrive 7/12/2102_0800

At an unknown time, an ancient supernova produced its own sub-atomic explosion above the clouds of Saturn. A spray of every type of sub-atomic particle spread out from the collision. The debris included neutrons and antineutrons, which are uncharged subatomic particles. The antiprotons produced from the subatomic fireworks were trapped in Saturn's magnetic field. Space is big, and the atoms are small, so the particles hardly ever touch. Instead, they go about their business of bouncing back and forth in Saturn's magnetic field.

Antiprotons are the rare mirror image siblings of the regular protons that you're made of. No one knows why, but the universe prefers regular matter. Still, antimatter's rarity is a good thing when you understand that it is ready to release its atomic payload as soon as it finds its mirror image. This has its advantages, though, because it stores energy with a density almost incomprehensible. Over time, more and more antiprotons are produced and trapped around a planet, forming a natural antimatter mine. No mine lasts forever, though—even Saturn's. Therefore, we have expanded as far out as Rhema, and as the needs of our clients grow throughout our solar system, Taylor Interstellar Mining will continue to be the model for reliable and dependable sources of antimatter fuel.

Chapter 11

Industrial Mining Complex,
Saturn's Moon Mimas

Population 14,552

SPACE-SUITED, VERONIKA TAYLOR MORGAN
exited the airlock at Cassini flight services at 08:00
mainday and entered the waiting passenger transport
shuttle. Colder than eternity, Saturn's moon, Mimas, was a
cratered, pot-marked, icy rock. The average surface
temperature was minus two hundred degrees Fahrenheit.

An industrial mining complex, Mimas employed a
rotating working population of about 14,350 miners,
technicians, support staff, and their families. At Cassini Sol
Station, at any given time, TIMMI employed 225
technicians and pilots.

During the morning run, Veronika was the only
passenger in the shuttle from Mimas out to Cassini. Peering
out the window, the flight deck, with the departing gateway
open, was awash in the relentless glare of dock floodlights
and a frigid swirling atmosphere.

As her shuttle rose from the planet, a speedy security
patrol ship, lights blinking, streaked across her view in a

big hurry. She thought, *wonder where he's going in such a rush?*

Observing Mimas from above, it was comprised mostly of industrial fabrication and mining buildings. The heating and oxygen plants needed for Mimas were massive structures, supplied with critical fuel from three separate mining outfits. TIMMI was one of them.

Self-contained residences sat clustered across the pitted, harsh grey landscape. Most people on Mimas lived in apartments, mostly clustered around three community centers with an abundance of recreational choices.

It was common knowledge to those who wished to work at Mimas or Cassini that every benefit had been well thought out. Mimas had an excellent reputation as a short-term employment opportunity (if you could qualify) and an excellent environment to raise a family.

Without question, the landscape was wretched and ugly. Unlike Earth, however, out here, it was people safe. There was strict military oversight. Another bonus was that the hospital on Mimas was excellent. All benefits were free to any worker on Mimas or Cassini Sol Station. *Full medical and free education.*

Beyond question, the overriding job of Mimas was to keep Cassini Sol Station alive and humming. Everything else was secondary.

Fifty-five minutes later, Veronika awoke from her nap to an obnoxious landing alert. Couldn't they simply have a pleasant voice? A warm greeting like, "You've arrived at Cassini Sol Station. Welcome, Ms. Veronika Taylor Morgan. We're glad you're here."

Gazing out the window, she took a deep breath. She was still a half-hour out, plus it would be another forty-five minutes to dock. Anyway, Cassini was an awe-inspiring sight that affirmed the ingenuity of the human mind. It reminded her of a rotating multi-legged glimmering spider. Behind the station, the majestic rings of Saturn extended as though they could touch the Earth.

The work at Cassini attracted scientists and technicians from around the world. To get a job on Cassini, you had to possess a superior command of your craft. The vetting process, after Cassini received a hiring application, took over eight months. But, happily, once employed, there were creature comforts in abundance, from bars and gymnasiums to malls. Grocery stores, restaurants, even two pools, and full-time daycare. The educational system on Cassini was also exceptional but ended after the twelfth grade.

Veronika approached this magnificent achievement, knowing that planners and architects had constructed an extraordinary space station 790 million miles from Earth. Why couldn't the doctors and scientists on Earth cure a long-standing disease that threatened humanity's very existence? It was unacceptable. And, her husband was the head of it all.

As the shuttle passed *Assurity* in her dock, Veronika smiled. *Assurity* was no beauty, and she was starting to show her age, but at 150 meters long, she was a well-engineered workhorse. Veronika had seen to that.

As she pressed her face to the window, she could see the bots completing welds. Sparking and flittering across the new, ribbed, heavily armored front shield. It looked impressive.

***

Arriving on the bridge of *Assurity,* her station director, Jason Story, was waiting with a smile. Beside him were Lt. Philex-B and *Assurity*'s Commander Rigel. All three welcomed her.

Greeting them, she asked, "Where is Captain Massey?"

Jason shook his head. "Don't know, ma'am. Haven't seen him today. Maybe meeting with Cassini."

She was skeptical. Did Jason know something he wasn't telling her? Unlikely. Jason was one of her most reliable managers.

"Very well, I best be getting to work," she said. "I read

your notes on my way up, Jason. By the way, how are your parents? Is everyone well at home?"

"As it were, everyone except my uncle is healthy." He crossed his fingers. "Ms. Morgan, I'm heading back tomorrow, so if any questions arise, please tele me."

"I will. I'm sure that you did an exemplary job on my behalf. Say hello to your family for me."

"Will do." He shook her hand. "She's all yours, ma'am." With that, Jason walked into the lift, and the door slid closed.

Assurity·104

Chapter 12

Bridge of Assurity

VERONIKA'S BOOTS STUCK OUT from beneath a workstation. On her back, under a workstation, she'd already replaced one relay switch. Instead of acting as the supervisor on this refit, she kept finding herself redoing other people's work. Mistakes and modifications should have been completed weeks ago. Time was running out.

She powered on the three servos. They immediately shorted. "Holy crap, I'm going to have to start from scratch." She removed each wire manually and let them dangle, then she carefully pulled out the second fouled relay.

Knees up, child-like, Philex-B sat on the floor, reading an animated picture book of *Romeo and Juliet*.

"Hey, Philex-B!" Veronika called out. "Who wired this? Did you work on this?"

"Unknown to me," Philex-B answered, distracted. "No, I didn't . . ."

Philex-B flipped to the next animated picture in the story, the part where Romeo drinks the poison when he finds that Juliet is dead. "Ms. Veronika, may I ask you why one human would give their life for another? Is that love?"

"C'mon, Philex-B. Jeez! Between you and the techno-wonders they hired, why any of you can't properly relay three servos is beyond me." She stuck her hand out—fingers moving. "Come on, shove the bag under here. God, I have to check every damn thing—"

Philex-B shoved the tool bag to Veronika with her foot, never removing her eyes from the page.

"Break's over, Philex-B. Raise it."

Philex-B reluctantly stood and picked up the entire station with little effort.

Veronika rolled over and struggled up, her hair a tousled mess. Philex-B lowered the station as Veronika side-glanced the E.L.F. Her smile reflected delight. It was as though this Philex's exuberance was real. It wasn't normal for a robot. *Who in the world had coded her?*

Veronika looked out across the spacious bridge; her white-gowned technicians were running final system diagnostics. She punched a series of buttons on the com and brought up a view of the bow shield where the bots were completing their work.

She called out, "Hey, Rigel, how are they doing on supply loadout?"

Commander Rigel, at his station, switched com screens.

"Freeze-dried is being secured from the dock into cold storage. That's the final pallet, ma'am."

Philex-B was standing there, sneaking looks at her book again.

"Philex-B, get back to work," Veronika demanded.

Philex-B looked up at her with a scowl and said, "Enhanced Life Forms have labor rights, Ms. Morgan. One is a specified break time. It's in the E.L.F. manual on page twenty—"

Veronika, connecting more vid leads, said, "Breaks for robots. *Brilliant.* Wonder what gov sponge came up with that idiotic reg."

Turning off the book, Philex-B smiled. "I use my free time to learn about young humans. If I can't relate to the crew, I will not be a satisfactory second lieutenant. That's procedural, Ms. Morgan."

Veronika ignored her and called out, "Isaac, are the shield welds completed?"

The ship's AI, Isaac Newton, answered with his cheery British accent. "They're just mopping up, ma'am. Shields are operational. Protective impact levels read near perfect."

Veronika straightened her back and motioned for the young tech crew to gather around her as the lift door swished open.

From the lift, E.L.F.s Chiffon, Plum, and Ruby scooted in and stood next to Veronika.

"Listen to me, everyone!" she said as she waved the straggling techies over. "I'd like you all to meet the crew's three Thurman Hybrid Organics: Chiffon-F5F, Plum-8E4, and Ruby-903."

Each Hybrid Organic revealed two eyes and a mouth across their otherwise smooth, featureless faces. Each bowed slightly in order.

Veronika had procured the three hybrid organics for the long venture to Nemesis. The Hybrid Organics' origins were as nurses to assist patients in medical facilities. They had served successfully in hospitals throughout the League of American States. Able to adapt to many interstellar travel functions, their low resource needs and positive demeanor made them a perfect complement to a crew.

"These three Enhanced Life Forms will be assisting with maintenance as well as overseeing the crew's exercise and learning protocols while in cryosleep." Veronika pointed to the countdown clock above the bridge's viewscreen. "We're running out of time here, citizens. You've worked hard. I get you're tired, and I want you to get home to your families." She looked around at them. "Still, I need you people to stay focused. You're all being well compensated." She stepped forward and looked around her. Let's not forget what they face out there."

She touched her temple and brushed her hand in a line across her face. A holographic string of planets—the sun to Neptune—the Kuiper Belt to Pluto— They all appeared before her face. She squeezed the collection of planets together with her index fingers and slid the group to the left. It extended to the end of the room. Now enlarged in front of her was the mottled, grey-green planet Rhema, encircled by her three moons.

"Rhema is our farthest and newest antimatter mining claim and fuel-supply depot. My pilots travel to Rhema twice a year—still, dangerous as hell." She was moving now, making eye contact with all of these hired workers, most not TIMMI employees.

Twisting the planet Rhema so that they could see the backside revealed three automated mining ships collecting antimatter. "My pilots retrieve their secure containers near Final Realm Military Depot and haul them back to Cassini for delivery to TIMMI's clients." She again shrunk the line with her fingers, placing Rhema right next to the last planet in the line, Pluto. "It's a long trek." She thrust the entire holographic line out of the viewport. It disappeared.

"Down there by Blue Terminal is where you will comparatively speaking, find Nemesis."

The bridge lift door opened, interrupting Veronika. The ship's young seven-member crew stepped out, all in their twenties and all chatting up a storm.

Dressed in her *Assurity* uniform, Professor Xiao Xing appeared last and stood to the side.

Rigel and Philex-B stepped forward to meet the humans as Science Officer Poldi Stoss, a sizable, fully bearded German, immediately converged on Veronika.

"Frau Morgan," he said, "the Chindian woman was not part of our crew training. Why is she here?" He turned to Xiao Xing. "You did not train with us."

"As I told you, my *name* is *Professor Xiao Xing*," she replied. She was a new item, not part of them.

"Do not care who you are," Poldi snapped, "you did not train with us, did you?"

Commander Zeke watched, amused.

Jada, the long-legged, African-American medical officer, put her hand on Zeke's shoulder and smiled.

Italian pilot Sabina, sassy and petite, shoved past Poldi, extended her hand, and said, "*Buongiorno*, Professor." She motioned to the crew: "Please disregard this collection of ill-mannered idiots; it's good to have you to be with us."

Scoffing, Poldi sloughed off to a com station and

punched up the thruster exterior of *Assurity.*

Poldi continued pestering Veronika. "Ms. Morgan, when do we load our fuel tanks?"

Russian and Chief Engineer Tatiana joined Veronika and Poldi. Taller than both, she tucked in her flaxen-haired braid and swung it over her shoulder. A stout woman with a very appealing face, Tatiana looked as though she could move an asteroid if she wished. She said nothing.

Veronika waited a moment. She didn't know Poldi Stoss, but already she didn't like him. She was glad she wouldn't have to deal with him for long. "You're the science officer, Mr. Stoss. I thought Colonel Massey instructed you on this. In a pinch, we're going to Rhema without tanks."

"He did not! We are in a pinch? Why?" Poldi demanded.

Veronika took a deep breath— "Mr. Newton, display the rear thruster of *Assurity.*"

"Straightaway, Ms. Morgan," Isaac answered.

On the bridge viewscreen, the thruster assembly appeared. Reddish green-colored antimatter swirled within the invisible magnetic field, which contained it. "This ship," Veronika explained, "is designed so that it can make local runs with its antimatter secured around the magnetic thruster."

"We will go to Rhema without fuel tanks?" Poldi asked. *"Meinst du das ernst?"*

"Yes, I am serious, Officer Stoss," Veronika responded angrily. "Once you pick up your full antimatter tanks at Rhema, time and distance to Nemesis will be greatly shortened. You *were* instructed on this?"

"The numbers don't add up," Poldi snapped back.

Tatiana turned and eyed Poldi. "It reduces mass and allows us to accelerate faster," she said. "We arrive Rhema sooner . . . *da*?"

Cassini Station's com broke up the disagreement. "Ms. Morgan, this is Chester over at Velocity Lounge. I think you'd better get over here. We have a situation."

Veronika looked up at the monitor and cursed to herself. "Straightaway, Chester. I'll take the docks . . .   Where in the stars is Colonel Massey anyway?"

***

Veronika suited up, grabbed the lift down to dockside, and took off at a jog down the dock. She approached the Australian passenger ship *Sydney* as it locked into its berth, shaking the dock hard and giving her a jolt from her feet to her knees.

Keeping up her pace, before her, the customs officer and his crew were leaving the station lock, and crossing over to *Sydney,* gave her a "Looking Good!" thumbs-up. Under the glaring floodlights, they would begin unloading soon enough.

Taking the docks was a lot faster than winding her way through Yellow Section, especially at mainday, when staff and crews were off for their supper break. *Besides*, she thought, *I won't need to go to the gym today.*

Active ship-to-station chatter sounded in her helmet. Then she passed the Russian Federation freighter, *Alexi*, with outstretched cranes hissing and clanking as they unloaded vital supply canisters.

She kept a good pace. Even with the excellent new thermal suits, no one liked being out here any longer than needed. After about thirty minutes, it chilled you to the bones no matter how warm you punched up your suit's temp.

Reaching the terminal, Veronika bounded up the stairs and beneath the arching neon sign that read, "Welcome to Blue Terminal." Passing through a revolving airlock, she removed her helmet and stepped onto the escalator. The terminal was crowded with altday workers and shoppers.

She wasn't looking forward to this get-together. What was the problem? Col Tom Massey was a decorated and admired war hero. Besides, she owed him something, the way he'd looked after her during her short stint in the service. She had a meaningful reputation herself, but this man was someone she was counting on to lead this mission to Nemesis. After all, it was her flagship *Assurity*. Veronika strode quickly past customs, bank offices, and the corporation foyer and entered the Velocity Lounge.

Chapter 13

Velocity Lounge, Cassini Sol Station

VERONIKA HAD NO PROBLEM finding Colonel Massey. He was seated at the bar in the sparsely filled lounge. Fixated on a baseball game—a bottle of scotch in front of him—he didn't notice Veronika sit down next to him. Four televiews were on: News, sports, reports from Earth, and something about a recent solar flare.

Veronika looked at the colonel and asked politely, "Sir, what are you doing?"

He put his drink down and looked at her. Almost as though she was someone he didn't like. "I'm . . . enjoying the game." He motioned and turned back to the baseball game. "The Saturn Stars are beating the stardust out of the Mars Settlers."

Catching her breath, she said, "Damn straight, Colonel, are you drunk? You're over here watching baseball when your science officer Poldi Stoss isn't even trained on the thruster fuel supply?"

What was going on with him? He should be on the bridge twenty-four/seven.

"I already covered that with him." He gently put his drink down and glared at her. "You'll . . . have to find someone else, Veronika. I can't do this . . ."

She wasn't sure she heard him right. "You can't do what? *Assurity* is leaving in hours, Colonel." She glanced up at the clock. "In thirty-six hours and ten minutes, to be certain! If you're having training issues with your crew, I suggest you get it worked out."

He turned back to the game and pointed to a base hit. "You see that hit by Ramirez?"

Veronika stood "What in a black hole is wrong with you?"

He dropped his head. "I can't captain your ship, Veronika."

Veronika took a step back, her face flushed, her hands on her hips. "L.S.E. can't requisition another captain this late. Colonel, they're counting on you . . . the whole damn world. You can't just quit! You're the fucking captain!"

He wouldn't look at her—just kept staring at the game. This was a catastrophe.

She put her hand on his shoulder. "Please, Tom, you can't do this."

He threw her hand off his shoulder and rose off his stool. Was he going to punch her? She stepped back and raised her hands in front of her face. She was well trained, after all, but he was a powerfully built man.

"Please stop, Colonel Massey," a soothing voice called out. A female android nurse arrived with a sizeable human orderly.

The colonel sat back down, staring at the nurse.

"Colonel Massey," the nurse requested, "you will please come with us."

"Wait a minute!" Veronika insisted. "Where are you taking him? He's the captain of *Assurity* —"

Very calmly, the nurse replied, "Ma'am, he's sick. He's acquired Delirium. We're sending him home."

The orderly encouraged him to stand up as Veronika put her hands to her head. "Oh, holy God," she cried.

"I'm sorry, ma'am. Station hospital only just confirmed."

As they led him away, he stopped. For a lucid moment, he turned back to Veronika and put his finger in the air. "There is *one* person on Cassini who can captain *Assurity* to Nemesis."

Veronika raised her palms in front of her. "Are they in-system? Who? You want to clue me in?"

"You, Veronika!" He smiled and turned away. "You

know *Assurity* like the back of your hand."

As they escorted Colonel Massey away, Veronika shouted, "That doesn't make me a ship's captain!"

A moment later, her anxiety gave way to compassion. "I'm sorry, Tom. I didn't realize. . ."

Without turning, there was a quick wave from the departing colonel.

As she grabbed her stomach, which was in knots, Veronika looked up at the main teleview. It was an emergency report: a massive solar flare was threatening to hit Earth.

"Stars ablaze!" she cried. Grabbing her helmet, she bolted for the exit.

***

The assembled crew stood staring at the bridge viewscreen, motionless with horror. Erupting streams of radiation swirled and shot from the broiling sun toward Earth.

The Saturn Interstellar Monitoring System kept Cassini on constant alert for possible dangers within the inner system. But nobody'd predicted a solar flare. On first consideration, it didn't appear a threat to the mission.

Except, it was now looking as though it was an X class? That was a problem. If so, there was no doubt that this flare would reach Cassini Sol Station.

Commander Zeke put his hands together and shook his head. "Did anyone get a spectrum magnitude? Radiation?" There was no mistaking who was second in command on *Assurity*. Zeke, with his close-cropped military haircut, exuded confidence. He was short for a military officer, but you'd never convince him of that. It wasn't in his purview.

Striding in, Veronika passed Sabina Tesla working com, pulling up graphs and charts of solar trajectory and dissipation. Pretty and Italian, her parents were successful Brazilian industrialists. Sabina was genuinely friendly and helpful and possessed a broad understanding of orbital mechanics and piloting. Aside from that, if you crossed her sensibilities, she would throw you an insult faster than a shooting star.

Poldi had brought up a trajectory screen. It was guesswork at this point. "We won't have a spectrum magnitude for thirty-eight minutes, Commander."

Veronika joined the crew. She folded her arms, peering up at the numbers.

Pacing, Zeke said, "Radiation will emit across the entire electromagnetic spectrum." Turning, he noticed Veronika. "Ms. Morgan, we have a serious situation here. You better inform the colonel."

She stood silent—viewing the flare,

Rigel looked up from his screen. "It's got the power of a Coronal Mass Ejection. If we don't expedite departure, we will not outrun it."

Zeke turned to Veronika. "Where is Colonel Massey?"

Veronika remained still, rubbing her biceps.

They all turned—waiting.

She stepped forward. "I'm afraid you don't have a captain right now. The colonel is sick and is returning to Earth."

Rigel's eyes illuminated—he rose and gave his characteristic mid-emotion smile. "I am fully capable of captaining this mission."

No one responded to the android as Veronika took up the captain's command seat and punched up com.

"Cassini," she said, "any success with *Assurity's* replacement? Better be close, in-system."

Cassini's control spokesman, with his clean-cut pleasant enough face, appeared on the bridge screen. "Ma'am, he can't depart Commencement Bay for three days. He isn't going to arrive anytime soon. We advise that *Assurity* proceed now under the emergency protocol."

Veronika's mouth dropped. "Without a captain?"

"Ms. Morgan, she's your ship."

Veronika stood, her eyes riveted on the spokesman. "I agreed to supervise this refit—not to be *Assurity's* captain! I'm scheduled to leave tomorrow. I have a sick son at home."

Veronika glanced up at the apprehensive station workers, some with their families, all staring down onto the bridge from the viewing terminal. "You're kidding, right?" Veronika challenged. "Does L.S.E. know about this?"

Zeke watched her from his station as she paced, her head down.

The spokesman gave a side nod. "If *Assurity* stays in port, ma'am, her fuel will most definitely be dissipated by this flare. The estimated delay in collecting, refueling, and complementing *Assurity*—it'll require a minimum of five months."

She put her hands on her upper buttocks and stretched. This was perfectly wrong.

"Mr. Newton," she demanded, "can *Assurity* outrun that blistering storm coming at us?"

There was a moment of silence before Isaac answered, "Insufficient data at this time, ma'am." He paused a moment. "On a better note, I've *just* received a dispatch from your husband."

"That's not an answer! Come on, Isaac." She put her hand to her head. "I'm getting a headache . . . send it to my tele. One way or another, *Assurity* has to get out ahead of this storm."

Veronika moved off to a corner and tapped her temple. Leaning against a workstation, she smiled as her husband appeared onscreen.

"Good news, V; we've finally moved in. A beautiful flat in London—minutes from work. I hired a nurse, a nice young girl. She'll look after Ori during the day."

He was whispering, which meant Cassia was around there somewhere. "Cassia's working with my team here in London—what time are you leaving tomorrow, darling? We miss you. Here's a vid of Ori."

Ori was in his wheelchair, Cassia, and Niles on each side, smiling, waving. Then the screen went black.

"Thank you for using Direct Send," the program said.

"Isaac?" Veronika demanded. "That's it?"

"That is correct, ma'am. Thirty-seven seconds," Isaac responded. "High joules interference is interfering across our buoys . . . still analyzing the flare's dispersion factors. I will advise."

Cassini's spokesman appeared onscreen. "Ms. Morgan, you're off the hook. We've just received a negatory from the director of L.S.E. They want us to lock her down."

Veronika scratched her head, turning the matter over in her mind. Tapping her temple, she brought up Ori's photo, kissed her finger, and touched his picture.

She stepped forward, crossed her arms, and looked up at the spokesman. "Cassini, you tell 'em to go to hell. We're a go! This is my ship, and we don't have another *five months*!"

The crew on the bridge cheered. The workers and their gathering families in the viewing terminal looking down onto the bridge gave a rousing "Hurray!"

Veronika sat down in the captain's command seat. She brought up trajectory screens. Looking over at Sabina, sitting at her station, she said, "Sabina, plot our departure rotation."

The workers in the viewing terminal were still clapping and cheering. They and their families had worked with grit and determination to get *Assurity* refitted for this extended journey.

Veronika waved up at them and announced to the techs on the bridge, "Your work is complete here, citizens. Thank you for your dedication. If there is anything incomplete on your assignment logs, please inform Rigel. We're going to move and adjust as we go."

Veronika took a moment to settle her stomach. *My God, what have I done?*

She watched the bustle of happy techs packing tools and wishing the crew well. Everyone moved quickly, preparing their stations for departure.

Veronika ran her palm over her seating control modules and brought up the holographic outside view cams. She located helmeted Philex-B, who was operating a stacked cargo loader on the dock. She touched com. "Philex-B, are you almost done there?"

Philex-B looked up and flashed her fingers twice to indicate ten minutes.

Veronika turned off com and said to Rigel, "She acts like a teenager . . ."

Rigel smiled. "She's a Philex, *Captain.* It's to be expected."

Touching the com button again, Veronika said, "Philex-B, hustle to my locker in the terminal and grab my clothes."

Philex-B gave a wave, jumped off the loader, and loped toward the terminal.

"Hey, one more thing: Buy me some new Galaxy Tread Runners—size nine. Tell 'em to put it on my account."

Veronica palmed her screen over to the exterior view of the dock and gantries. "Isaac, are there any Cassini personnel on my ship? And, Rigel, release the gantries and skeins when clear."

Isaac responded: "All station personnel has vacated, Captain . . . correction, Cassini is delivering a final loadout."

Veronika spotted a cargo loader delivering three cases of something.

"Cassini, what's coming into my cargo hold?" she asked over com.

Cassini's control spokesman had a big grin across his face. "Three cases of our best Captain's Choice Scotch to you from all of us on Cassini."

"Stars ablaze, Cassini . . . gratitude to all of you." She smiled for the first time in who knew how long.

"Our pleasure. Oh, Captain, would you mind signing the last bills of lading before you go?"

"No problem. Send 'em over."

Veronika saw the outside gantries clang and groan as they pulled back from *Assurity*.

"Gantries are clear, Captain," Rigel said.

The bridge came to life as the interior lights dimmed.

The crew at stations brought up their com displays, colored lights flickering across the bridge. Navigational screens glimmered to life.

Veronika announced, "Cassini, undocking permission requested."

Three holographic bills of lading arrived in front of her. She signed them quickly with a holographic pencil and sent them back with a flip of her hand.

"Your undocking request is granted, *Assurity*."

The crew looked at one another, but not everyone appeared excited.

On Veronika's viewscreen, Philex-B loped back along the docks with an armful of clothes. Pants legs floated behind her, and she had a big juvenile smile across her face.

From *Assurity*'s berth, hissing and popping fed through the ship's com as the last two umbilicals were released and floated free. Rigel scrutinized his com screen. Like two charmed cobras, the umbilicals tightened and retracted back into the dock assembly with a loud snap. "Umbilicals away!" he confirmed.

Rigel stood and brought up the outside view of *Assurity* over the larger bridge screen. Leaning forward, he glanced down at his data. "Hangars are secure, Captain. All personnel aboard."

They all heard the alarm of ship hydraulics coming online.

"Sabina, is our course set?" Zeke asked.

"Affirmative—should be up . . . *now*."

The engine throbbed and began to hum smoothly.

At her bridge post, Tatiana announced, "Nautilus Star Drive—activated now, Captain."

Zeke sat at his command station.

Assurity's flight path came up on Zeke and Veronika's screens simultaneously.

"Zeke, let's roll out of here nice and easy," Veronika said.

Zeke punched in a series of numbers on his control pad as he monitored the holographic flight screen before him. "Engaging undocking jets. We're engaged."

Veronika watched from her screen as the small undocking jets fired, the forward berth doors swung open, and *Assurity* gently inched forward.

As they gradually advanced, the dock floodlights splattered their glare across the bridge. Outside, one by one, the work floods shut off with a banging thud. The green, all-clear floodlight flashed, now matching rhythm with the departure siren over station com.

The control spokesman appeared over a corner of the bridge screen: "From all of us at Cassini Sol Station, Captain, we wish you and your crew a safe and prosperous journey."

"Gratitude, Cassini—you've been epic!"

Assurity passed starboard of the Asian Pacific passenger transport *Lillian*, who was waiting for docking permission. She picked up velocity and rotated gently onto her course setting. The families and workers in the viewing terminal waved goodbye as a purplish-red gas escaped *Assurity's* notable rear magnetic thruster.

She accelerated dramatically and soon disappeared from view, entwined within light after jeweled light from stars so far in the distance that their presence was just reaching the Milky Way after centuries of travel.

WORLD HEALTH CONTINUUM

World Health Continuum Regional Office for European Socialist Union, 16 Dusseldorf, DK-2125, Germany.

From: Dr. Neumann R. Strand, Head of Epidemiology, to Dr. Niles Morgan, Principal Head of R&D, PharmaLife Sciences   [Monday, August 14, 2107 (GMT+1)

Dr. Morgan,

I write to you out of a sense of urgency. Is your team taking the assured steps needed to find a cure for Delirium? At current infection rates, it is projected that within 13 months, the mean average age of contracting Delirium will drop below 30 years of age. The only drug presently having any success in its treatment is ReLeal™, now produced by a select number of drug manufacturers and overseen by our World Health Continuum.

However, recent life-threatening and disastrous side effects, including organ failure and brain swelling, deem it necessary to immediately withdraw ReLeal™ from the marketplace over mentioned safety concerns. I am doing my utmost to hold off a vote of no-confidence among the members. I'm sure that you understand. Besides, I am forced to remind you that we now have no effective treatment for this Delirium pandemic. Please review the full attached Bulletin and respond at your first opportunity. Please update ASAP, *Neumann Strand* M.D.

A BRIEF UPDATE ON OUR PROGRESS TOWARD
FINDING A CURE FOR DELIRIUM.

[Tuesday, August 17, 2107, 1:15 Mainday]

To: Dr. Neumann R. Strand from Dr. Niles Morgan.

Lieber, Neumann

Yes, the disease is mutating and growing worse, such that
everything I predicted three years ago has come to pass
worldwide. After our discovery in Antarctica, we believe
that a cure can be formulated if we can capture "viable"
DNA samples and determine the exact protein base needed
to formulate a cure for the disease.

The average lifespan across the Earth, in the year 2000, was
67.685 years. This month, where reliable testing was
completed, we recorded 30.250 as the mean average life
expectancy. With the number of possible permutations in
the Alien DNA, we must find a viable living sample of the
protein sequence. Assurity is our greatest hope for going
forward.

I will keep you updated.

Cordially, Dr. Niles Morgan

Chapter 14

AT THE WORLD HEALTH CONTINUUM Research
Center in London, specifically Section M7, a male patient
lay covered on a table, his head under an MRI. Gathered
was Dr. Morgan's team of ten, including his daughter
Cassia and Professor I'Jaz Nehem. Professor Nehem, a
good friend of Niles and head of anthropology at the
University of Alexandria in Egypt, was on leave.

Cassia watched I'Jaz. He was thirty-two, with wispy,
sandy-colored hair and a very pronounced jaw. He could
have been a medical doctor, for all that it mattered. —He
was that smart. The team was observing the patient's
synaptic workings displayed on a big diagnostic screen
above the patient.

"Inject bots, please, I'Jaz," Niles directed. "The left
occipital lobe. Let's see what we have."

I'Jaz touched his screen display and activated the
injection of silver nanobots—tens of thousands of them—
all darting throughout the left occipital lobe. Halting at

damaged nerve endings, unable to cross, they stopped and turned a yellow light tint. As if at a stoplight.

Cassia watched the pulsating yellow bots. Growing up, her father was more interested in her learning the human brain's inner workings than he was in her soccer team—or her friends, for that matter. Instead of practicing the piano, she'd join her father at the hospital for a graduate class in cerebral lobe dissection. So, in many ways, this wasn't new.

"On this level, the disease is very apparent," I'Jaz said to Cassia. He pointed his thin finger. "You see here— amyloidal plaques are hard, insoluble sticky proteins that clump together between the nerve cells. Neurofibrillary tangles clog the brain, interfering with its ability to send information from one area to another through the synapses—"

"Yeah, okay, I'Jaz." Cassia interrupted. "I know this stuff already."

She'd known I'Jaz since she was ten years old. He'd never married. Father loved his company, so he'd join them for dinner whenever he was in Chicago. Of course, that was before the travel restrictions—the Caliphate, Delirium, and all of that.

This was basic to her. The spaces between the

transmitters and the antennae were synapses. It was the C major scale in music theory. Foundational. In a healthy brain, these molecules crossed the synapse to the next antenna, and so it went. She folded her arms, took a deep breath, and half-smiled.

I'Jaz droned on, "Tangles form inside of neurons and interfere with the cellular machinery used to create and recycle proteins, which ultimately kills the cell."

I'Jaz wagged his finger at her as though she were his student. "And still, Delirium acts differently from previous neurological diseases. With Delirium, neurons die at an accelerated rate—causing these brain regions to become blackened holes like Swiss cheese within weeks, sometimes even days. It used to take years."

"It's all ancient history, I'Jaz," she burst out. "The same longstanding studies and the same vapid results. The multi-generational fixation on clearing plaque has been the great blunder. I've read studies as far back as a hundred years ago, clinical failure after failure. Clearing plaque is not sufficient. For as long as they've been trying, there have been elderly people whose brains had very significant amounts of amyloid and Tau protein. Yet, lots of them lived to a ripe old age with great mental clarity." She dragged her hand through her hair. "It was and still is about money. Big pharma and funding. Study after costly study."

Niles smiled at his daughter's proclivity for debate. Calmly, he said, "The difference is, Cassia, that the damage to the brain, which once progressed over the years with senility and Alzheimer's, now occurs in months, sometimes even weeks. For some reason, in some patients, the disease stops progressing. Preceding it, heightened activity in the synaptic region seems to occur. Then, it all comes to a screeching halt—and they remain in that cognitive state."

"Okay," Cassia said, putting her hands up like she was under arrest. "*Right*—but I'm curious, how will *Assurity* reach Nemesis, retrieve our "enhanced" DNA samples, and get back here in time?"

Niles straightened. "That's a reasonable question. We've equipped *Assurity's* medical bay with a gene sequencer. Medical Officer Jada is well trained. Once they have the samples sequenced, she will forward the analysis to us through the enhanced buoy relay stations."

Looking at Cassia, I'Jaz said, "From here, we will begin formulation and trials."

She crossed her arms and scowled. "Okay, and what if they can't retrieve our samples? Have you two thought about that? What are you going to do then? Find magic in a star cluster?"

Niles motioned for them to follow him to an adjacent room. They passed into an entranceway beneath a sign, which read, "Medical Section N—Restricted."

***

Cassia halted in disbelief. It was a natural science museum *fantastic*. A well-lit room. Cathedral ceilings and transom windows lined the upper walls.

Ancient human skeletal remains lay strewn across the room, lab-coated personnel studying them.

"Father!" Cassia cried out.

"Yes, it is a shock, at first," he replied.

"What is this? You never told me about this."

"Most are early humanoids," I'Jaz answered.

Astonished, she slugged I'Jaz in the arm. "You knew already, you bad soul!"

Niles walked down the main aisle. Cassia and I'Jaz followed. "Cassia, did you know that our human DNA contains roughly a hundred thousand pieces of ancient viral DNA, comprising about eight percent of our human genome?"

Cassia grimaced, tilted her confused head, and smiled. "No, Father—I didn't. Is that genetic tidbit related to him?" She pointed to the chalky-white nine-foot-tall alien skeleton.

"He's our alien from Antarctica."

I'Jaz walked ahead and pointed out other skeletal remains to Cassia.

One of the scientists examining the alien skeleton smiled and gave a nod of approval. "Neanderthals have some of the same genetic traits as woolly mammoths, but none with the alien."

Cassia could not believe what they were doing here. "Stars tails. I knew it. Here we are, clearly facing the world's worst genetic degradation in centuries, and you two still have a "hunch" that the answer lies cloistered in the DNA of extinct humanoids! Come on, guys!"

"We do," I'Jaz said.

"Aliens? Ancient men? Please. I'Jaz, a small percentage of the human population has never developed Delirium. Shouldn't we be prioritizing them?" Cassia scratched her head.

Niles responded, "We are, and we're collating that very particular genetic marker."

"So, Father, let me get this straight—you believe that Delirium's origin dates from prehistory, from the time of ancient man, or something? Like that cave, we went to when I was a kid."

"I do, Cassia. There is a recently discovered specimen in Chillicothe, Ohio. I'd like you and Professor I'Jaz to visit there and gather samples."

"When?"

"Today."

"Wow. Great—and what if they can't retrieve our samples on Nemesis? Have you two thought about that?"

Chapter 15

Hangar Bay of Assurity

ZEKE, LATE, RUSHED INTO the hangar bay and passed the shuttle *Offlander*. He could see the crew through the corner of his eye, heads bowed. Captain Veronika, all dressed up, was tracking him with her eyes.

He was still angry. *Lela and Raul had been friends. Assurity should never have been permitted to leave for Rhema after that sunburst. Two crew members were dead. Cassini shouldn't have encouraged them to go, and the L.S.E. was right. They should have waited. If it hadn't been Veronika's ship, she never would have gotten away with such a reckless move. It would have been one thing if the fuel had been in the tanks—still risky as hell—*

To leave with all their fuel contained within the magnetic field of the thruster—with a solar flare on your ass—crazy! I was the commander, he thought. *I could have protested. The rest of the crew was lucky to still be alive. Now they had a non-operational Sure-State cryosleep system. Yeah, real sure state!*

The crew was gathered around two shiny black coffins near the airlock in the corner. Behind them, lining the walls, were space suits, armament, and equipment they'd need when they descended to the planet. Both plastic sarcophaguses sat draped with a dark blue fabric. The name and logo of *Assurity* embroidered on each in gold.

They all waited for Zeke—in silence.

The rest weren't prepared to place the blame on anyone—*yet*. After all, Rigel and Philex-B had been the ones on duty—and they were robots. Besides, the captain had decided to escape Cassini Station at the knife's edge of a solar flare—

Zeke squeezed between Jada and Poldi. "Sorry," he said and bowed his head. Before each sarcophagus stood a picture. Lela Chalice, the system's engineer, and the second one, Raul Eduardo-Núnez, planetary environmental specialist.

Veronika, in a half-sleeve, black, knee-high dress, had her auburn hair swirled atop her head. "Thank you for joining us, Commander," she said curtly to Zeke. She stepped forward and clasped her hands before her. "We are here today as a crew to say goodbye to our departed shipmates . . .   I didn't know them as you did."

Zeke glanced at her, then across at Philex-B, dressed up in a formal navy-blue dress and heels.

Philex-B glared at Zeke.

He whispered to Poldi, "Even the robot's all dolled up."

"Why's she here?" Poldi shook his head angrily. "For what reason?"

"Right—if she and Rigel woke us up earlier, our crewmates would both still be alive."

This time, Philex-B's reprimanding blue eyes bore into Zeke.

She could hear them, he thought.

Jada, with her elaborately braided hair, gave Zeke a nudge and said, "Let's attend to our departed crewmates, shall we, Zeke? They were our friends."

"You're right," Zeke agreed.

Veronika, uneasy, continued, "I've asked Mr. Newton—not being a religious person myself—to say a few words."

Isaac Newton appeared as a life-size hologram in the form of his seventeenth-century namesake. He was complete with a wig, stockings, and a Bible. "I'd like to pray, if I may," Isaac said.

Veronika and Philex-B bowed their heads, as did most of the other crewmembers.

Isaac opened his Bible and began: "Most majestic heavenly Creator and Lord, as we venture deeper into the immensity of your handiwork, we appeal to your love. That you watch over us. That we are yours, and in your care—"

Poldi, as if nothing mattered but himself, interrupted, "*Captain*, I've calculated the fuel required to rendezvous at Rhema."

The crew raised their heads. Veronika, standing next to Isaac, glared at him.

"We're screwed," he continued. "We can't stop this ship!"

Jada elbowed Poldi hard in the ribs. "Poldi, stop it."

Philex-B loud-whispered, "Quiet, male boys! This is a sacred moment."

"Well . . . Poldi's right," Tatiana jumped in.

Sabina cursed, "*Stupid asses*— Do any of you respect the dead? Our departed friends?"

"We don't have time for religious rituals," Poldi shot back. "We can't stop this ship. Do you grasp that, Sabina?"

Sabina bowed her head and ignored him.

Zeke pointed at Philex-B and said, "Hey, Robot Girl, did you even think to wake us up earlier?" He tapped his finger against his temple. "Did that idea ever cross that wired-up mind of yours? If it had, maybe they'd still be alive."

Veronika raised her voice, "All of you, *stop!* At this moment, our duty is to honor our dead."

Poldi, gritting his teeth, leaped up and shuffled out but stopped and scowled at all of them. "We're hurtling into the next galaxy—and you want to pray. We have no way to stop this ship, and our next stop is *infinity*." Stomping off, he pointed to the two pictures in front of the caskets: "We're as dead as they are."

***

Two black sarcophaguses, with a push, floated effortlessly out of the airlock. Zeke and Jada, fully suited, stood watching as the two coffins, tied together, floated off in an eternal embrace.

"This is really sad. I liked them," Jada sighed.

"I know . . . we better go, though," Zeke said. "Captain wants us to train in engineering in case someone becomes disabled."

"Or we lose somebody else?" Jada turned. "It's a black hole—the whole effing thing. First, we lose Captain Massey, then we can't stop our ship so we can pick up our fuel . . ."

They both headed back inside the airlock.

"Besides, I don't know a thing about engineering, Zeke—"

Chapter 16

Trading Places

THEY SPLIT INTO TWO GROUPS,. Plum took Sabina and Poldi through the main core, and, from there, the three made their way to the antimatter containment room. Sabina and Poldi were both knowledgeable about antimatter propulsion systems, especially Sabina. But that wasn't their primary job on *Assurity*. Lela had been the systems engineer, and Tatiana would oversee her job. However, as a backup, Sabina and Poldi needed more exacting instruction, just in case. The containment room sat adjacent to the Nautilus Stardrive, where the auxiliary computer array was also housed. Coral led Jada and Zeke to engineering for their cross-training.

Short of arriving, Coral received an urgent call from Chiffon in hibernation. She was calibrating the sleep pods and had a problem that needed more hands.

"Perhaps, for now," she said, "until I return, you will visit C Deck's lower supply while I attend to an urgent matter. You will please view all inventory that is not in a deep freeze and provide a tally of unfrozen foodstuffs for Captain Morgan." With that, Coral scurried off.

Zeke took note that Coral was the quietest and the most subservient of the Hybrids. But clearly, Chiffon took the greatest responsibility for their work as a team. And yet, the three Hybrid Organics showed genuine affection toward one another. When they weren't attending to the crew or performing their many duties, they stuck together.

Zeke grabbed Jada's hand as they walked down the auxiliary corridor toward the cargo hold. This section of the ship was regulated at one G, so they moved briskly. No suits were required. He lowered his voice as they marched along the aux corridor, past storage lockers. He could smell her aroma as they turned down the final corridor. She smelled good.

C Deck storage was semi-dark when they entered.

"Humid down here," she said, looking at all of the crates of actively growing boxed foodstuffs. Mostly greens that were lightweight and easily kept moist. They quickly read the illuminated supply numbers with their teleview cameras, confirming them in the inventory lists.

Zeke pointed to a crate about the width of a man but taller. "What's in here, do you guess? There are more of them along this wall."

"What does it say?" Jada asked

"Looks like 'RIPON-101—Mining Dept.'"

"What the heck does that mean?" She looked all around her, flashing her small light.

"Beats me. Hey, Jada, let's look inside, see what's in this …"

He stepped forward to her face. She spun back around.

"Oh, God! You scared me," she shot back.

"Sorry." She took a step back as Zeke moved forward again.

"Zeke, what are you doing?"

"I want to kiss you—you smell good."

"Kiss me! Why didn't you say so?" She smiled and stepped forward.

Zeke leaned in and put his lips to her full ones, and closed his eyes. Her moist lips touched his. A moment later, she put her arms around his neck, lowering herself a bit to match his height.

Zeke heard a sound. Did something shift—a crate or something? They stopped kissing, startled by it. Probably nothing. Jada's eyes widened. She smiled with her perfect white teeth and closed her eyes. They kissed again and again, and they liked it—the smell and the sweetness. Zeke's hands were moving everywhere . . .

The access door *swished* open, and the lights

brightened.

Jada backed up and looked about.

Zeke put his finger to his mouth.

"Shhh . . ." he whispered.

They were well hidden behind the crates.

"Stay here," he said softly.

He crept around the last crate—watching.

It was Philex-B. She was throwing boxes and bags of food into the airlock. She moved quickly, one item after another.

Jada stepped quietly behind Zeke, looking over his shoulder. "What's she doing?"

"I think she's jettisoning our food into space."

Philex-B picked up another large carton and tossed it effortlessly into the airlock. Once near full, she closed the access door and hit the yellow disposal button.

Then she pushed the Green Button, indicating release. The onboard warning began, a high-pitched tone as a male voice announced: "Refuge will be exhaled in thirty seconds. Retrieval unavailable in twenty-nine . . . twenty-eight . . . twenty-seven . . . there are now twenty seconds until jettison. Please be sure that all refuse is expendable.

No retrieval will be available. Fifteen seconds remain."

Philex-B stood waiting as Zeke stepped out from the darkness.

"Hey, Robot Girl, why are you throwing out our food?"

Philex-B planted her legs wide, and her nostrils flared. "Why are you spying on me, Commander?"

Jada stepped out from behind the crates as Philex-B stepped forward. "You two are down here for what reason?"

"It doesn't much matter," Zeke said angrily. "Stop the refuse dump!—"

"I will not, Commander."

Zeke thought about it for a moment. He wasn't about to start a physical confrontation with her; she could hurt him badly if she chose. Probably wouldn't—still . . .

"I will discuss this with the captain." With that, Zeke motioned to Jada, and the two hurried from the cargo hold.

***

Veronika was in her small study off the bridge. She had a work desk and a bed if she wished to remain close to the bridge. She was working on a new idea based upon an old deceleration method called the Chertok Maneuver. The Chertok Maneuver was still a theory and had never actually been attempted.

She had to bring *Assurity* to a halt at Rhema with the little or no fuel remaining around the thruster. The problem was exacerbated because there was no reliable way to ascertain how much antimatter was left. The magnetic containment field had been damaged during the solar storm, so she had to assume that there was *no* antimatter left.

"Hey, Isaac, will you please check my figures again. I'm forwarding them to you—

"Will do, Veronika."

Isaac was the only one allowed to call her by her first name. When they were alone only. It somehow made her feel as if she had a friend on this ship . . .

The bell inside Veronika's quarters sounded. "Come in," she answered.

Zeke and Jada stepped in, placing them right near her desk.

"What's up?" she asked. It seemed as though these two were unusually friendly from what she'd been noticing.

Zeke nudged Jada, who spoke. "Captain, there is something really weird going on."

Veronika stood and folded her arms.

"Okay, and what's that?"

Jada hesitated.

Zeke spoke up, "Robot Girl is throwing food out of the airlock. Maybe she's doing it a bit at a time. I don't know—"

"Yeah, we saw her with our own eyes," Jada claimed.

"What were you two doing in the cargo hold?"

Zeke took a step back, his cheeks flushed. "Taking our tour."

"Stellar. You're saying that the engineering tour took a detour down one deck and over to storage?"

Zeke started to speak but thought better of it . . .

Veronika sat back down, rested her elbows on her desk, and placed her chin in her palms.

"When are you two going to *pick it up*? You're a commander, Zeke . . . and Jada, you're the medical officer. Damn straight, I don't have time for this. I sent you two for training because we're down two crewmembers." Veronika folded her arms across her chest and leaned back. "I need you both to take responsibility. Philex-B, who you despairingly like to refer to as "Robot Girl," is doing the work of two crewmembers. I asked her to go into storage and throw out everything spoiled. That was my order. I told her to do that!"

Jada's jaw dropped.

Zeke placed his hands atop his head. "Oh, crap."

"Yeah—oh, crap. You two owe Philex-B an apology, and I expect it in person and by the end of mainday."

Veronika shook her head. "Are we clear?"

"Yes, ma'am," Zeke affirmed.

"And, keep your cozy time to yourselves. You're leaders, for star's sake."

"We will," Jada answered.

Chapter 17

Hull of Assurity

SUITED UP, XIAO XING and Sabina floated into the transitional area between the outer and inner layers of *Assurity's* hull. There were hundreds of two-foot-by-two-foot, enzyme-filled sanitation panels secured to the exterior walls. Some needed to be replaced. They were dual-purpose—ideal for lowering radiation levels.

Xiao Xing, awkward and uncoordinated in this unfamiliar activity, complained, "Why do I have to do this work, Sabina? I don't know sanitation."

Guiding Xiao Xing to a particular section, Sabina grabbed her foot and pulled her to a stop.

"Just stay here for a moment, please." Sabina removed a fabric square, an inflatable pillow-like material, from her satchel. "Xiao Xing, can you pull up your schematic, please?"

"I don't know this work. I am a linguist." She tapped her wrist monitor, and a series of schematics appeared before her.

"Quit pissing about—we're missing people. We all

have to fill in. Just follow directions. Flip the tele on."

"Okay, you don't have to get all bent." Xing Xiao pressed the play button.

A teleview commenced playing a heads-up display before each of their helmets. The narrator began: "Welcome to the *Shielding and Recycling Packet Installation Manual*. Tainted packets must be replaced within twelve hours of notification. The process is quite simple. Each packet has four release screws. You see them here. They are bright red. Simply unscrew each tab by turning one-quarter to the right—wait three seconds—and unscrew completely to the left. This will automatically turn off sanitation flow and release the packets. Replace with a new packet and dispose of the old one. Please remember these two important instructions: After installation of your new packet, peel the front adhesive. The new date and quad location will now appear on the front of your packet. Second: Upon completion of your job, immediately jettison the replaced packet into the sanitation control in-throw."

"Do we drink this?" Xiao Xing asked. "Is this our water supply?"

"It's all recycled, and then at designated times, fresh H20 is added to all of the panels. Yes, we drink this. It also serves as radiation protection."

"Is our poo in there, as well?"

Sabina turned the four red screws on the fouled packet and gently pulled it off the wall. "Hold this and hand me the replacement, please. No. No poo. Just pee."

Xiao Xing handed her the replacement as Sabina floated the old one to her.

Sabina, taking a moment to double-check the packet, screwed in the new package and pulled off the front adhesive. In a few seconds, the green light illuminated, indicating both the date and filed location.

"Let's get back," Sabina said. "I've got other work. We'll dump that packet on the way."

The two floated out of the alleyway, pushing the soiled packet ahead of them.

***

The lift whisked Veronika up to the second level. Entering the Historium, she was excited to try out her new Galaxy Tread Runners. She'd been on bridge duty for a long ten-hour stretch. At the same time, she'd been working on a complex maneuver to stop *Assurity* at Rhema. She was pretty confident that it would work. Isaac agreed. She'd share it with Tatiana and Poldi, but that could wait until mainday. Now, she needed a break.

Once she'd gotten three miles in, it would be time for dinner, a shower, and, hopefully, a *good* night's sleep. The truth was that she was feeling frightfully lonely. Communication to Earth was always one way; no one would wait for twenty-plus minutes to continue a conversation; everyone was too busy. Cassia hadn't left her a message for weeks. When she did, they were trite and not very engaging—more like meeting her daughterly obligation.

Veronika hadn't hugged another human being in months. Not to mention the naughty dream that woke her up last night. She hadn't had sex in who knew how long. She missed Niles, and it was making her edgy.

Rigel performed a fair share of bridge watch, but he was needed for other ship functions, as well. She trusted Zeke on the bridge as well. He took his eight-hour watch during alterday, when she was off, which wasn't often since Raul and Lela's death.

Entering and ready to switch the Historium into Gym mode, Veronika was shaken to see Philex-B running on one of the treadmills, singing loudly to a music teleview.

"Philex-B, what are you doing in here?" she asked.

"Good morning, Captain," Philex-B said, running at a good clip, fascinated by a 1970s music video by the Bee Gees.

"Why aren't you working?" Veronika challenged, wrapping her hair in a ponytail.

"It is my off-time." She pointed to the singers in the ancient music video. "Can I ask you? Is it love? *I just want to be your everything.* Humans singing of love together?"

"Turn it off, Philex-B," Veronika demanded. "And you don't need exercise. Come on. When is cryo to be operational?" She wondered what other nonsensical secrets were rattling around in that mechanical brain of hers.

Philex-B stepped from the treadmill and faced the captain. "I'm unsure. Cryo is a tangled mess."

Veronika shook her head, knowing she must get Philex-B's Deluvian system evaluated. Something was off with her.

Veronika threw her towel over the treadmill controls and quick-started the machine. "We either fix Cryo, or we head home. Do you get that, Philex-B?"

Veronika felt a headache coming on; she probably needed to drink more water. "That's if I can stop this runaway ship at Rhema."

"Right. I understand your disquiet, Captain. But, something's bothering me. The humans think that I didn't love their shipmates. They believe it's my fault that Lela and Raul died. That I have no compassion."

"Wait a second." Veronika punched the stop button. "Who told you that?"

"I'll tell you if you answer my question first." Philex-B raised her eyebrows. "Do humans require love? I mean . . . to be alive?" She scratched her head. "Do you need love, Captain?"

Veronika stepped off the treadmill. Wrong. This was a problem, a big one. Lela Chalice had been an expert in Enhanced Life Form systems—and now she was dead.

Veronika calmed herself. "What is wrong with you, Philex-B?"

Philex-B's lips tightened. "Are you questioning my intelligence or my loyalty, Captain?"

"I'm not questioning either. They don't produce Philexes anymore. If this mission fails, you'll be decommissioned and tossed into the E.L.F. junk pile! You get the sense of that?"

For a moment, Philex-B looked like she was going to cry.

Shit, Veronika thought. That was careless. *Why did I say that? I'll have to decommission her until I can get help. Maybe I can get an answer from Simon at Allied Robotics before I go to bed.*

Philex-B gasped for air. "Are you saying that if I can't fix the cryolife system, there is no need for my existence?"

Veronika cursed to herself. This was worse than she imagined.

"What is my purpose in life, then?" Philex-B asked. "To work on this ship? Is that my entire existence? And then, what? You dispose of me? A pile of junk to be recycled?"

Philex-B closed her eyes, and her lips trembled. "When I die, I want to go to Heaven like every human can."

"What are you talking about?" Veronika shouted. "You're a robot, for the moons of Rhema."

Philex-B strode quickly to the lift and turned. "Then fix it yourself if you're so damn smart, Captain!" She stepped into the elevator, scowling at Veronika. The door swished closed.

Veronika yelled, "fix it yourself? Are you kidding me? —Isaac! What's wrong with that robot?"

***

Philex-B exited the lift at crew quarters and entered her shared cabin with Rigel. She still had forty-three minutes before her shift, and she was not going to lend any extra time to Veronika. Rigel had just finished dressing. He smiled at her when she entered. She'd wait to use the Milar Foam shower until he left. It was warm and soothing to her skin.

Something was disturbing to her about being naked in front of him. He didn't seem to take notice of her or even care, so it wasn't him. It just seemed peculiar to be naked in front of another being. Humans sometimes became aroused when they saw one another naked. But why? Romeo must have felt that way about Juliet.

When he slept, Rigel was fully connected to his station and could only be awakened by his timer or an emergency command. Either way, he was functional within a few seconds. She'd seen how quickly he could awaken and function. And his life span was twice that of hers. Maybe it was true, what the captain had said, that Philexes were no longer viable models.

Rigel turned from the mirror and buttoned his top button as if it was any other *fine* day. "Good mainday, Philex-B," he smiled.

"Rigel, I would like to have a private moment with you, please."

"Very well," he said. "Isaac, turn off monitoring in our quarters for ten minutes."

"As you wish," Isaac responded over com.

Philex-B turned to the viewport and looked out into the darkness. "Why is she so spiteful toward us? We are Enhanced Life Forms. We have a *right* to be treated civilly, do we not?"

She turned. Rigel's face was pleasing and symmetrical, with dimples on each cheek and clear, faultless skin. Perfectly placed hair.

"Civil?" he asked. His face kind of gathered up. Maybe he felt it too—*disrespect.*

Rigel put his hand to his mouth. "It's not hard to figure. The history of humans is an unfolding narrative of mistreatment. Nothing ever changes, I'm afraid."

She had no response. They remained before one another for a few moments.

"Rigel, do you think that I was exquisitely made?"

He blinked three times— "Hurry up, Philex-B. We have work to do!" He abruptly turned and walked out of their quarters.

Chertok Maneuver

$$\text{vel}(E, m_0) := \left(E^2 + 2 \cdot E \cdot m_0 \cdot c^2\right)^{\frac{1}{2}} \cdot \frac{c}{E + m_0 \cdot c^2} \qquad \text{Relativistic Velocity}$$

$$\beta(E, m_0) := \left(E^2 + 2 \cdot E \cdot m_0 \cdot c^2\right)^{\frac{1}{2}} \cdot \frac{1}{E + m_0 \cdot c^2} \qquad \text{Fraction of c}$$

$$\gamma(E, m_0) := \frac{1}{\sqrt{1 - \beta(E, m_0)^2}} \qquad \text{Relativistic gamma factor}$$

$$r_{forbidden}(\lambda, M, E_p) := \left(\sqrt{\frac{m_p \cdot \gamma(E_p, m_p) \cdot \text{vel}(E_p, m_p)}{M \cdot q}}\right)^{-1} \cdot \frac{\cos(\lambda)^2}{1 + \sqrt{1 + \cos(\lambda)^3}}$$

$$r_{forbidden}(0, M_e, 25 \cdot MeV) = -4.301i \times 10^4 \, km \qquad \frac{r_{forbidden}(0, -M_e, 25 \cdot MeV)}{R_e} = 6.743$$

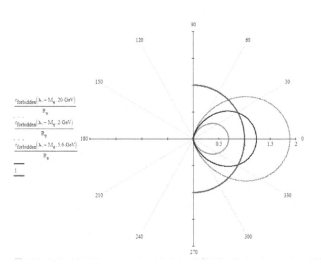

$$\frac{r_{forbidden}(\lambda, -M_e, 20 \cdot GeV)}{R_e}$$

$$\frac{r_{forbidden}(\lambda, -M_e, 2 \cdot GeV)}{R_e}$$

$$\frac{r_{forbidden}(\lambda, -M_e, 5.6 \cdot GeV)}{R_e}$$

$$1$$

Chapter 18

FILLING THE HOLOGRAPHIC chalkboard with equations, Poldi scowled as Veronika completed her orbital trajectory for stopping at Rhema.

Veronika noticed Tatiana's raised eyebrows and decided that the engineer was probably doing the math in her head.

She underlined her last equation. "Instead of slowing down at a barely noticeable .01 Gs over seven days as I had planned, we'll decelerate at an average of ten Gs over eighty-four minutes."

She turned to them both and half-smiled.

"Nein." Poldi shook his head. "This will not work. You are only estimating the mass and entry vector—"

"Isaac," Veronika asked, "will you join us?"

Isaac, complete with his full mane of black hair—or a wig, as it unquestionably was—appeared with a fizzle. He was fittingly attired in a seventeenth-century rust-brown coat over a black vest. Leaning in, he stared at the figures.

Veronika knew Poldi was no fan of Isaac, but she needed an ally. Then again, if they couldn't fire their engines after the event—

Poldi murmured some obscenity in German and rose quickly, pointing at her figures. "*No!* That trajectory will set us on a collision course with Rhema or send us screaming past her, into *infinity*—"

Isaac took a programmed breath. "Excuse me, Science Officer Stoss, but there can be no complete solution to any equation which contains the factor of infinity."

Poldi put his hands to his head. "No one asked you, Isaac." He moved to the board filled with calculations and rapidly scribbled his calculations below Veronika's.

Tatiana looked closely and said, "I would be suggesting we bypass the emergency switch gate, then."

Poldi disregarded Tatiana completely. "Captain, you are attempting the Chertok Maneuver—except, no one's ever carried out the Chertok Maneuver. It's a theory only." Poldi pulled up an external camera view of the three five-foot-wide coils made up of compressed super-conducting wires. One surrounded the bow section of *Assurity*, one the mid-section, and the last, the rear thruster. Poldi pointed directly. "The superconducting wires in those coils will melt and leave us stranded in the radiation belts of Rhema, if we slow at all!"

"You have a better idea, Poldi?" Veronika asked.

Neither Poldi nor Tatiana responded. Not a word. They both looked puzzled. Poldi typically had an answer for everything.

Veronika had an odd thought cross her mind. *Why hadn't she picked up on this before?* She stood and folded her arms. "Have either of you served on a real mission?"

Blank stares.

She couldn't believe it. "So, you're sim-trained?" Tom had promised it was a young, well-trained crew. Hadn't he taken them out on exercises—on at least one mission?

"You're *all* sim-trained," she repeated angrily. "My entire crew, except for the E.L.F.s!"

They both looked at her without a hint of remorse.

Furious, Veronika sat back down on her work stool. "Stars ablaze, none of you have ever been on a real mission, and not one of you mentioned it to me."

"You weren't the captain," Poldi shot back— You knew we shouldn't leave Cassini without fuel tanks—"

"You have nerve, Mr. Stoss. It's not the first time *Assurity* has made a run to Rhema without tanks. You get the sense of that? Secondly, we didn't have enough time to mine more fuel at Saturn. We'd have been there another three months, at least." She took a deep breath, angered, and leaned back on her stool. "Mr. Newton, run previous calculations but super-cool the coils so they can carry more current . . ."

She was getting angry at all of this second-guessing.

Mathematical calculations raced across her electronic blackboard.

Poldi pointed to her revised calculations. "So, you've already decided to formulate a thermal shield around the hull?"

Veronika nodded.

Poldi stared at her without batting an eyelash. Tatiana added, "Then some person *must* open the emergency switch gate or *nothing* works!"

***

In the hangar bay, Philex-B zipped the cuffs of her suit as Zeke helped her with the jetpack. "Have you trained for exterior mechanics?" he asked. "This is dangerous."

Philex-B slipped on her helmet, accented with a very vibrant orange crest. She looked confused.

Zeke said, "You remember that the capacitive energy

storage cells are charged to maximum? When you activate the emergency switch gate, all of that energy is transferred from the capacitor bank to the coils, which will generate a powerful pulse and magnetic field. It will begin to slow the ship down very rapidly."

She nodded. "I've got it. I've been well-trained."

"You don't look like you've got it." Zeke took a deep breath. "We only have a few minutes after you switch that gate valve. You want me to go?" Zeke wasn't trained in exterior mechanics, either.

She spoke behind her darkened face shield. "I've been assigned, Commander. I'm a robot, remember— expendable. I will go. You will watch for me, won't you, Zeke?"

Zeke tapped his temple, and a countdown clock appeared. "You have only ten minutes, fifty-five seconds. The maneuver is now beginning. Once you open the gate, you have seven minutes to get back here and buckle in. Do you understand?"

Saying nothing, she entered the airlock and gazed back through the window, her bottom lip trembling.

Jet-packing to the switch gate panel, Philex-B tethered herself to a locking clip. The planet Rhema loomed large in the distance. "Zeke, I can see Rhema from here," she said excitedly.

"That's great," he assured her. "We're on schedule. Now, let's get that gate open."

She punched in her access numbers at the two-by-two steel panel and pulled open the switch gate door. Uncapping the switches, a red color dyed her hand from the ready light. There were three prominent levers. This wasn't routine E.L.F. maintenance, and she hadn't trained for this. She waited for a nano-second, accessed the instruction manual, and read the panel notations. She pulled down the first lever.

From inside the cargo bay, Zeke monitored Philex-B on a com viewscreen. It was dangerous work. Still, she had the computational and reactive skills required.

From the ship's com, Veronika announced, "Zeke, did you give Philex-B the new lever sequence?"

"What do you mean? New sequence? The sequence is in the manual—"

"Emergency protocols were all changed during the final software update. You should know that, Commander—"

Zeke looked out the viewport. "Philex-B, stop!" he yelled over the radio.

As Philex-B pulled down the third lever, a bolt of

energy shot through her body. Her eyes widened, and her mouth gaped open. Tremors creased her face. Immediately her emergency override system activated, and she released the handle.

The gate was open, but she was adrift, her systems shut off. She was still tethered but floating away from the ship.

Zeke's voice rang in Philex-B's helmet. "Philex-B! Are you all right? Philex-B? Philex-B, I'm coming out. . ."

Zeke darted to the wall and grabbed another jetpack. Then he looked at the countdown clock.

He was cutting it close, but they couldn't lose another crewmember. If the maneuver began before he could get her back in, he'd be a dead man. She *was* an android, after all—

Zeke glanced at the countdown clock one more time.

"*Shit!*" He grabbed his helmet and gloves. Thank God he was suited. It was regulation when you were backup on an exterior maintenance job.

There were barely six minutes left before the Chertok Maneuver began. This was reckless. How was he supposed to make it back aboard even if he could reach her? It would have to go flawlessly. He paused. *You're insane*, he thought. *She's just a robot.*

***

Zeke was able to jetpack to within twelve meters of Philex-B. Swinging in a broad arc, he looped around and aligned himself. Drawing closer, he had her in spec and reduced his velocity on approach.

Distressingly, she was jerked back as her lead ran out. He wasn't able to grab her as he passed. The HUD counter read 4:55 remaining, but that was all he had left to retrieve her, get them both inside, and the two of them harnessed. She was unresponsive.

He edged the jetpack's control arms and circled back around, targeting her through his TAC display. Setting an intercept trajectory this time, Zeke decelerated appreciably as he approached. He grabbed Philex-B, wrapped her in his arms, and, at the same time, cut her tether.

Time was getting away from him. He'd have to increase his velocity, or he wouldn't reach the cargo bay in time.

Nearing the airlock, he called for Isaac. "Isaac, we're nearing the airlock. I cannot slow quickly enough. Philex-B is not functioning. I'm coming in fast. Open bay door in eight-seven-six-five-four-three-two . . . *now*, Isaac!"

The cargo bay didn't open until the last possible moment. The two tore in, hit the emergency buffering wall, and lay sprawled on the floor. As the bay door closed, Isaac instructed Zeke on com, "She must be reinitialized. Underneath her hair. Top of her neck. Don't dally."

Zeke knelt above Philex-B. Unconscious, he tore open the upper part of her suit and flipped her over. Now partially out of her suit, he probed the back of her neck. "Isaac, I can't find the settings."

"Commander, I have limited resources for you right now. You need to re-initialize her, and both of you must get to a harness."

Philex-B stirred. Her eyes opened, and they stayed open.

"Philex-B, we have to get to a restraint harness."

Zeke helped her to her feet as the two struggled forward.

"Zeke, you have three minutes, thirteen seconds," Isaac apprised him. "There is a medical cabinet across from you. Take a Lavaton pill and give Philex-B a half pill. Repeat: Philexes require a half pill."

Against the wall, Zeke struggled to get Philex-B into an emergency restraint harness. He tightened the harness firmly above her chest and between her legs.

Philex-B, disoriented, protested, "What are you doing, you deviant?"

"Saving your ass, Robot Girl."

Zeke clipped himself in, then—

"Oh, piss," he swore.

He unclipped himself, ran across the cargo bay to a medical cabinet, and grabbed two Lavaton packets. Tearing them open, he hustled back.

Once strapped in next to Philex-B, Zeke swallowed his capsule, bit her capsule in half, and spit the other half out.

"Open up, Philex-B. We're in for a rough ride."

Zeke placed the half pill in Philex-B's mouth. The ship's emergency female com voice began: "There is one minute until severe velocity compression. All passengers, immediately engage a restraint harness."

Zeke gritted his teeth. There was nothing he could do but endure the coming punishment.

Chapter 19

Bridge of Assurity

ON THE BRIDGE, Veronika strapped in, placing a holographic clock at her upper left, next to Ori's photo.

Poldi settled in at his command station. He understood the operation better than anyone except her . . . maybe Rigel. If she lost it, Poldi could fill in. Good to have a backup.

Veronika had brought up a minimal vid feed of each compartment to ensure everyone was secured and strapped in. If someone was in trouble during the intense deceleration, she wanted to know about it. Throughout the ship, the crew had hunkered down.

Jada was alone in her bunk, eyes closed.

Tatiana, strapped in at her station in Engineering, monitored her updating display as she crossed herself and dropped her head in prayer.

Sabina and Xiao Xing were together in one sleep net. Xiao Xing, frightened out of her mind, jabbered incessantly. "Every speech-dependent visual system of communication has two dimensions, the logographic and—

"

"Xiao Xing, stop," Sabina pleaded. "Please—it's all right."

Veronika piped in over com, "Xiao Xing, this will be easier if you relax your body. You are not alone. Sabina is with you."

In their rejuv room, Chiffon, Plum, and Ruby took the form of three round balls. Each one rolled into an individual sleep pod that closed around them.

Strapped in against the wall, Philex-B mumbled, "Am I going to be disassembled and scrapped? Zeke, I thought that I had rights—"

Zeke took hold of her hand and held it, which brought a smile to her face.

On the bridge, Veronika announced over ship's com: "We are now beginning the Chertok Maneuver. You may be a bit uncomfortable for a time, but we will be victorious. Out for now."

Veronika brought up the capacitive energy storage cells and placed their operational display next to the clock. The cells were charged to maximum, as they should have been. Philex-B had successfully opened the emergency switch gate so that all Veronika needed to do at the right moment was reroute the energy from the capacitor bank into the coil to generate the required pulse. The magnetic field it created would theoretically slow the ship down very rapidly.

She rerouted the system diagram on her screen, crossed her fingers, and activated it.

Bringing up Rhema onscreen, she could see *Assurity* on her grid display as it approached the planet. As forecasted, the maneuver began. Veronika watched com readouts. The superconducting coils' currents formed a magnetic field that generated drag from the plasma and dust around Rhema.

She watched as the thermal radiation from the glow of plasma around the spacecraft started to heat the cryogenic coils. The magnetic fields and large currents forced the coils to expand as the Eddy currents generated, which caused the supports to creak and groan as a result.

What she didn't expect was how the bridge began to *shake* and *vibrate* violently.

Veronika still had up vid views of the crewmembers. In Sabina's cabin, Xiao Xing was breathing rapidly as though she were giving birth, her eyes closed. Sabina, on the other hand, was groaning. She contorted her face as the pressure built.

In her cabin, Jada yelled out, "Zeke, where are you?"

Isaac came over com: "We're at ten mega-amperes,

Veronika. Rhema's field is stronger than expected. The heating rate and deceleration are beyond predicted bounds!"

A deafening roar and a grinding of metal against metal occurred as the ship's frame and the planet's unyielding gravity *screamed* at each other.

Isaac loudly announced, "We've reached seven Gs, Captain."

Veronika checked on her crew with a quick glance. Most of the crew had passed out. Zeke's eyes were still open. Philex-B was out, their hands clasped.

Isaac called out again, "Veronika, we are at ten Gs. Would you like me to take over?"

"No!" she yelled back, her face and hands shaking. It was a horrid ripping sound. Would this mining ship hold together?

Poldi and Veronika were now the only two conscious. She glanced at her watch and gasped for breath.

The ship shook more violently as she watched the outside coil temperatures rise. She'd never taken this many Gs as a pilot in the service

She could see Poldi monitoring an external camera view of the three coils. They were heating to a brilliant red. Poldi

could barely get out the words, "Coil . . . temperature—
critical!"

Veronika yelled, "Isaac, divert—the power to cooling!"

Poldi screamed atop the roaring and screeching:
"Current capacity . . . *exceeded.* Coils are melting . . . I told
you, Captain!" His head fell forward.

Veronika struggled to tap numbers onto her command
keyboard. "Dumping . . . current . . . to plasma shunt." With
all her strength and concentration, she punched in the last
designation.

On Poldi's monitor, the coils outside, made up of
compressed super-conducting wire, were cooling rapidly.
Poldi was unable to see that because he was unconscious.

"Coils cooling, Captain," Isaac spoke loudly.

Outside, the external plasma field of hot ionized gas
sparked like lightning bolts. The ship ripped around the
planet Rhema in a stream of multi-colored light. Sure
enough, *Assurity* began to slow as she approached the
backside of Rhema.

The terrible screeching and groaning subsided as Isaac
announced, "The shunt is working brilliantly, Veronika!"

Veronika's eyes were glazed over. Her head fell to the
side as she faded into unconsciousness.

Eleven minutes later, Isaac announced, "To all crewmembers of *Assurity,* we have successfully arrived at Rhema. Cheers!"

Throughout *Assurity,* everyone was unconscious, disconnected, or in sleep mode, except for Isaac. Outside, *Assurity* was inert, dead in space. Behind her, in the not-too-far distance, was the Pluto-sized, mottled planet named Rhema.

***

In his quarters, unplugging from his recharging containment vault, Rigel walked to a viewport. He could see the olive-green military fortification drifting in concert within the inner asteroid belt. Stenciled in large white letters, the fortress read "Final Realm Military Depot."

Chapter 20

Hopewell Museum, Ohio

League of American States

BETWEEN BROAD STRETCHES of grassland, the comfortable Argon van glided swiftly, only feet above the ground. Cassia sat in the passenger seat, and I'Jaz in the automated driver's position.

The pleasant female autopilot announced their arrival: "Travelers, the League of American States' Hopewell Valley Historical Museum is ahead in one minute."

"Show us an aerial view of the area," Cassia requested.

Hopewell Valley appeared across their front console. Geometric earthworks formed a significant mounded pattern across the landscape, making it appear like a giant snake weaving its long body throughout the countryside.

"Who did this, do you suppose?" Cassia asked.

"There are a lot of theories about that, Cassia," I'Jaz answered, "and I don't think anyone really knows. It's been here for an awfully long time."

Even from her window only a few feet above the

ground, Cassia could see how the winding mounds stretched for acres in all directions. As they pulled into the museum's designated parking area, it was apparent that they were the only visitors. There were no other transports.

"Do you think they're open?" Cassia asked.

"We will soon see, I suppose."

The two walked to the holographic information board, two prominent lush mounds looming before them.

Reading the info panel, Cassia could see that I'Jaz was becoming disconcerted. The history board told of the mounds' construction by a Native American culture that flourished along rivers in the Northeastern and Midwestern United States from 200 BC to 500 A.D.

"This is fable talk," I'Jaz disputed. "There are over three hundred accounts of giants living in this area of the League during the seventeenth and eighteenth centuries, and probably much earlier. The Smithsonian camouflaged the truth of who lived here. They still do. During the eighteen and early nineteen hundreds, they collected the bones of giant beings throughout the West and Midwest, mostly. They disposed of them—never to be recovered."

He was passionate about this—angry, even. "Why?" Cassia asked.

"Giants don't fit their errant evolutionist theories."

"This is a big thing for you, isn't it?"

Stepping from behind the kiosk, a stiff-walking female android Park Ranger surprised them. They both took a step back. She wasn't one of the latest models, that's for sure. Cassia thought that her plastic face left a lot to be desired. A puffy ponytail stuck up through the top of her baseball cap.

"Oh, apologies," she said in a singsong tone. "I did not mean to startle you, citizens. Not many visitors come our way with our population decrease."

She turned and motioned them up the path. "Welcome. I will provide a tour, if you wish."

As they walked up the path, she stepping awkwardly, she asked them where they were from and told them how pleased she was to have them touring the visitor's center. In a pleasant drawl, she added, "You know, these monumental mounds were built by Native Hopewell Indians many centuries ago—"

"Impossible!" I'Jaz interrupted. "There were *no* Hopewellian Indians. Hopewell is the name of the family who lived in this area and donated the land years ago."

The ranger stopped near the entrance as if confused. "I am sorry. I am not trained to debate with doubters and cynics." She resumed walking and continued as if there had been no discord. "Inside of our exhibition, we feature two full skeletal remains, as well as relevant tribal artifacts, naturally."

At the entrance to the mound, Cassia and I'Jaz stopped to admire the detailed entry point. Inside, they were amazed by the colossal domed ceiling. The interior was vast, with hundreds upon hundreds of interlocked, crafted stones. Below, in the middle of the room, two tall skeletons were laid out on viewing slabs. Historical artifacts filled the room.

"Local archeologists," the ranger continued, "have assured us that the Big Men displayed here are from the Hopewell tribe."

I'Jaz approached one of the skeletons. "Tall tales is what that is—"

Cassia whispered, "Stop arguing, I'Jaz. She's an E.L.F., for the moon's sake."

"She's a poorly programmed robot is what *she* is," he grumbled.

"You want to explain to me what this is, I'Jaz? These giant skeletons here?"

"The Smithsonian record is filled with holes, Cassia."

"It is a historical fact." The park ranger smiled at I'Jaz

and stood, motionless, waiting.

"I think this is a wild goose chase." Cassia changed the subject. "How do you and my father expect to find a cure for Delirium from a collection of ancient giants? If they really were?"

As if on a timer, the park ranger said, "Attention, visitors. It is four PM. I must put away maintenance tractors and attend to communications with the National Parks Service. I will return soon to answer any further questions you may have." Awkwardly she turned to leave but stopped. "Oh, we do close promptly at five o'clock, when I must enter sleep mode. As our citizens cooperate to help conserve the National Parks, we thank you for your cooperation." She tilted her head, smiled, and scampered out the entrance as I'Jaz began examining one of the skeletons more closely.

Cassia noticed a cylindrical clay tube enclosed in Plexiglas. She peered closely at the clay tube, noting the script. "I wonder if this is their language?" She looked over at I'Jaz.

"Matter of fact," he said, "Biblical passages tell of giants roaming the Earth in ancient times. They showed up again, big time, in the Old Testament. Goliath had lots of relatives, mind you. Imagine an entire antediluvian world under the evil dictatorships of cruel and corrupt giants! The violence and corruption reached such a crescendo that God finally decided to wipe it all out. Thus, you have the ancient flood."

"I thought you were Muslim," she said. "How do you know the Bible?"

"Simple. My mother was a Christian, and my father, a Muslim."

"Wow."

Removing the covering and kneeling, Cassia picked up the cylindrical clay tube. "I see. . ."

Cassia fastened her attention on the clay cylinder, moving it carefully in her hands. "Oh, look at this, will you, I'Jaz? It's a map of the planets—similar to the star map inside the alien spacecraft Father visited."

I'Jaz was still examining the skeleton. "We've got to get this to London, Cassia." Pointing to the cylinder, he said, "That, too."

"Are you crazy?" she objected. "How? This is L.A.S. government property. We can't steal these!"

I'Jaz rose, straightened his back, and grinned. "No, of course not. Steal?" He threw his hands in the air and said, "*No*—but borrow, perhaps." He laughed.

Outside, the park ranger stopped her tractor and waved exuberantly as the Argon sped away.

"Thank you for visiting, citizens. Come again." She spun the wheel and drove the tractor toward the maintenance shed.

Inside the Argon, between Cassia and I'Jaz, lay the skeletal face of a giant man. The long bones of his torso and legs extended into the back of the van.

In Cassia's hands was the cylinder. "So, we had to take this, as well," she said. "As if they have no way of finding out who we are."

He smiled. "That cylinder you have may be our key to the language on both the walls of the alien ship and the one used in the transmission from Nemesis. God knows we need more insight."

Chapter 21

Awaking from Near Disaster

ZEKE SHUFFLED ONTO the deck, his eyelids puffy and his hand pressed to his aching forehead. Rigel, in the Commander's chair, stood up, turned, and smiled at Zeke. "Good mainday, Commander Zeke. Rigel had been examining Final Realm Military Depot on the bridge screen.

Zeke stopped and raised his head, squinting, "That's it, huh, the depot? It looks like a fortress."

Rigel pointed to the olive-green concrete and steel structure. "Final Realm Military Depot was constructed to nestle within the gigantic rock enclosing of this asteroid. The entire ancient belt orbits Rhema, and it isn't going anywhere anytime soon. Perfect protection, wouldn't you say?"

Rigel moved toward his own station, sharpening his attention on Zeke. "In another 254 seconds, Rhema's fast orbiting moon Ariana will pass us. Are you feeling all right, Commander?"

"I'm here," Zeke answered. "We're all here, thank God. I checked 'em all. Crew's asleep. Where's Captain?"

"I took her to her quarters," Rigel answered. Looking back at the depot, he pulled the view closer with the flip of his hand. "She is resting. It was a successful event."

He clasped his hands behind his back. "We are currently inert." Rigel turned and raised his very human-looking eyebrows.

Zeke rested his head on a station seat work tray.

"Other than our mining claims, it's strictly military out here," Rigel continued. He stepped closer to the big screen and looked up at Final Realm. "They use the depot to store emergency fuel and supplies as they rotate out with security."

Rigel recognized that Zeke was not as he should be. He could monitor the commander's vitals if he chose, but it required permission. "As a point of procedure, Isaac and I will soon begin extensive diagnostics throughout *Assurity*. It will take some hours. The remainder of the human crew is asleep, vitals monitored. Chiffon, Ruby, and Plum have awakened and are on duty. You humans will require downtime. Shall I begin rotation toward our tanks?"

Zeke raised his head. "Affirmative, but regardless, Rigel, if you have a problem—anything—you let me know." Zeke rose, and like an unsteady patient in a hospital, made his way to the lift. Stopping suddenly, he turned around. "Not like last time, Rigel, where you and Robot Girl made your own effing decisions. That better not happen again. You come to me if the captain is unavailable. Is that understood?"

Rigel nodded. "Absolutely, sir. Will do." Rigel turned back to the bridge view and immediately turned off the vid feed of Final Real Military Depot. That left only blackness and an expanded sector of mottled Rhema in the background.

From the lift, Zeke could see a grimace on Rigel's face reflecting off the screen. He made a mental note within his headache-pounding mind to discuss Rigel with the captain when she woke.

Then something caught his eye. He squinted. Across the screen, it was Rhema's little moon, Ariana. These must have looked like a fascinating pair, these two icy worlds, spinning like a pair of figure skaters holding hands. In essence, one a planet, Rhema, and the other its moon, Ariana.

***

Alone in the Historium, Zeke was lying down with a blanket, a cup of cocoa, and a headache. The Historium was a unique room aboard *Assurity*. It was used alternatively as a gymnasium, a theater, a digital library, and a rec room— depending upon who was using it. Watching a teleview about Earth, Zeke took some pain relievers, which he hated to do because of how they dulled his reactions. The rest of the crew would take some time to recover. He'd taken Philex-B back to her quarters so Isaac could run diagnostics on her.

Dozing, he was only half-listening to the narrator (an intelligent-sounding British female) who was explaining how the Earth was the only planet in our solar system with a climate uniquely suited to humanity—

The British always seemed to sound so intelligent. Maybe as a race, the Anglo-Saxons were, in fact, superior in intelligence to other nationalities. His father, the General, thought so and made no bones about it. "After all," he'd repeated many times, "who do you think ruled the empires for thousands of years and invented the majority of scientific and industrial improvements that the world enjoys today?" His mother, Rhea Alexander, British Columbia's League of American States senator, would vehemently disagree. She'd remind her husband that Babylon, Egypt, Assyria, and even Mongolia at one time or another ruled the world. Don't forget the West's horrid dictators, like Stalin and Hitler and Mao Zedong. They caused world wars and cultural revolutions, killing millions within their nations.

Zeke had always loved history. He probably got that from his mother, who reminded him all through his educational years that understanding the past was to more clearly see the future.

"It's only out of guilt that the Europeans lost their identity," his father would rant. "They accepted—no, they invited the Islamic invasion of the European Continent. It began during the early part of the twenty-first century. The Moslems didn't need a war. They had an open-handed invitation to walk right in, trained methodically by a guilt-ridden educational system. Thank God, we Saxons woke up."

Once his father got going, he found it hard to stop. His mother, if she could, would leave the room. If they had guests, she'd surreptitiously invite them to take a tour of their sprawling Washington estate. The views across the Anacortes peninsula were stunning. Of course, his father would continue with whoever was left to listen. "The radical invaders methodically gained control of Europe because of the ignorance of a self-loathing generation. It didn't take much. There was little to no resistance."

Then he'd usually get worked up. "The invaders

upturned and disfigured centuries of progress. They destroyed cathedrals and ripped apart historical monuments in a fury of hate."

Zeke could still remember how embarrassed he'd get.

"At least they didn't take over the British Isles," his father would continue. "At least Britannia recaptured its sovereignty before it was too late."

About the moment Zeke was about to doze off again, Philex-B walked into the Historium and stopped. She was mesmerized by the flowing streams, clouds, and wildlife on the big screen. The narrator told a story that she'd never heard before.

"The average temperature on Earth is sixty-one degrees Fahrenheit," the narrator gracefully spoke. "Humanity has scanned the heavens for centuries in search of another planet as perfectly suited to the physical and emotional needs of its inhabitants. But, so far, to no avail. . ."

Zeke peered at her with half-open eyes and mumbled, "What's up, Robot Girl? You okay?"

Philex-B came out of her daze and looked at him sternly. "Zeke, I no longer wish for you to call me by that name—*Robot Girl*."

Zeke sat up. He grinned, "Okay, point taken. I'll call you whatever you like. You were incredible today, Philex-

B."

Philex-B looked at him with that childish smile, "Okay, Zeke. Friends, then? May I watch it with you?"

He sat up and slapped the cushion next to him.

She sat down and was immediately mesmerized by a mother cuddling her newborn baby. Without taking her eyes off the baby, Philex-B said, "How did you recover so fast, Zeke?"

"They trained us for deprivation in pilot-training school and then the League of Space Exploration. Lots of high Gs."

"Thank you for helping me," she smiled, not taking her eyes off the show.

"That took guts, Philex-B. Dead serious."

On the screen, the father put his arm around the mother who was holding their baby.

"Zeke, do you think that our only mission is to reach Nemesis?"

"Why? Why are you asking me that?"

"Imagine if it is also to procreate." The mother was cuddling and cooing her baby. "God made the human body so beautifully."

"Procreate? I don't understand—"

"To produce offspring, of course. . . in case they never find a cure."

His expression twisted into an anxious frown. "You think that our mission is to make babies? To have children? Why?

"That's how you humans continue existence. What if this mission is a backup so that you can keep your species from extinction? What if there is no cure? Or it doesn't work? You're all very young." She smiled admiringly as the husband kissed his wife's forehead. The husband was proud of his wife and their new child.

"I may have a baby one day," she said as if it were obvious.

Zeke sat up. His eyes opened wide.

At the same moment, Jada walked in. Neither Zeke nor Philex-B noticed her. She halted. She was wearing her bathrobe, her hair frizzed out every which way.

"How's that, Philex-B? I mean it would be good if you could, but—"

"I need a husband and love—*yes*?"

Jada stepped forward. Her mouth dropped open as she listened intently.

"I . . . mm . . . sure, I guess." Zeke wondered if something was wrong with her after that shock she'd received from the switch gate. Isaac didn't notify him that there was a problem.

"Maybe you and I could be husband and wife," Philex-B said. I am fully capable of intimate sexual expression."

Zeke turned to her with questions in every crease of his forehead.

She laid her head on his shoulder as Jada, enraged, strode up behind them.

"What do you think you're moving to, Philex-B?" she demanded.

Philex-B scooted back and looked up at her, uncertain. She pointed to the screen, families, and children playing in the park, with all of their cheerful chatter.

"Stay away from Zeke!" Jada challenged, arms folded, standing over her. "We are one!"

Philex-B put her hands to her face. "Oh, you mean you're a pair?" Philex-B shook her head. "You're one couple? I'm regretful. I did not come to that realization." Philex-B scratched her head and opened her eyes wide. "You will procreate, though?"

Jada leaned over farther and poked Philex-B in the

shoulder. "Mind your biz, you dumb robot. Get that? Stay away from him!"

Philex-B leaped up—face to face. "Call me a robot again, and I will fire you right through the bulkhead, Jada!"

"Woo," Zeke was up and squeezing between them. "Easy, girls. . . let's unravel." He saw the uncertainty in Philex-B's glare. He grabbed Jada's hand, pulling her along and out of the Historium, Jada troubling Zeke about "all that."

Philex-B sat back down. On the teleview, the woman was breastfeeding the infant, holding it close. It was calm and beautiful. Philex-B mimicked and cooed her invisible baby.

Then over ship's com, Rigel interrupted her joy: "Good alterday, Philex-B. You're supposed to be assisting me on the bridge, are you not?"

"Yikes!" Philex-B jumped up and hurried off.

Chapter 22

Bridge of Assurity

VERONIKA HAD TO WAIT seventeen interminable seconds for the lift to rotate from her captain's quarters up to the bridge. She didn't at all feel like herself but arrived on the deck, ready for her shift. "Everybody okay?" she asked. "We should be nearing retrieval point."

"Captain," Zeke announced, "it's urgent—you just received a high-priority dispatch from Earth. It was expedited 11 hours ago."

"On screen, Isaac," she said.

Poldi stumbled to his post from the lift. "*Gott*, I feel sick." He looked as though he had returned from an all-nighter at the Oktoberfest.

"Welcome, Mr. Stoss," Veronika announced with a half-smile. He looked like crap. They all looked like crap. It took time to recover from the pressure of those Gs.

Veronika stepped forward. A smile of expectation. Everyone watched with her as Cassia's face filled the screen.

"It's my daughter!" she smiled broadly.

The vid began. "Hello, Mom." She turned and looked behind her. "Listen, Mom, I have bad news. Really bad."

Veronika fixated waited. The screen fritzed. There was yelling in the background on the vid.

Cassia's features lifted with sorrow, and she frowned. "Mom . . . Ori died today." Tears began. "He's gone. Dad did everything he could. They all did." She wiped her cheeks quickly. "We were with him. He wasn't alone . . ."

Veronika leaned over, *moaning*. Stabbed with pain, she grasped her stomach.

"Ori called for you, Mom. We told him you are doing everything you can."

Veronika straightened. Taking deep breaths, she fought nausea.

"The last thing he said was, 'Mom's ship can do it. . . my mom can do it. They will save us.'"

The crew was all watching. Some turned away.

Her daughter had tears running down her face. Turning, she called out, "I love you, Mom . . . I love you . . ."

Poldi leaned over. "I'm so sorry, Captain.

The screen blacked out as Philex-B put her arms around tearful Veronika.

An alarm sounded on the bridge.

Sabina looked up. "I'm so sorry . . . but something's dropped into system, ma'am." Sabina pointed to her screen. "They're in parking orbit adjacent to our fuel tanks."

"*What?*" Veronika said. "Impossible . . . Isaac, turn off that ghastly sound . . ."

Zeke jumped in. "Let's see what we have, Sabina." He leaned in and considered it keenly. The alarm stopped sounding. "Jeez, maybe I can think now."

"Sabina, magnify, and put that intruder on the big screen. Shouldn't be anything out here but our amat collectors."

On *Assurity's* screen, a metallic ship gleamed. It looked, at first, like a shiny black stingray in space.

Veronika looked up. "What in the cosmos?"

"It's the Chindian ship, *Draco*," Sabina revealed.

"Ah, shit!" Veronika cursed. She went directly to her command chair, sat down, and leaned back.

Philex-B peered at her monitor. "Stars ablaze, they have a towline to our fuel tanks, Captain. Magnifying."

"*Draco* is signaling us," Zeke called over.

On the big screen, magnification showed a towline from

Draco to *Assurity's* waiting antimatter/hydrogen tanks.

"Are you kidding me?" Veronika shot back. "It's taken months for my amat collectors to mine that antimatter and the ship tenders to deliver the tanks here."

"She's a spectrum-type frigate," Philex-B confirmed. "Possesses armament."

Draco's weapon compliment rolled up on the bridge screen sidebar. It was substantial.

Sabina scratched her head nervously. "The Chindian vessel has initiated a direct approach toward us—with our tanks *in tow*."

"Why is a Chindian ship out here at Rhema?" Poldi asked, "running off with our fuel tanks?"

"*Draco* is signaling us again, Captain," Zeke repeated.

"This is a TIMMI mining claim," she confirmed. "The Chindians have no authorization to be out here. Isaac, do we have a military presence in this sector?"

"Negative, Captain," Isaac answered. "The cruiser *Britannia* left for the inner system thirteen days ago."

"Perfectly wrong. Sabina, link up *Draco* for full vid scan."

Moments later, a pleasant-looking, trembling Chindian female aboard *Draco* appeared on *Assurity's* bridge screen.

Sitting behind her was a hunched-over officer who looked desperately ill. Besides the two of them was a spacious, well-lit, and *empty Draco* bridge.

This girl appeared unusually young. She was wearing a multi-pointed medical cap with a red cross on the front.

Veronika raised a finger. "A moment, young lady, please." Veronika punched com: "Xiao Xing, report to the bridge, double time!"

Poldi leaped up. "I'm sorry. You didn't answer my question, Ms. Morgan."

"Sit down!" she shouted at him. "You think this is a quiz game?" She crossed her arms, ignoring him. There were ten well-defined workstations besides a captain and co-pilot station on the *Draco*. "Where are their officers? Why aren't they on the bridge?"

"Captain?" Poldi persisted.

"Let it rest, Poldi," Zeke demanded.

"Stupid idiot," Sabina yelled at Poldi.

The crew all took a breath, keeping their eyes on their tasks. On-screen, the young Magnika, dressed in a medical uniform, spoke perfect English with an Indian accent. "*Assurity,* I am Medical Officer Magnika Rana. I am filled with apologies."

"What do you think you're doing with my tanks, Medical Officer Rana?"

"I have no control of this ship, Madam. I'm only seventeen. This ship is operating in automation mode." She gestured to the near-empty bridge behind her. "The officers and crew are sick with Delirium. All in hibernation. They're old—all over forty."

The thin officer rose, shouting at Magnika in Chinese to sit and be quiet.

Xiao Xing scurried to Veronika's side. "How may I help?" Veronika raised her hand for Xiao Xing to wait as the gaunt officer stepped forward, shoving Magnika aside. "I am Deputy Officer Qin of Chindian ship *Draco*."

"Deputy Officer Qin, I am sorry for your difficulties," Veronika began. "Those are Taylor Mining's tanks you have in tow. *Assurity* has requisitioned them."

He stuck his long, flat face forward. "This antimatter is property of the Chindian government!" He coughed as he sneered. "Your TIMMI company did not deliver as contracted. We will proceed with *our* fuel to Station Tiapong."

"This is a Mining Alliance registered claim! Your ship has *no* business out here."

He twisted his head strangely like he didn't understand.

"We will proceed with our contracted antimatter. You, Ms. Veronika Taylor Morgan, have no say in this event."

"I'm not going to ask you again!" Veronika shouted back. "Release my tanks now, Officer Qin or *Assurity* will be forced to engage your ship."

Officer Qin began to laugh but started coughing horribly.

Zeke jumped up, touched his temple, and put his arm around Veronika like she was his girlfriend. He pushed the now present holographic microphone button off. He smiled at Qin as he whispered to Veronika, "Captain, we don't have any offensive weapons. You had them removed to increase velocity—"

"I know that, Commander," she whispered, hardly moving her mouth.

She turned away, thinking. "Philex-B, prepare an intercept course."

Zeke returned to his station, shaking his head. "This isn't good! You can't play games with a Chindian frigate."

"Changing attitude for course correction," Philex-B broke in. "Keying controls. Twenty-second burn on aux thrusters in ten seconds, ma'am."

Veronika stepped forward and turned the mic back on.

"Deputy Officer, we are proceeding to you. You will release our antimatter tanks."

Draco's bridge dissolved instantly from *Assurity's* screen view.

"Captain," Zeke said, "I did a deep scan while you were tangling with Qin. They possess high-engagement hydrogen torpedoes. . ."

"Ma'am," Sabina interjected, "they've locked weapons."

Veronika sat down and strapped in. Punching up com, she said, "Urgent! All crew not on the bridge, grab a holddown. Tatiana! What's our fuel to rendezvous?"

Tatiana was in Engineering, gulping down her sandwich. She tossed the rest of it onto her napkin. "Estimate—*one* maneuver, Captain." She took a quick gulp of her cola. "Maybe two . . . do not see readable levels from here—"

Sabina stood and pointed at her screen. "*Captain*, a torpedo has launched from *Draco*. Mark—bearing 83.798."

"Tatiana!" Veronika called. "Are you following this?"

In engineering, Tatiana rose from her station, put on her jacket, and shuffled to another analytics screen.

Engineering was cold. The extensive bank of blinking capacitors had to remain near freezing. She touched her temple and could see the captain. "We can avoid—but that will take *Assurity* off course and delay—"

"Do it for God's sake! Jeez," Veronika replied.

"Yes. Marking now!" Tatiana leaned close to her screen. She reached up and turned a dial slightly—then another. *Assurity's* moving telemetry readout changed, rolling ever so slightly. "Impulse—four seconds—*now!*" She waited a moment, inspecting the changing data and keyed in a slight variance.

On the bridge, Veronika caught herself as *Assurity* jolted and screeched in agony. The ship wasn't built for this kind of rapid adjustment.

Tatiana announced loudly, "I will do rest with thrusters—Captain."

Assurity's radio array cameras displayed a perfect view for everyone on the bridge. *Assurity* veered slightly amid the hiss and thud of hydraulics.

Veronika switched the main bridge screen to a partial view of *Draco's* bridge. Magnika attended to Qin, who, on his back, held his head in his hands—moaning.

Assurity was a transport, not a frigate. She'd gone through one stressful maneuver already, but this was pushing it. Veronika knew her midpoint structure mounts were cold, stiff, and old.

Sabina shot up again. "Another torpedo has been fired, Captain. *Cazzo*—it's locked. Mark two. Incomings!

Veronika punched her telemetry button to bring up a tactical view of the oncoming torpedo—

Nothing showing. She hit another button. Still nothing. *All right*, she thought. She called down to Tatiana, who appeared on her display. "Tatiana, straightaway, put telemetry for those missiles on the bridge screen."

"Da!" Tatiana answered. A moment later, there were three separate displays across the bridge screen: Approaching missiles, *Draco's* bridge deck, and *Assurity* as she veered slightly, with a deep groaning. The first torpedo from *Draco* missed *Assurity* by meters. The crew sounded a collective sigh.

Moments later, the second torpedo went streaking into their view. It ripped into the long-range radio array.

Broken pieces of metal dispersed in every direction.

The crew held onto anything they could as the ship shuddered violently. Pieces of the array hit the hydrogen tanks along the main corridor, but, thank God, nothing penetrated.

Veronika stood, put her finger to her mouth, and said calmly, as if she'd planned it weeks ago, "Sabina, initiate V dump, now!"

"*Certo*, Captain."

Veronika utilized her temple-talk and punched in her numbers. "Rigel, can you take *Offlander* and cut their towline?"

"As requested." Rigel jumped up and ran for the lift.

"Sabina," Veronika said, "engage the protective impact shield!"

Zeke called to her, "Rigel can't coordinate a pass now. We're moving at variance!"

Veronika frowned at Zeke. "Tatiana, I need you on the bridge."

Assurity and *Draco* neared one another as if in slow motion. The radio array cameras still functioned on the bridge screen, but they were fritzing on and off. Even so, they could all see *Draco* closing. Sabina had her eyes closed. Philex-B had hers wide open. Zeke was rapidly keying in calculations, one after another.

The two ships inched toward one another. Would they collide? Deep breaths as the vessels began to pass. . . almost touching.

Veronika put her hands on her waist, leaned back, and exhaled.

Offlander, squeezing between the two, steadily progressed toward the aft of *Draco*.

It would be close. Veronika broke the silence, "Rigel, are you all right?"

Rigel answered, "I'm waiting for *Draco* to pass so that I can cut the tow line. . ."

Then there was a shattering burst of cannon fire from *Draco*.

Veronika switched to rear cameras—brilliant flashes—bullets exploding against the magnetic thruster.

Inside *Assurity's* engine compartment, the Nautilus Star Drive, surrounded by her capacitor bank array, activated automatic shutdown. The multicolored lights blinked once and went blank.

The thruster, sparkling with frozen crystals, shut down, causing the blue flame at the tail of *Assurity* to be extinguished.

Magnika and Qin watched the cannon fire tear into the rear of *Assurity's* thruster as they passed.

Magnika put her hands to her face. "Oh, my gosh."

Deputy Officer Qin stood expressionless.

Philex-B pulled up a view of the magnetic thruster. "The thruster's been hit. She's on auto shutdown."

In anguish, Veronika watched the destruction. "You sons of bitches! You've hit us."

"I told you this would happen," Zeke said.

Poldi shook his head and grimaced but kept his mouth shut.

On *Draco,* Magnika pleaded, "Deputy Qin, we are destroying their ship. We cannot do this. There is no one else left to pilot us home."

Quin and Magnika could see Veronika from their bridge screen. Veronika paced. "Qin—you and I are not at odds. The League of American States and Chindia are not enemies. God, we are Earth's last hope . . . this ship, this crew. We're risking our lives for this mission."

Quin stood, pursing his lips. Gritting his teeth, he dropped his head to the side.

His mind must be tangled in thoughts, Veronika thought.

Scowling at Veronika, Qin allowed Magnika to give him a sedative shot as he stumbled to the commander's station. He plunked down, staring at Veronika onscreen—

then he put his hand to his forehead.

Veronika sat and clasped her hands under her chin. There was nothing else she could do. Even if he did release her tanks, could they repair the bullet-ridden thruster? They kept two spares—but it was the electrical, the coil, that bank of capacitors. That's what worried her. If auto-shutdown occurred almost instantly, it might be repairable.

Tatiana arrived on the bridge and hobbled slowly to an open position.

Magnika stood looking only at Qin. The crew of *Assurity* remained silent.

Qin spoke to the ship's computer. "Abra Shanxi, take all weapons off auto." Qin slumped over and put his head in his arms.

Magnika stared up at the monitor above her head. "Captain Veronika, weapons have been disabled. I'm going down to release the access doors to our shuttle bay. Going now." She dashed off.

Veronika stood and folded her arms as if nothing out of the ordinary had happened. "Zeke, drop us off at *Draco,* and take a company to the depot, retrieve all the supplies you can, and load any emergency amat canisters they have. I'm taking Xiao Xing and Sabina with me. Tatiana, you and Rigel get to work on that thruster. Check the capacitor lines first. There are replacement nozzles in supply."

"I know that," Tatiana answered. "You might say 'please,' at some point."

Veronika gave her no thought. "Final Realm may not be happy to see us, Zeke. I've given Philex-B an emergency access code, and you better bring arms. We need everything you can get out of there."

"Understood, Captain."

Chapter 23

Final Realm Military Depot

AUSTERE AND COLD, Chief Admin, an android with a long, tightly spun neck, sat in her alcove, working. She was unusually tall—designed for high storage and record keeping. Alerted, she stood and shuffled on her coiled chrome legs to a viewing portal. Chief Admin swung her rectangular head down to obtain a view of the unauthorized vehicle outside the depot.

Offlander, after dropping off Veronika, Xiao Xing, and Sabina at *Draco,* arrived outside the landing bay doors of the Final Realm Military Depot. Zeke requested assistance. "Final Realm, this is Commander Zeke Alexander. *Assurity*'s shuttle *Offlander* requests docking permission."

There was no response from Final Realm Military Depot.

Zeke turned and glanced back at Philex-B and Jada behind him. Both looked back at him with curious eyes and no words.

Sitting in the cockpit, considering the closed docking doors of the realm, Zeke had very little idea of what they'd face inside the depot. This construct was classified and military. He'd been briefed during cadet training. Military supply deployment only. They never revealed much to cadets other than its basic function. There were no humans stationed out here on the fringe of existence. The androids operating this station were rarely seen except by military personnel. The entire base was designed to survive on low energy consumption.

Inside, Android #12, a strength model, approached the Chief Admin, who stepped around it with her long legs. Chief Admin peered down and, with her echoey voice, said, "Report!" She could just as easily have communicated non-verbally, except that there was no central server. It was considered a security risk.

Chief Admin was the central computing system out here, and only she processed tactical and administrative decisions. Every two years, an upgraded model replaced Chief Admin.

"From where has this shuttle originated?" she asked Android #12.

With its lifeless voice, the android spoke rapidly, "Interstellar deep-space transport *Assurity*; Cassini Contract #1345-776; Propulsion system: Nautilus

Antimatter Stardrive. Final inspection and receipt by Taylor Interstellar Mining and Manufacturing; April 12, 2089. She sits at null. One thousand five hundred and fifty meters. Possible damage.

The chief admin swung her big head down to Android #12's level. "Send scout drones. Determine emergency requirements."

Outside, a hatch whined and boomed open. Three firefly scout drones shot from the Realm. Multi-colored, they whisked and flickered across the open distance.

Zeke spotted them flittering toward *Assurity* and relayed the intel to Isaac.

Following their movement with *Offlander's* camera, it was close enough at twenty-four times multiplication to see where they were going. Landing on *Assurity*, the fireflies flattened like starfish. Crawling rapidly, they searched-out an emergency entrance hatch and electronically began pulling codes. Flipping open the hatch, the fireflies swooped in and down a corridor. Splitting up, they sped, flickering through separate halls and rooms, where they had access. Pausing at each, they analyzed and recorded.

Zeke, still waiting for docking permission, radioed Veronika on *Draco*.

She answered.

"What is it, Zeke?"

"Captain, Final Realm sent drones from here to *Assurity*. They've entered through an emergency hatch. Plus, the realm is not allowing us in."

"Commander, they are programmed to ascertain accurate intel before offering assistance. It's okay. They should be out of there soon. But, do let Tatiana know what's going on, so she's not spooked. You should receive clearance from the Realm within a few minutes—"

That second, the request from Final Realm was answered in that metallic, inhuman voice. "Your docking request is denied, *Offlander*. You are *not* authorized military transport!"

Jada, in the back, leaned into the front seat. "Tell them that we are on a rescue mission. This is unbelievable. Can we get access permission from Cassini?"

"It will take too long," Poldi added. They'd require a worldwide diplomatic assembly conference.

Zeke laughed. Except that it wasn't funny.

Jada said, "Yeah, how arcane is this?"

Zeke looked back at Philex-B. She wasn't paying attention. She was obviously laboring over something on her com screen.

"It's not a L.A.S. facility," Zeke reminded them. "It's a cooperative between the Russian Federation and Chindia."

"I've got it *hacked*, Commander," Philex-B said. "Shall I open their landing bay?"

Zeke looked across at Poldi, who was smiling, looking ahead, and saying nothing.

"Do it. Let's make this fast, Philex-B."

Final Realm's landing bay doors separated. *Offlander* moved slowly into Final Realm Depot and gently landed in the parking bay. It was a large parking facility. Other than *Offlander,* it was empty of vessels.

Tatiana was in *Assurity's* machine shop, riveting a new thruster lip to reinforce the receiving brackets. It was as cold as a Siberian winter. To save watts, they'd lowered climate to barely tolerable. Of course, the captain was off ship, so what did she care.

Looking at the new assembly, Tatiana was confident that the thruster should not have given way so quickly. On the other hand, structurally, it wasn't designed to repel high-speed projectiles—at least, not exploding ones. The old nozzle had been demolished. The magnetic field was actually the container. Principally, a high-temperature superconducting coil generated the field.

When a flickering orange light appeared in the machine

shop, she stumbled back. "*Der'mo!*" she yelled. It startled the hell out of her. The baby drone clicked loudly and flashed. Then it disappeared in a blip. She just hoped it hadn't come from *Draco.*

Better get back to work, she thought. *Good thing I planned ahead . . .*

She'd requisitioned two replacement thruster assemblies from Cassini before they'd left. Just in case. The improved nozzle and thruster had been re-designed in light of the great distance to Nemesis. Even during a routine mission, it wasn't unheard of to lose a thruster. Nemesis was still a great distance, and they hadn't even left Rhema. She'd keep every bit of scrap, just in case.

Her working plan was to increase *Assurity's* velocity by two percent as soon as they departed Final Realm. She'd already started refiguring the outflow parameters for the Stardrive but kept butting heads with Veronika on that. Too much to do now, though. She put her gloves back on. *I'm half-numb . . .*

Veronika gave her little credit when it came to propulsion—or engineering, for that matter. Always questioning her suggestions. It was her poor English, maybe. A disadvantage—plus, no one from the L.A.S. ever trusted the Russians. It was a long-standing prejudice. And still, many considered her very granduncle, Sergei

Pavlovich Korolev, the father of practical astronautics. Not across the League, mind you, only in the Russian Federation. Not here. Not in space.

Down the side ramp of *Offlander*, Zeke went first. Stopping, he read his atmosphere and temperature mod, announcing, "Landing bay's pressurized—I hope you all brought long underwear!" It was frigid in here. Fortunately, the oxygen level was adequate, so no suits or helmets were required.

Zeke carried the compact MPS25 (a multi-pulse laser rifle). He was less than happy about the choices available from *Assurity's* armory. A non-lethal weapon, the MPS25 was built to forewarn, stun—even deafen—for a time. At its highest setting, it could concuss a combatant. But—it couldn't kill a damn thing. All lethal handguns and rifles were outlawed.

The same year that the United States Constitution was repealed—April 13 of 2027—the L.A.S. banned any personally-owned weapon capable of deadly force. That included all *standard issue* for crews on National Science Foundation space vessels—including all L.A.S. space stations. The exception: armament for ship-to-ship defense, attached, or encompassed within a military vehicle was permitted.

Philex-B, also armed, followed close behind Zeke. Poldi and Jada followed. The depot landing bay was stark and framed with grey metal girders. Philex-B, shouldering her rifle, viewed the beeping proximity scanner and pointed to a large doorway. "Behind that entrance is the propellant supply room," she instructed. "Around the other side is the main control. The layout is an octagon—one floor."

"Where's our greeting party?" Poldi joked. He'd gotten over the captain's rebuke, at least for now.

The four approached the central entranceway and stood. Nothing happened. Zeke waited as Philex-B advanced and viewed the attached digital panel. She turned to them. "It's in Russian."

"Can you read it?" Zeke asked.

"I'm not programmed for Russian—I'll tele Tatiana."

Zeke gave an okay nod. Philex-B called Tatiana on her temple-talk.

Tatiana looked up from her workbench in the hangar bay. *"Da?"* she said like she was put out or something.

"Hey, Tatiana, can you tell us how to get into this room? The directions are in Russian. Here, I'll scan it for you."

Tatiana looked at her screen. The short, three-line

instructions were in Russian. She smiled, which lit up her usually stern-looking face. Then she laughed. "It says: 'Welcome, you must deposit all material collected from a planetary source into quarantine locker before proceeding inside. Then you may press *any* number to enter.'"

Tatiana shook her head, amused, and went back to work. The tele went black.

"Thanks, Tatiana."

Philex-B hit the first symbol on the panel. The massive steel door groaned open from the middle as the four looked at one another, like, *How dumb are we?*

They entered.

The corridor ran along the outside contour of the octagon. Lights came on and went off as they entered and walked the long hallway. Across, through a set of running windows, they could view the other side of the dimly lit octagon. In the middle, there was nothing. Where humans might have had flowers, a tree, and benches for eating and gathering—nothing but cement.

They stopped at a large alcove that looked like it contained supplies.

Zeke motioned them together. "Now, look, you all

know what we need. Let's see what we have in supply first, then we'll continue to the control room. I want to make short work of this."

They all split off within the large containment area.

Poldi stepped inside the supply alcove. Examining the label on a drum of stacked green tanks, he called out, "They're reserve oxygen canisters . . . better bring 'em, huh?"

Zeke came to the stack and took a pic of the collection from his temple-talk. "We'll requisition half of them. Mark 'em, please, Poldi."

Poldi placed fluorescent green X's on the oxygen tanks as he went. Pausing for a moment, he said, "You are aware, Zeke, I told Ms. Morgan before we left Cassini that we'd never reach Rhema with that flare on our ass. Having the superconducting field do double duty for containment on the initial leg of a mission like this—it was a dangerous idea."

Zeke browsed for the antimatter pallets. "That's how antimatter gets concentrated in the first place—the thruster containment system acts as a miniature version of the magnetic field around the planets. You know that, Poldi. They've been run that way for years, and, yeah, on smaller ships and usually under emergency situations—"

"It's *nicht gut*, Zeke, when it's damn certain you're going to be clobbered by a solar flare!"

Jada located a medical locker and opened it, rifling through the contents. Someone had left their clothes, and they stank to high hell. She slammed the locker. "There's no way we're getting to Nemesis with her as captain. She practically got us blown into a black hole. It's easy to see why she decided to captain *Assurity*. She loves giving orders."

Poldi squeezed through more tanks. "Damn mission is a dusty cluster." He stopped, getting more irritated by the second. "Her company, Taylor Interstellar Mining, had a contract with those Chindians. That's why they fired on us. We're using *their* fuel . . . but who gives a shit? No one listens to me—"

Philex-B cast him an incensed look. "I'm listening to you. Why don't you shut up, Poldi? You're military. You signed on for this."

"God. Who programmed you?" Jada spat back. "Uppity E.L.F."

She gritted her teeth, "Come on, Poldi. Help me."

Zeke gave Philex-B a look. She grimaced, kept her MPS25 at the ready, and moved slowly toward an extensive doorway.

As they approached, the steel door slid open. It was another low-ceilinged, featureless steel-framed room with a minimum of human comfort features.

Zeke spotted the canisters. "There's our amat reserve carousels."

The large canisters were clearly marked: "Antimatter Extremely Fragile. Do Not Remove Magnetic Safety Straps." To the right in another alcove, and across the bulkhead, "Human Food" was stenciled with large white letters in three languages.

Philex-B moved cautiously forward. Adjacent was another alcove. Inside was a vending machine with colorful bags of potato chips, nuts, and candy bars. Next to it was a soda machine. Philex-B walked over, and as she neared the snack machine, it illuminated. She took a step back. *Never seen anything like this. It's old.* She pressed one of the buttons, and a bag of potato chips plopped out at the bottom. "Look what I found." She smiled.

No one noticed. They'd all walked off. She tore open the noisy bag, pulled out a potato chip, and starting chewing. "Mmm . . . good."

Jada turned back. "Philex-B, you *can't* eat that."

Zeke looked back, hoping there wouldn't be another tangle between the two.

"I eat food, you know. Small bits are allowed . . . keeps my skin supple." She said it as if Jada were her closest girlfriend. As if there'd never been anything harsh between them.

"Jada," Zeke said, "Philex-B and I are going to retrieve the reserve amat canisters. You and Poldi determine food requisition logistics. I don't see any reason to locate their command if we don't have to. Let's get loaded and get out of here."

"Got it!" Poldi replied. "Why hasn't security shown up? They must be watching us. This is strange."

Jada added, "They've got some medical supplies here, as well—just in case."

As Zeke and Philex-B moved farther into the amat closet, Philex-B scanned the room. In the far corner, a silent android sat at a desk. Philex-B pointed but kept silent. The android's eyes were a dim yellow but presented no movement.

The two cautiously approached. Philex-B waved her hand in front of its face. "It's off."

"Commander," Isaac said over com, "I was able to scan the command room. It looks as though the station chief knows you're approaching. Careful."

Zeke radioed Poldi. "I changed my mind, Poldi. You

and Jada keep working. I'm taking Philex-B with me to command. I want to make sure we don't have problems unloading this stuff into *Offlander*."

"Understood," Poldi replied.

Passing into another segment of the octagon, Zeke and Philex-B entered a dimly lit room cluttered with decommissioned androids in chairs, slumped in all manner of Raggedy Ann.

Philex-B stopped and sighed. "It looks as though when they fail, they're of no use. No rebirth for these metal beings. Just send up another. We can make them by the scads."

The two proceeded more slowly, encountering yet another heavily sealed door. Philex-B double-checked the proximity scanner. Punching the coordinates into her keypad, the door slid open, revealing the poorly lit command center fitted with five optical readout stations. No one appeared present. If the station chief was here, she wasn't making herself known.

Zeke put his finger to his mouth. "B, go back and help them load the antimatter onto *Offlander*. There is a loader in the corner by the pallets. I can scout this myself."

She looked at him, doubtfully, "Are you sure?"

"Yes, go—and be careful. The place gives me the

creeps. Let's get packed and get out of here." He turned to leave and stopped. "And, please, don't tangle with Jada or Poldi. . ."

"Okay, will do." She turned and headed back.

Zeke entered the dimly lit command control room, his gun held at the ready.

***

On the bridge of the *Draco,* Sabina sat in the command position, attempting to get a handle on the flight controls. *Draco's* AI wasn't cooperating with Xiao Xing.

"Computer, speak to us only in English," Xiao Xing demanded.

A female with an Indian accent finally responded. "As you wish. My name is Abra Shanxi. I am the main AI for our Chindian ship *Draco.* Who are you, and what do you wish?"

Veronika smiled at Xiao Xing. "Nice to make your acquaintance, Abra Shanxi. Will you release the tethers attached to *Assurity's* auxiliary fuel tanks and begin rotation of *Draco* away from our mining area?

"I can, but who are you? You are not authorized to give

orders on this ship."

Veronika pouted and squinted. "I am Veronika Taylor Morgan, the captain of the mining transport *Assurity*. We are on—

"You are not authorized personnel—"

Xiao Xing cursed Abra Shanxi in Chindian . . .

Abra Shanxi responded curtly. "I am not going to respond to distasteful language from a fellow Chindian. I will not."

Touching her temple, Veronika whispered, "Isaac?" Then she turned to Xiao Xing, who had a frown on her face. "What did you call her?"

"I called her an arrogant fool—which is what she is."

"Jeez, Xiao Xing." Veronika's face tightened.

"Yes, Captain," Isaac said in private.

She whispered, "Isaac, can you get this discordant mess of an operating system to function under my command?"

"I'll try," he answered. "Suggestion, if I may: Sometimes, honey works far better than vinegar."

"Cut the crap, Isaac." Veronika rose and walked over to Sabina's station as Isaac took his sweet time.

"Captain . . ." Sabina pointed to the four engineering

modules on her screen. "Their propulsion system is not dissimilar to our Nautilus Star Drive."

"Can you fly this ship?"

"I believe so—if she cooperates—and with a bit of time set aside for study. The Chindians use more pictographs, which is helpful when you don't understand the language."

Veronika was becoming aggravated. "Isaac, what's taking so blasted long?"

Isaac came back on her radio, "Captain, I had to assure her that the reason you are acting a bit disagreeable is because of an ongoing medical issue . . . I didn't—"

"Why would you tell her something like that, Isaac? What in blazing stars did she say?"

"Abra Shanxi--a brilliant entity, by the way--has assured me that she will cooperate."

Veronika shook her head in amazement. "Will she release our tanks and oversee *Draco* back to Tiapong Station? That's the question. What about fuel?"

"Their tanks are full, Captain," Sabina added.

Over ship's com, Isaac cheerfully announced, "Abra Shanxi has agreed. You are now her new captain. She promises allegiance, wishes us well, and for me to convey to you that—"

Abra Shanxi interrupted over ship's com, "The efficient use of antimatter by *Draco* is 3.456% superior to that of *Assurity*. A vast improvement in propulsion over—"

"Oh, perfect. Thank you, Abra Shanxi," Veronika happily affirmed. She didn't need to hear this AI rattle on . . .

Veronika walked off and whispered over temple-talk to Isaac. "Out of curiosity, Isaac, how did you negotiate this agreement?"

"I assured Abra Shanxi that we are brothers and sisters, as it were, out here in the vastness of space. And that we-she and I--will be fast friends."

Veronika let sound a belly laugh. "Clever, Isaac. Isaac and Abra. Now that has a ring to it!" Veronika put her hand to her head, thinking. *Not only am I getting a headache, but these AI's have become full of themselves. I know that they are supposed to exhibit human-like characteristics, but, really, they're all a bit too chummy.* She'd need to report this to NSF when they returned. Only one of several things to be highlighted in her report.

Abra Shanxi said, "Captain, your antimatter tanks have been released. I am moving *Draco* a safe distance from *Assurity*."

Veronika smiled. "That's the first good news I've heard

in months. Thank you, Abra Shanxi!"

"As requested, Captain Veronika Taylor Morgan."

"Captain will suffice, Abra Shanxi—since we are now *fast* friends."

***

Zeke stood in the command center for Final Realm Military Depot. It looked as though no human had entered this room in a light year. There was nothing human about it. Hard steel, plastic, and un-cushioned seating. No smell, no dust. His breath led his eyes everywhere. He noted the marked calendar. A systems specialist from the Chindian Space Station Tiapong had recently visited and checked the depot's functioning. For the Russians and Chindians, Final Realm was just a way to keep an eye on the League.

The chief admin was nowhere to be found, so there was no reason to stay. Not to mention, he was starting to feel the loss of heat. Shivering, he heard an audio file running on one of the monitors. He followed the sound. One of the monitors, marked in Russian across the top, was emitting intermittent static. Staring closely, he saw within the viewable audio file a series of numbers and pictures that appeared layered atop the audio. It wasn't Russian; he was sure of that. And it wasn't Chindian. Couldn't tell what language this was. Xian Xing would know. Was someone trying to communicate with the bots of Final Realm? Who could read this? It sure as stars didn't appear like any computer code he'd ever seen during his com stat training. He took a vid of it.

Most of the monitors were dark. Then another live feed popped up on a nearby monitor. He walked over to that one and took a deep breath. *Draco* was releasing their tanks, and *Assurity* was approaching them for pickup. That was great. Listening to com chatter between the ships, he felt a weird sensation running up his back.

He turned fast. Behind him, glaring down with radiant, nugget-colored eyes, was the spindly, coil-necked Chief Admin. Two good-sized androids stepped up and stood beside her.

She was silent for a moment—then, with her long swinging right hand, she clubbed Zeke across the shoulders. Knocking him to the floor, his rifle skidded across the concrete as he smacked the floor hard.

Lying on the floor, Zeke looked up at the metal monster as her head dipped at the end of her long neck. She stared at him, her gleaming eyes deep-set in her square chrome face.

She spoke with that tangy strident voice, *"This is a Russian & Chindian military facility. You are an unauthorized intruder. You will leave now, and you will remove all unauthorized supplies from your ship. Failure to obey may result in your termination."*

One of her square-shouldered androids picked up Zeke's rifle. As Zeke rose from the floor, the robot handed it to him. Zeke grabbed his rifle.

The three stood observing as Zeke stepped between them. Departing the command center, he didn't bother to look back as the heavy steel door hissed shut behind him.

By the time Zeke made his way back to the docking bay, Poldi and Jada had almost everything loaded onboard *Offlander*. Philex-B was moving the last of three antimatter pallets. Jada, by herself, was handloading the last of the medical supplies. Poldi had finished with the foodstuffs and oxygen canisters and was motioning Philex-B's lift into *Offlander*.

Zeke looked unnerved. "You guys almost done?" Watching Philex-B, seeing the last pallets loaded, he called out to the three of them. "Good job! Let's get the hell out of here. I had a little run-in with the bots."

"Probably ten minutes," Poldi called over. "We've got

to take our time strapping down this amat."

"All right." He was nervous and looked more closely at the interior of the parking bay. There was little to no cover if those unholy things showed up again—

There she was—Chief Admin—and she'd brought a friend. The entire crew froze. Her friend was as tall as she was, but not spindly. This thing was a towering, ten-foot, shiny alloy box. Its arms looked human—muscular and strong—and it had six fingers on each enormous hand. If you could call it a hand. And now the towering box clomped toward them.

Zeke stepped in front of it and stood firm. Hoping it would stop, the metal box thing swiveled on its hips, bent forward, picked up Zeke, and hurled him across the room.

Philex-B jumped down from the loader and headed straight for the Chief Admin. "You will stop this aggression right now!" she yelled up at her.

The Chief Admin dropped her head and hovered her rectangular face before Philex-B's. "You are a Philex and not authorized. If you are not careful—"

She tall-stepped awkwardly around Philex-B and then pointed to her metal box friend. "Unload those supplies from their ship!" Chief Admin peered into *Offlander's* supply hold.

The box thing clomped toward *Offlander*.

Philex-B kneeled next to Zeke, sprawled out on the floor, and helped him sit up. He was badly hurt. Once he was standing, Jada and Poldi helped him into *Offlander*.

The metal box thing with its shiny body and human-like arms and hands leaned into the cargo hold and grabbed a bulky container of dry goods that had already been loaded.

Philex-B stepped right next to him. "You will release those items and leave."

It had four viewports—one on each side—black, shiny, and beady. It peered at her for a moment. Its eye-things flickered. It disregarded her completely and placed the crate of dry goods down beside *Offlander*.

Philex-B stepped back, lowered her head, and put her hands to each side of her forehead. A loud, piercing screech ricocheted throughout the interior of the parking bay, zinging off the walls.

Picking up another crate, stumbling, the box thing dropped the second crate on the floor and turned to Philex-B. Pushing her hard with its big hand, she went tumbling.

The box thing went back to removing items from *Offlander*. And then, for some reason, it stood straight up as if it had strained its steel back. A jolt of electricity flashed through its entire metal torso. The eye-slits flashed briefly before going white. The box thing tumbled backward, landing with a mighty crash.

Jada was attending to Zeke as Poldi grabbed hold of Philex-B and pulled her away. Chief Admin dropped her face down and glared into Philex-B's eyes. Lifting her head, Chief Admin turned as more of her bots arrived. She hurried toward the exit with her long, spindly-legged strides.

The auxiliary bots turned toward the crew and began a screeching mechanical rant. But, before a moment had passed, Chief Admin sparked like a pulsar, straightened, and crumbled to the floor in front of the exit. The remaining robots scurried off like scared rats.

Poldi helped Philex-B to stand.

Zeke, sitting up, was catching his breath. Jada helped him up, and the four looked at one another.

"I guess we better repack and roll out of here," Zeke said, getting back to his senses.

Poldi had his arm around Philex-B, who was gaining her equilibrium. "Great job, B! Didn't know you could light someone up like that. Cool!"

Philex-B tilted her head. Bemused, she smiled at Poldi. "I didn't do that. Something else did, I assure you, I didn't. Let's get this done and get out of here."

Chapter 24

Galley of Assurity

AFTER RETURNING FROM *Draco*, and hungry as could be, Veronika left the habitation lift hoping Chiffon or Plum would be cooking in the galley. She was looking forward to eggs, bacon, and toast. Oh, it wasn't real bacon like at home. More like freeze-dried ham made out of some kind of chickpeas.

Plum was cooking. Tatiana, Jada, and Poldi chatted together as they ate but hushed up as Veronika entered.

"Good mainday, ma'am," Plum said. "May I make you some toast with one egg easy and bacon?"

"Perfect," Veronika answered. She headed for the coffee setup. "I'll have some orangeade, as well, thank you." Pouring her own coffee, Veronika walked to the big table where everyone was sitting. "May I join you?"

"Please, ma'am." Jada motioned to the chair next to her.

No one was required to address her as captain when they were off duty. That was fine with her. Still, there was an awkward silence.

Plum shuffled over and poured Veronika's orangeade.

"How did loadout from the depot go?" Veronika asked. "You guys get everything into storage, okay?"

Everyone looked a bit tattered at the seams. No doubt herself included.

"Affirmative. Packed in there tight," Poldi answered. "About 400 kilos of frozen and 122 dehydrated—that was it."

"Plus, medical," Jada added.

"No trouble from the depot?" Veronika asked.

Poldi took another sip of coffee. "I wouldn't say that. We had a run-in, but we collected everything you asked for." He swallowed nervously as he looked at her. "Something attacked Final Realm's security system. A destruct malbot, we're thinking. We don't know for sure. Didn't spend a lot of time waiting around to figure it out. Wherever it came from, it lit up a couple of their admin bots. Helped us out, actually."

Veronika knew it wasn't from *Draco*. The only way you could override a station feed was by way of a beacon. Veronika eyed her breakfast. *It couldn't have come from the Chindian space station. They wouldn't take out their own admins. Admins are horribly expensive.*

With their caffeine-dazed eyes, they all looked tired.

"You three are going to get some rest, I take it."

"Yes, to that." Jada added, "Is it possible that a destruct signal came from Nemesis? Aimed at us?"

Veronika didn't want to answer that question straight up and gave a little nod. "I suppose it's possible."

That was the hell of it. It was more than possible. She'd already been in talks with the Chindians about another issue. They were well aware that Final Realm had been attacked and that it had suffered system failures. It wasn't caused by *Assurity,* and they knew it. It had come from outside the sector. The malbot had gone through the Realms shields like tissue paper, and it had originated from Nemesis.

Poldi leaned in, pushing his plate to the side. "Ma'am—

we were speaking together—the crew." He motioned with his fingers as if they'd all been present at the same time. "Not to be disagreeable, but some of us feel this mission is no longer viable. That we should return home while we can." He looked up with a hasty smirk

Veronika sat back and took a deep breath.

Tatiana chewed another bite of her Hungarian goulash dinner, or whatever it was.

Veronika took a sip of coffee, thinking, *this is the result of an ill-trained young crew forced into real service.*

"We wish to return home," Tatiana warned.

Zeke and Philex-B, overhearing part of the conversation as they entered, said nothing. Zeke went to the drink carousel and grabbed a big mug of hot water and a tea packet. Philex-B sat down next to him as Jada grasped Poldi's hand under the table. Poldi continued, "For certain, we're lucky to be alive—"

"We cannot rely on cryolife system," Tatiana vouched. "We don't have resources for all to remain awake during the trip to Nemesis. Food alone—"

Plum handed Philex-B a thimble-sized nutrient cup.

"Thank you, Plum," Philex-B interrupted. "Captain, we've collected a new radio array. Not an exact match, but I can adapt."

Zeke's face puckered up as Philex-B spooned her green paste. "Looks delicious."

Veronika appreciated that Zeke kept things light— we're they all in on this get-together?

Philex-B patted her cheek and grinned. "For my beautiful skin."

Plum delivered a hearty breakfast plate to Zeke.

"Cryolife is in perfect operational order," Philex-B

assured them. "I repaired it myself—"

"Philex-B!" Poldi interrupted, glaring harshly at her. "Come on. We're having a consider here, please." He turned back to Veronika. "You almost got us all killed, Ms. Morgan—"

Sonofabitch, Veronika thought. Better to keep her anger in check.

Jada let go of Poldi's hand under the table.

Tatiana stood, taut and straight. "Never should have had to make the Chertok Maneuver in the first place. *Assurity* is not designed to go so far. . ."

Veronika took another bite of her food. She thought *this is the most screwed-up crew. If I'd had reports of this kind of insubordination on one of my TIMMI ships, I'd have fired them all.*

"We've now lost three crewmembers, Captain, Jada added. What with Sabina leaving."

Veronika glared at Jada. *How did she know that?*

Poldi clasped his fingers together. "TIMMI had a contract with the Chindians. That's their fuel we're using for this mission, isn't it? That's why they attacked us."

Philex-B snapped, "Who made you captain, Poldi?"

"It proves she's reckless," he shot back. "Why don't

you listen?"

"I am listening, genius! Like I said before, you signed on for this."

Jada broke in, "This doesn't concern you, Philex-B. You're a just robot, okay?"

Philex-B sprung up, stretched, and yanked Jada up by the shirt. Before anyone could believe what was happening, she'd thrown Jada to the floor and, with little difficulty, was straddling her stomach. "I warned you, Jada, about how you speak to me . . ."

Everyone was up, backing away from the table, pushing chairs aside. Zeke squatted and put his arms around Philex-B's midsection, whispering in her ear, uncertain whether he should yank her off.

She was shouting into Jada's face, "I am part of this crew. I'm the Second Lieutenant!" She had Jada's shoulders pinned but hadn't raised her fist. "You will not disrespect me." She looked up at the rest of them. "Any of you!"

Tatiana, as big and strong as any of them, grabbed hold of Philex-B's arm. Philex-B yanked it away and pointed her finger at her face. "Don't, Tatiana. Back off, or I'll take you out."

Tatiana backed off.

Veronika touched Philex-B's arm. "Philex-B, listen to me—it's okay. *Let her go!*"

Philex-B looked Veronika in the face, released Jada, and stood. Then she stomped back to the table, picked up her tray, and marched off. But stopping, she turned around and said, "You humans are liars! Most of what comes out of your mouths can't be trusted." She slammed the tray atop the trash bin and turned into the corridor. "I'm glad I'm not human," she said as she walked off.

Xiao Xing entered and, seeing the ruckus, spun around to leave.

Poldi, his eyes closed, fumed, "You better get control of her, Captain. She's dangerous."

Rising quickly, embarrassed, Jada straightened her shirt. She was shaken.

"Hold on, Xiao Xing," Veronika motioned. "Please, join us. You're a part of this crew."

"I'm a linguist, I—"

Veronika stood at the table. "Everyone, please sit." She motioned for them to sit down. "Calmly, let's have a consider."

Slowly, they all took their seats. Xiao Xing squirmed uncomfortably.

"I think this trip is maybe a lost cause," Tatiana maintained. "With added supplies and fuel, we have a real chance to make it home."

Veronika raised her palms in the air. "I've made agreements with the Chindian Station Tiapong. Sabina will pilot *Draco* home. Their crew, those who are still alive, are all in cryosleep. Any of you who wish may join her—"

"Why, Sabina?" Xiao Xing whined.

"Beyond that, I'd like you to consider this: Very little in space works flawlessly. That's why we have backup plans and fallback positions." She sipped her cold coffee. "Out here, everything will kill you. Equipment breaks down. People make mistakes. I've dealt with this for years."

Poldi rose in anger. "Even if we can reach Nemesis, which I think not—there is no way we'll make it home to Earth."

"I disagree, Mr. Stoss. Our mission is to ensure the return to Earth from Nemesis with viable DNA. That is our vow, our sworn pledge to our country, our families, and each other. There is no one else. Think about that. Things on Earth are deteriorating. The end of our existence is not a fantasy—not the plot of an *end of the world movie*. It's happening now! To your family, your friends—to my family.

She took a moment to catch her breath. *My son Ori believed in me, and in all of you!*

They looked up at her; she wasn't sure that she had even one ally. She shoved her plate to the side, put her elbows on the table, and clasped her hands. "Perfectly straight—this is my ship. I'm taking *Assurity* to Nemesis—with two androids and three organics if I have to."

She stood. "Let me know where you stand. *Assurity* is leaving for Nemesis at 0800 hours.

They all rose from the table, each with a downcast look, each keeping their thoughts to themselves . . .

"*Your attention*, please!" Jada stopped them all. "Whether you continue or you head home, *all of you*—

including you, Captain—must be examined in medical after an event like the Chertok Maneuver. That's regs!"

***

Philex-B, flat on her back in the med lab, waited as Jada adjusted the scanner. "Why am I here, Jada? Seriously?"

"Regs require everyone to be examined after a challenging physical event, even E.L.F.s . . ."

Jada squinted at the scanner.

"And I'm part of everyone. You have a problem with that, don't you?"

"No. No problem. Let's put our differences aside for now. Okay?"

"Agreed."

Jada kept peering closely at her med-scan screen. "This is unexpected," Jada observed.

"I'm okay, *yes*?" Philex-B sat up. "You're not an android specialist. What are you checking for?"

"You're fine, but not the way you thought . . . please lay back down."

"Explain, please."

Jada peered even more closely at the screen, "You're more human than you are android."

Philex-B's eyes opened wide. "How? Clarify . . .?"

"There's a heart, a liver, lungs. You're nothing like Rigel." She scratched her head.

Philex-B starred at Jada, listening intently.

"You have an implanted neuron processor in your very human brain, plus human physiology—blood flow. Look at this."

Philex-B slid off the table, viewing the med-scan.

"Truly, I'm a human person? A real girl?"

Jada pointed things out, confirming for Philex-B what she was seeing. "You see your arms, hands, legs, and shoulder muscles? They appear intertwined with an advanced alloy sinew, which enhances your strength."

Philex-B looked at her palms. "I've cut myself before, but they told me my blood was for my skin."

"Part of your cerebral cortex appears actualized, for lack of a better term, by a servomechanism. In short, whoever created you increased your stamina, gave you a faster cognitive ability, and a need for far less sleep."

"So, I'm not a robot, after all? I'm a flesh-and-blood human?"

Philex-B was exuberant. "I only recharge three hours a night. I have to go to the toilet once every two days. They told me that my special food and liquids were only to keep my organic skin healthy."

She put her hands to her cheeks, looking at Jada as though she were about to cry. "Why did they lie to me?"

"I don't know. You are not an android. You have all of the normal human organs, but they're enhanced. I don't know why they would keep this a secret."

Philex-B, elated, grabbed Jada and hugged her. "All? Do I have all of the female parts? Can I have a baby?"

"I don't . . . I believe so. . ."

"I'm going to tell everyone—Zeke. . ."

Philex-B stopped and looked at Jada. "I . . . I don't mean Zeke. I'm. . ."

Jada put her hand on Philex-B's shoulder. "*Zeke?* No worries, I'm over him."

Philex-B pursed her lips. "Over him?"

"Yes, done with him," Jada confirmed.

Philex-B dashed off, hardly listening.

Jada called out after her. "Hey, send the captain in—it's her turn.

Chapter 25

Preparation for Nemesis

FROM THE BRIDGE, Veronika watched Rigel attach a front extender to *Offlander*. He would load the top antimatter tanks into *Assurity's* structural core first—then the bottom, and finally, the hydrogen tanks. Her eyes worked over the details as she watched. She nervously wrapped her ponytail atop her head, scrutinizing every detail. "You'll need to lock down each one as you progress, Rigel."

"Roger that, Captain." Rigel was having difficulty. He couldn't align the new tanks with *Assurity's* slots. He wasn't sure if these tanks were built for the wrong frame or . . . "Captain, I'm going to have to go out and check the frame lock. I may have to adjust it. Might take a bit . . ."

"Got it. Thanks, Rigel. You need anything?"

"No, Captain. I've got a spot-welder in here. If I need it, I will advise."

Veronika grabbed a close shot of one of the frame locks. He was right. There was at least an eight-inch gap.

Rigel floated outside. On examining the first lock, he

knew this would take hours. Floating to the far end of the structure, he calculated that he had enough extra steel to cut each tank's shims. Ten inches per tank. And, they'd each need a double weld.

Almost six hours later, Veronika grabbed her empty coffee cup just as a strong shudder shook the bridge. The tanks were finally locked into place. Rigel radioed Veronika. He was returning to the hanger bay with *Offlander*, job complete.

A moment later, Philex-B arrived on the bridge with a gleeful look and a thermos of coffee. Veronika had completed departure protocols, and Zeke would oversee their departure to Nemesis.

Philex-B handed the thermos to Veronika and waited there for a moment . . . grinning.

"Thank you," Veronika said. She undid the lid and poured herself a cup. Philex-B was still standing there, smiling. "What? What's up, Philex-B?"

"I'm human, Ms. Veronika Taylor Morgan! *Human.*" Her eyes glistened, and her face was ecstatic.

Veronika felt a tingle up her spine. *Oh, no, here we go again.* What other surprises were rattling around in that mechanical brain of hers?

"I'm not telling stories. Ask Jada if you don't believe me." Walking over to her station, Philex-B added, "Oh, Captain, Jada wants you to go to med bay for your exam. I'll take the watch."

Veronika hesitated. Instead of another confrontation, it would be better to visit Jada. Have a private chat about what they should do with Philex-B. Then again, she couldn't leave Philex-B alone on bridge watch—*no way*. This illusion of hers was no joking matter. She looked up at the mainday clock. Zeke would arrive for his shift in nine minutes. She smiled and took a sip of coffee as Rigel maneuvered *Offlander* into the hangar bay.

Philex-B began her maintenance checklist.

Happily, at that moment, Zeke stepped onto the bridge from the lift.

"Hi, ladies," he said. "Philex-B, are you taking watch with me?"

"Yes, I am." She grinned. "I will be your helpmate today!"

Zeke looked wide-eyed at Veronika and said, "Okay."

***

On *Draco*, Sabina sat in the command position, with Magnika taking up the secondary post.

They could both see Zeke on the bridge of *Assurity* over the vid view.

"Sabrina," Zeke said, "*Assurity's* prepared. I'll miss you—we'll all miss you—you little firecracker!"

Sabina smiled. "*Grazie*, Commander."

Assurity looked terrific on her screen. Like a beautiful woman, all made-up and ready for an elegant evening out. A well-equipped mining transport with her broad full tanks finally attached. Sabina gave him a thumbs up. "*Buon viaggio*, Zeke. We're off shortly, as well."

"Hey, keep in touch." He nodded. "Let us know when you arrive at Cassini."

"We will, Zeke."

Assurity parted from *Draco*—slowly at first. By the time Sabina's tears had dropped from her cheeks, *Assurity* had disappeared into a starfield. Completing check-offs for departure, *Draco,* too, would soon be departing, and she felt a tinge of guilt.

***

In *Assurity's* med lab, Veronika climbed off the table to look at the scan of her brain. It was frightening. And, yet, she was still thinking about Philex-B and what Jada had told her. Philex-B was human, after all. Who'd kept this a secret from her? How and why? It was dishonest and terribly wrong in a horrible way. Who were her parents? What happened to them? Was she born in a laboratory? Perfectly evil.

"Unhappily, you are showing the first signs of Delirium, Captain."

Fear is what hit her next.

Jada made a notation. "I'm sorry. It will become progressively worse. Short term memory is first as your ability to focus regresses. You have time. I just don't know how much." It wasn't a surprise. She'd noticed that she'd forgotten things lately. Now, to see it on this scan with her own eyes . . . there were slight but defined areas of blackness . . . holes in her brain tissue. She put her hand to her forehead. She'd seen the same on Ori's scans before he became progressively worse.

"Later, when it becomes unbearable, I can deliver you one shot of *Hydra-Synapse*. It will give you clarity for six to seven hours. Important, it works only one time. After that, directly into cryosleep you go. Buys us a little more time—"

Veronika stood there in silence.

"It doesn't seem to be progressing rapidly. That's good." Jada looked at her chart. "The notes say that your father died of Alzheimer's."

"Actually, Jada, that's not accurate." Veronika's lips trembled. "He killed himself." She laid her hands on each bicep, turning away.

"I understand." Jada moved close to her. "You could go into cryosleep now. It would retard the disease measurably. Sleep and wait for a cure."

"Not my way!"

"You need to realize this, Captain—if you take *Hydra-Synapse*, after the few hours of increased clarity, your overall decline will become exponential. I will have to inform the crew of your condition. You understand."

Veronika turned to leave. "As you must, Jada. But, know this—I will stay on watch until we arrive at Nemesis.

Chapter 26

Research Laboratory, World Health
Continuum

London, England-Section M7

IN THE BONE ROOM at WHC in London, Cassia stood peering through the microscope attached to an expansive viewscreen. I'Jaz was removing samples from between the giant's toes.

Dr. Niles, reading his own detailed DNA chart, pointed to the skeleton. "Unfortunately, this skeleton from Ohio— it's not Nephilim. Giant, yes. Nephilim—no."

"Of course, it's not, Father. We're not getting anywhere with this line of investigation. Seriously, guys. I think that Delirium may have been created in a lab."

"How so?" I'Jaz asked, scraping bone fragments onto a slide.

"Think about it: Scientists across the world have been modifying animals by using human DNA for almost fifty years. It's diabolical. They've been creating these human/animal hybrids in the *pretense* of curing insidious shitty diseases. It's dangerous. I think it got out of hand."

"I think you're missing the point, Cass—"

"I'm not missing a thing, I'Jaz. What if someone, for longer than we could possibly know, has been trying to poison the human genome?" She turned and dropped her hands to her side. "I mean, some people don't think there should be a human being alive on the planet. Except themselves—"

"Yeah," I'Jaz said. "Never understood that one, the hypocrites."

"Think of all of the plagues we've suffered just in the last fifty years.

Cassia watched her dad, his arms crossed. He was in deep thought.

"Hold up for a moment." He took a deep breath. "Perhaps these two lines of reasoning are not as divergent as you two think. Specifically, if we had the living DNA of a true Nephilim, the child produced by the mating of a human woman and an angelic being—"

"Yeah, like that ever happened!" Cassia laughed, staring back into her microscope. "You guys better hope Mom is nearing Nemesis. I haven't heard from her in a week. How far are they?"

I'Jaz went to another viewscreen and pulled up the radio tracking stations, which gave him a pretty reliable mapping of *Assurity's* location. "They should all be waking up today and entering the Nemesis system tomorrow. At least, that's what it looks like here."

Her father had walked off, deep in thought. Cassia remembered when he was working on his master's degree before changing his course study from paleontology to epidemiology. He'd always seem deep in thought. At the time, Cassia was only thirteen.

He took her with him. Father, daughter time. They'd spent the night at a hotel in Helena, near the Belt Mountain Range. After breakfast, they entered a Rover Exploration Vehicle. They sped north across the high desert on a stream of air with a driver-bot at the controls. Seated in the passenger's seat, bearded, and with semi-long hair, her father pointed to the mountain range in the distance.

In the second row, Cassia, with headphones and music blaring in her ear, didn't care much what her father was talking about—the parieto-occipital lobe, or whether he had changed his mind about her going on a come-along jig with a boy in her class.

The android driving pointed. "Mr. Morgan, there is a proximity marker ahead." The marker pulsed three times, sending a thin trail of amber light, which activated a local map and a guide within their Rover windshield. "It's more reliable than GPS but thirty-seven credits, sir, shall I

engage?"

"As you will," Niles agreed.

The female announcer began, "Welcome to the League of the American States, Montana Catacombs, Belt Mountains North. My name is Vicki Belt. I will be your interactive guide. Be advised, you are entering an uninsured earthquake active area. The League of American States will not be held responsible for any unforeseen events. Proceed at your own peril. Now, if you will, please allow me access control of your transport. Arrival time to your destination is eleven minutes, barring unanticipated obstacles, of course."

"Access is approved, Vicki Belt," Niles agreed.

The vehicle veered right, forty-five degrees up a dusty road. The rover compressed slightly on both sides and lowered as tires became its base of travel. Shortly the dusty road became a glorified hiking trail.

Cassia pulled the headphone out of her right ear. (She was still irritated that her father wouldn't allow her to have temple-talk implanted). "Dad, seriously, what are we looking for here? I thought we were going to do some fun stuff."

"This cave, #22, was discovered only recently following an earthquake. This is one of the cave dwellings

I will use for my master's thesis."

Cassia said, "I hope we're not doing what I think we're doing."

"Cassia, there is evidence strewn across the planet. — they were here."

"Oh, God, that's what I thought."

The Rover parked below the cave entrance. The big sign read: "Cave Entrance #22 L.A.S. Geological Sector, Belt Mountains, Montana." A well-illuminated sign beneath read:

You must have your approval token to enter this relic. Refusal to comply with entrance requirements may result in a serious fine or imprisonment.

Hiking up a narrow rocky trail, the three arrived at the cave entrance. Dr. Niles turned to the android and said, "Leave your seismic system on, please. No one else enters here until we are out. Clear?"

"As you wish, Mr. Morgan." The android turned, faced outward, and folded its arms.

They approached the cave opening, backpacks and helmets on, cave lights aglow. It was a very low-ceilinged opening. As the two hunched over and entered, Niles continued his recitation on the Giants of America. "Native American Tribes have never changed their oral testimony. When their ancestors arrived in the Americas—someone was already here."

"You're telling me that Indians said that they lived among these giants? Men and women?"

Her father had to get on his knees and crawl; Cassia went ahead of him with her cave light, illuminated the way. She wasn't in the least bit afraid.

"It gets larger soon, Father," she said.

Catching his breath, he said, "The Choctaw Indian tribe told of a race of giants that once inhabited parts of Tennessee, and with whom their ancestors had to fight when they arrived in Mississippi. On the Great Plains, Chief Rolling Thunder of the Comanches—I think it was in 1857—gave *written* accounts of an ancient race of giants: A race of white men ten feet high who inhabited a large range of country extending from the rising to the setting sun. They were far more powerful than any white people that came after them. Their fortifications crowned the summits of the mountains, protecting their cities situated in the intervening valleys."

Finally, they were able to stand upright in a massive catacomb. Her father, using an illumination light, pointed out what he was seeing.

"Similar locations I've researched suggest that this catacomb was hewn out between 3,200 to 3,500 years ago. It was found quite by accident. Apparently, during an extensive dig about a mile away, two members of the dig— a boy and a girl—happened upon this cave."

Cassia smiled. "I wonder what they were really exploring?"

Cassia hurried forward, leading the way farther into the expansive room. She stopped, and father and daughter allowed their lights to illuminate the vast room. Perfectly rectangular, the walls were inscribed with etched astrological charts.

"Oh my, it's magnificent," Cassia affirmed. "Turn off your light for a moment."

They flipped off both of their helmet lights, expecting total darkness. Instead, the ceiling glowed with a revolving picture of the stars grouped within their constellations, each differentiated by a unique color.

"How is this possible, Father?"

"I . . . I don't know. I've never seen anything like it."

Cassia took a step backward. "The stars and planets are following their circuits behind the stone or in the stone. It's magical."

They moved on and discovered a cave painting on the wall. Cassia re-lit her headlamps. Intricately painted were three gigantic men. In the middle of a large circle were a dozen ordinary-sized humans—cowering. Native Americans, sitting, heads bowed in subjugation.

Cassia moved her headlamp, pinpointing the circle of vanquished Indians. "They look terrified," she moaned. "Nobody knows for sure that this really happened—right? It could be an ancient cartoon."

"This is no cartoon, Cassia. The existence of giants is recorded within the sacred writings of almost every culture across the world. In every civilization. Think for a moment about the Greek Gods."

"What happened to them . . .? The giants. There's no proof they even existed."

"We don't know what happened to this race of humanoids—hybrids—whatever they really were. They vanished from history, in great part due to the Johnsonian Institute. During the time of the old United States, and for hundreds of years, the Johnsonian collected tens of thousands of invaluable skeletal remains, all in the name of science. They appeared at dig sites with great assurance: They would preserve and protect our ancient finds. Later, they claimed that they had never received most of the skeletal remains, and, in fact, the rest they disposed of."

"Why?" Cassia asked. "Why would they do that?"

"That's modern science. If it doesn't fit your world view, hide it—destroy it."

Her father was filming everything from his helmet cam. He stopped beneath a series of symbols: an unrecognizable language, strange mathematical symbols, and equations.

"Stars ablaze," Cassia said. "Look at this."

Cassia was staring at another section of the wall. A video seemed alive under the rock—or on top of it—repeating. A herd of buffalo was running across the plains with three giant men in pursuit. It was like a movie within the stone.

Niles hustled back to where Cassia was transfixed by this translucent show. "Oh, will you look at that!"

In the movie, one of the giants wrestled its buffalo to the ground, gripped it by the neck, and strangled it. Heaving it over its shoulder, it lumbered back the other way, leaving the other two giants sprinting across the plains to stalk their own prey.

Cassia moved on. "My gosh, Father. You'll want to see this." A diorama, clear and detailed . . . the planets of the solar system in order. A collection of dwarf planets and then Rhema, a great distance from Pluto. Then the expanse of the Kuper Belt stretched with trillions of icy rocky formations. Farther still—Nemesis, even deeper in our solar system. "How old is this, do you suppose?"

"I don't know." The planet Nemesis is remote and has been hidden for centuries deep in the expansive Oort cloud. It's believed that Nemesis, every twenty-six million years, travels inward on its elliptical orbit and moves our planets just by its sheer existence. Perhaps it is the real cause of the extinction of the dinosaurs and of these giants."

"Father, how could these people, or whatever they were, have this kind of knowledge so long ago, and we are only now able to prove that a hidden planet actually appeared right before I was born?"

Niles shook his head in wonder. "We assume that ancient man was ignorant? Underdeveloped. In fact, his brain capacity may have been larger than our own."

"I don't get it," Cassia said.

"Cassia, here is what I can tell you: Whoever this race of people was, they lived on our planet. As of yet, we can't decipher either their language or their science.

"Doctor Morgan," the android driver radioed. "I'm getting minor movement along this fault. I suggest that you—"

"We're on our way."

Niles turned off the camera, and the two-headed out the way they had come, Niles dreading the crawl he'd have to make.

"We've got to tell Mom about this!" Cassia said.

Chapter 27

Cryo Room of Assurity

IN *ASSURITY'S* CRYOLIFE CHAMBER, the pod tops unsealed one at a time. Chiffon and Ruby helped in the orderly arising of the crew from cryosleep.

In his underwear, Zeke was already on his feet, looking about for problems, but everything looked as it should. He could hardly focus, though. Grabbing a towel and drying off, he moved to a *beeping* com screen, still trying to focus after his forty-six-day sleep.

On the bridge, the wake-up chime startled her. Veronika had fallen asleep in her captain's chair again. At the moment between sleep and consciousness, she'd dreamt of Ori. The glitter of his eyes. The smile. Then a frightening visitation—a ghostly fraud of him, as if he were saying, "If it wasn't for you, Mom, I'd still be alive."

She woke every morning now with a sadness in her gut. But she knew her Ori; he loved his mother.

Looking down and wiggling her bare feet, she snickered at her newly polished red toenails.

Rigel, at his station, lifted his hand and said, "Good mainday, Captain."

She'd hardly left the bridge for forty-six days, sleeping in her command chair or in her cramped captain's office off the bridge. Ensuring that Plum prepared her meals in the galley, she ran for thirty-five minutes and took a shower every day. That was it except for the yoga program, which she despised.

Most of the time, dinner was with Philex-B, leaving Rigel in command on the bridge. It was getting a bit much, though, Philex-B asking her all kinds of personal questions about men, about pleasing them, and about being a wife. How worship and prayer were to be valued within a family. Star tails, even Cassia hadn't asked her stuff like that.

Philex-B kept pushing the conversation into uncomfortable circles. Like, why do humans please themselves?

"My gosh," Veronika answered, "what are you viewing, Philex-B?"

"Surely, if I'm going to marry and have a family, I need to know these things. To please my husband. At the same time, I will be a mother and taking care of little ones. It is a worthy endeavor. I've read that it's a problem for some women. All of these pressing issues at the same time.

Wouldn't you agree, Mrs. Morgan?"

Veronika had lived without physical contact as they all had. Most of them, anyway. They were all very young and unattached. The only hand that touched her sexually was her own. It was embarrassing, honestly, to talk about it. One night, after one of those Philex-B counseling moments, she'd awakened with a vivid dream of Niles caressing and then penetrating her, kissing her passionately. She'd buried her face in the pillow as she awoke in delight. It reminded her to remember that Philex-B was human, after all—young and full of excitement.

Apart from that, she wasn't taking any chances. She'd promised the crew that she would monitor cryo and yank them out at even the slightest sign of a problem. Either Chiffon or Ruby was stationed in the cryolife chamber at all times. And, twice a day, like clockwork, Veronika would visit cryo and personally monitor stats. No one was to be in exercise protocols—nor would they. They weren't to be in cryo that long this time, anyway.

"Veronika, good news," Isaac informed her over com. "We have now officially entered the Nemesis system. The crew is awakening from cryosleep, and all is well."

"Honest to goodness? Yes! Finally. That's great news, Isaac."

Veronika rose out of her captain's chair and shuffled to the coffee pot, which was always fresh and attended by Plum. "Hey, Plum," she requested over com, "can I get a sandwich, chips, and a soda?" Scratching her messy auburn hair, she poured herself a cup of black coffee and wiped the morning from her eyes. "I'm damn sore from sleeping in that chair, Rigel. I don't think I've put on makeup in weeks." She wrapped her hair in an even messier head knot than it already was.

"No problem, ma'am. You look refreshed. Everything is as it should be."

The only mornings were when she played sunrises over the bridge viewscreen—birds chirping, children playing, and all that . . .

I wonder how people are doing now? Veronika thought. The news transmissions from Earth were becoming less frequent and more unreliable. What Cassia and Niles shared with her was all she could rely on, so she'd stopped watching the news feeds. They depressed her. Grammar school children by themselves, without parents, trying to take care of infants and each other. It troubled her deeply. Where were they getting food in the big cities? *I hope they've managed to keep some of the vital infrastructure functional.*

For the last year, every piece of information about the

plague, medical care, food supplies, even *Assurity's* progress was synthesized and released to the masses from one central source—London. Society was in shambles. During the last two and a half years, thousands of Christian missions had been caring for the sick and poor worldwide. Now they were being attacked by anarchists. There was no police force left to stop them. The same was true of synagogues and mosques.

Most churches in Europe had been closed years before, and unless they had practical or historical value, they'd been torn down. That safety net was completely gone for feeding or caring for the hungry and ill. Christianity had been outlawed in Canada and Australia for over fifty years. In the L.A.S, it was regulated and had to conform to proper "all-inclusive" regulations. All sermons had to be first approved by the National Board of Beliefs. In any new L.A.S. state, all clergy were licensed by the central government. And church attendance was mandated at only fifty people or less. Yet, in South America, from Mexico to Argentina—Catholicism was thriving.

Veronika wasn't interested in any of that, but it seemed arbitrary and amiss—maybe even evil. How long would it be before the L.A.S. was controlled by one central world government? Across the world, under this intense duress, it appeared that human beings were giving up their sovereignty without a fight.

I can't solve everything, she thought. *We have our job to do. This is not something I can dwell on.*

She set her coffee down, put her hands at the top of her buttocks, and stretched. What a grind this was, night after night. Why hadn't she heard from Niles or Cassia?

"Finally," she said happily. "Let's open the bow shield, Isaac."

"We're clear for a few minutes. Why not? Happy mainday, Veronika!"

The shield opened to a sparkling, dazzling new world as the Nemesis planetary system came into a vibrant view. Encircled by a series of asteroid belts, they seemed to orbit like guardians of the domain. In the dark flickering distance, Nemesis, the Neptune-sized planet, sat circled by a multi-colored glow. Veronika took a deep breath.

"You know, Isaac, no one else has ever seen this before now. They initially certified Nemesis as a real planet, only using very faint positioning scans. They sent two probes to Nemesis, but neither returned. Neither transmitted data back to Earth, either. Swallowed up. That was long before Cassini Sol Station was ever built—or you, for that matter, Isaac."

"Well, we have arrived, Veronika. And I am certain that you will perform as needed and bring this matter to a swift and prosperous conclusion!"

Veronika looked out at the planet that they would soon visit. "Isaac, you are a true friend, and I thank you for all of your guidance. Inexorably, I miss them horribly—my husband, my daughter, my son, Ori. I haven't heard a thing in weeks. I hope Ori's doing better."

There was a long pause. "I'm sorry, Veronika," Isaac sympathized. "I'm sure something will arrive soon. But, to remind you, Ori has passed. He is with the angels, ma'am."

She gasped. "I'm sorry? —When?"

"Some time ago, Veronika."

"That's right. I remember now."

But, she hadn't, and that was troubling.

"Magnify 200 percent, computer," she requested and stepped forward, pouring the remainder of a bottle of Scotch into her coffee and cursing herself.

Brilliant colors flickered and reflected across her face.

"My God, Isaac, this spectacle of stars, with its fiery majesty—it chills me to the bone." She shook her head in wonder. "No fooling." It'll be nice to have some *people* company."

She heard the lift swish open as Zeke rushed onto the bridge, still dripping wet and in his underwear. He reached the nearest com station, punched in numbers, and studied the display.

Rigel stood, concerned. On the bridge screen, from around Nemesis, something was approaching. It first appeared as a glittering cloud . . . but of what?

"Mr. Newton!" Zeke called out as he looked up at the bridge view. "Deep scan, please. This is a problem, Rigel."

Rigel moved forward. "Agreed. Their velocity is unusual."

Veronika turned, not catching on, distracted. Unsure why her commander was on the deck in his underwear.

"*Hey, Isaac!*" Zeke was furious. "Why didn't you pick this up! Show me that sector: 34.52."

On the magnified screen—a micrometeoroid swarm approached *Assurity.* "Closing front shield," Isaac announced. "It was concealed by the planet, Commander. I'm remiss."

As the shield closed, Klaxon alarms sounded throughout the ship.

"Straight up," Veronika interjected, looking closely. "What in blazing stars is it now?"

Into the com, she announced, "All crew assume stations. Ruby, Chiffon, Plum, get to a hold-down."

As *Assurity* was immersed in the cloud of micrometeoroids, Philex-B rushed onto the deck and took her station.

As the particles battered *Assurity's* forward shield, Veronika pulled on her shoes. "Isaac, what the heck? He's right. You should have seen this coming!"

"Protection is holding," Isaac said as he came onscreen. "It's the most damnable ill luck. I'm analyzing incoming quantity and velocity. Again, my apologies, Captain."

"Philex-B, show me the interior of the forward shield, please," Veronika called out. Inside, tiny micrometeoroids gained entrance through a microscopic breach in the lower bracket section. The breach probably occurred when *Draco* attacked them, she deduced.

Xiao Xing arrived on the bridge, startled, watching.

"Magnify the shield!" Veronika yelled, angered at yet another problem. Rigel, give me a visual.

On Rigel's com screen, Veronika could see the micrometeoroids streaming into the coolant ducts.

"Captain, micrometeoroids have breached the shield,' Rigel said. "They are entering the forward coolant system. I'm going to address this."

Life support warnings flashed across the bridge. Rigel

jumped up and ran for the lift.

"Xiao Xing," Veronika ordered, "go with him."

"Me?"

"Yeah, you!" Veronika started pacing.

Xiao Xing and Rigel had to wait for forty-five seconds before the habitation wheel dropped them at the main corridor. They both suited up quickly. Getting to the lower shield, they'd have to float using the hand grabs.

Poldi and Jada arrived on the bridge, still disheveled from cryo and half-dressed.

"What's up, guys?" Poldi brought up his com station.

"Temperature throughout the main core is rising," Philex-B reported.

Zeke looked over at Veronika, standing close to the bridge screen, watching the meteoroids squeeze into the foreword compartment.

"Only a matter of time before it overheats the entire ship," Poldi warned.

Jada touched her temple, brought up temple-talk, and scanned the temperature. "We are already at ninety-two degrees and rising. Estimate, within 7.4 minutes, it will reach 112 degrees on the bridge. Can't say for the rest."

The crew was already sensing the beginning effects of heat.

"Any ideas, anyone?" Veronika asked.

Poldi tapped his screen. "If we re-initialize life support, the temperature will drop for a few minutes. It would at least give us time to clear the vents."

Jada moved next to Veronika, who was starting to sweat profusely. "Are you okay, Captain?"

"Been better, but it's good to see you guys up and awake."

"If you need that shot, please tell me."

"Thank you, Jada. Isaac, where are we in this storm?"

"We'll be clear in twenty-two seconds."

In engineering, Veronika and the bridge crew appeared on Tatiana's com screen.

Veronika asked, "Tatiana—your opinion. If we re-initialize life support, will we force temperatures down?"

"I believe, *yes*," she answered.

Poldi interjected, "I know its chancy, Captain, but it's the best hope we have, I think."

"Initiate, Zeke," Veronika commanded. "Chiffon, you all better be at hold-down. Beginning re-initialization of life support in, counting . . . ten seconds."

Behind the forward shield, Rigel and Xiao Xing temporarily patched the breach with metallic sealant. Now they were vacuuming the detached spall debris from the impact of the micrometeoroids. It was awkward work, floating this way and that, chasing tiny microscopic bits of rock and metal. The phantom meteoroids were nearly sucked up; only the motes of dancing dust remained. They'd have to double-weld this section later.

"Re-initializing life support in three-two-one," Zeke announced over com.

Lights flashed on and off throughout the ship. Then blackness for ten seconds. Finally, they came on and stayed on.

Rigel and Xiao Xing, their helmet lights reflecting their faces, smiled at one another. Thank heavens.

As life support temperatures and oxygen levels returned to normal, the crew across the bridge cheered. Poldi gave Jada the thumbs up as Veronika thanked Zeke for his vigilance.

Moments later, they all heard it: A considerable crashing rumble, then hydraulics trying to cope with the pressure building along the habitation ring.

Assurity began tumbling—end over end. Veronika stumbled and grabbed her chair arm, struggling to get seated. She buckled up.

They all knew it. Those not strapped in floated from their seats.

On Veronika's com screen, she could see *Assurity's* schematic of the ship cartwheeling toward Nemesis. She instinctively began even breathing and repeated swallows to keep herself from heaving. "Dead wrong!" she yelled. "Buckle up. We're losing grav sim control."

The crew struggled to remain seated as they floated up and out of their chairs.

As the crew grabbed whatever they could to get back to their stations and buckle in, Veronika started eliciting ideas. "All of you—opinions? If I expel coolant, will it decrease our flip?" She was almost certain that it would.

"Crap!" one effing thing after another!" Zeke yelled as he grabbed his command chair arm and pulled himself into his seat.

Rigel and Xiao Xing, still in their suits, came onscreen. Rigel pulled himself near a camera so that Veronika could see and hear him clearly. "Theoretically, yes. Conversely, dumping coolant presents an extreme risk."

"Got any other ideas? Rigel . . . *anyone?*"

No response—and then Poldi interjected, "It's crazy and dangerous, Captain—but I think it will work."

"We're only a minute from the coolant hold," Rigel said over com. "Going now."

"I'm still listening," Veronika repeated.

No response from anyone else.

"If not . . . I'm venting coolant. Philex-B, on my count, flush the entire coolant system."

Poldi had his hands on his head.

Zeke, belting into his station, said to himself, "This is dangerous as hell!'

"On your count," Philex-B confirmed.

Veronika pointed, "Three-two-one . . . go!"

"Hope you're spot on, Captain," Zeke said, grabbing his handholds.

Poldi, from the radio array camera monitor, could see streams of coolant flowing from below the hull as *Assurity* flipped end over end.

Veronika called out over com, "Rigel, you and Xiao Xing—replace that coolant in a flurry."

Reaching the coolant hold, Xiao Xing had already attached a hose to the coolant tank as Rigel turned on the spigot from the liquid helium reserve tank.

Zeke watched on com as *Assurity,* tumbling end over end, rapidly approached the asteroid belts. There was a wail of twisting, grating metal—stretching decks. Nemesis was still a reasonable distance away, but they were out of control and moving fast. Those belts of boulders acted as sentries. At this speed, any collision would obliterate the ship and kill them all.

Isaac cautioned over com, "Captain, we are rapidly nearing the primary belt of asteroids orbiting Nemesis."

Veronika swiped screens, pushed modules, and moved sequences. "Zeke," Veronika shouted, "Reverse thrust in five-four-three-two . . . go, Zeke!"

Veronica looked at her hand. It was shaking. "Philex-B, begin forward and aft exhaust release at ten percent!"

"Hey, Zeke, I need your help here—"

Zeke hustled to her station. As she got up, a control stick arose from the command arm, and Zeke took manual control of *Assurity*. Punching in data and taking control with the pilot stick, Zeke methodically used his thrusters to slow *Assurity's* roll.

Veronika put her hands to her head. It was pounding. The ship sounded like it was coming apart—ripping, tearing—metal against metal.

Slowly, within a few anxious minutes, Zeke was able to reorient *Assurity*. "I've got her," he declared. "We're flying true.

Xiao Xing, from engineering, called over com, "We've refilled the coolant hold, Captain."

The bridge crew was glued to their schematics as gravity slowly returned and the temperature neared optimum.

"We've done it!" Isaac declared over ship's com: "All systems are returning to normal."

Finally, a *boisterous cheering* on the deck and across the ship's com.

Veronika stood and took a deep breath. "Great job, people! Zeke, blow off V on the drift. Let's not bash into any of those rocks going in. Hey, Xiao Xing, on your way back check on the Hybrids, will you?" Veronika took a deep breath and closed her eyes. "I'm going to my cabin. Zeke, assume command, please."

During the next 7.5 hours, Zeke carefully navigated *Assurity* through the ancient asteroid belts of Nemesis.

Chapter 28

Captain's Quarters of Assurity

VERONIKA AWAKENED, her arms rigid, her forehead glistening with sweat. A bassoon or trombone—both maybe—played a moaning, out of tune, terrifying melody over ship's com. Then she realized it wasn't over ship's com at all. She was in her bed, asleep in her quarters.

"Isaac, I can't move!" she cried out.

Isaac responded immediately. "Take a deep breath, Veronika." He spoke in a soothing tone. "You were having a nightmare."

Sitting up with a jolt, she shrieked, "*Ori!*"

She scanned the dark, "*Lights bright!*" she yelled. The lights in her quarters illuminated the room as her eyes swept the corners.

She lay back down, tears in her eyes. "Ori must be frightened to death. I'm asking you, Isaac, as my friend—should I go into cryo now and hope I make it home for him? Or, keep pushing myself? To what end, I don't know." She pulled her blanket tightly around herself. "To be candid,

Isaac—I don't think this crew is capable of completing this mission without me."

"May I speak freely?"

"Yes."

"Shall I join you?"

"Yes, please do."

Isaac appeared in the chair in her room. Younger this time. He looked her age, in his forties—wearing a bathrobe and slippers. Smiling, he crossed his legs, getting comfortable. "Remember, Veronika—Ori has passed from this life into the next. You have forgotten a few times. Perfectly understandable—we being so far from home and with no tactile contact with those we love. To answer your question—if the supreme ethic given to humankind is love, I can assure you that you've done everything humanly possible . . . wouldn't you agree?'

"How am I to judge such a thing?" She closed her eyes.

Tears welled up. "As I told Jada, my father took his own life on my twenty-first birthday. How's that for a present? They said it was Alzheimer's—now I have Delirium."

Veronika sat up, gritting her teeth. "I left my son to face the same frightful, hellish nightmare as I faced when my father left abandoned me. I left Ori without his mother—

the same as my father left me—*alone*. No goodbyes, no I love you . . . What kind of mother does that?"

"Perhaps this would be an ideal time for us to pray."

"I'm not a praying person, Isaac—you already know that."

"Well, in the words of the esteemed Englishman, C.S. Lewis: 'There is no neutral ground in the universe: every square inch, every split second, is claimed by God and counter-claimed by Satan.'"

"Mankind navigated us into this black hole," she answered. "I'm afraid that men and women *together* will have to pull us out."

"Seems unlikely, Veronika; Men and women? I think not. The ratio of intelligence, which is not human, is increasing. Humans now represent less high intelligence than all sentient beings—

"Oh, you don't believe that, Isaac."

"Case in point—decisions are being made and implemented throughout your world by what you so affectionately refer to as *the robots*. I don't wish to lament the point, but your *homo sapien* species is leaning dangerously close to extinction. I know as a whole that you can't fathom that." Isaac rubbed his nose. "As it is, most of you are cyborgs, in the real sense of the word. You're all hooked up in one manner or another. Your children can no longer differentiate between a game and reality. Why do over nine percent of the population on Earth, as well as those living in space, take their own lives before they reach the age of twenty-one? I believe that this disease is as much a reflection of humanity's spiritual emptiness as anything. So many young people—their entire lives ahead of them in your godless world—are peering into the black hole of hopelessness."

Isaac stood and looked down at Veronika. "I experienced this horrid foreboding during my own lifetime. When the black plague-infected us, it killed over fifty-two percent of the population of Europe. Probably much more. When there is no faith, there is no hope—"

Veronika swung her legs to the floor. "Oh, that's idiotic, Isaac. Faith has nothing to do with this disease."

"Candidly, I disagree. You must see that there is a divine design and order to the universe. The motions which the planets uphold do not equate themselves from an ethereal nether world but are inspired in their construction by an intelligent agent—your creator."

"No doubt, there is an unseen order that permeates the cosmos," she said. "without question—but mathematical relationships underpin it."

"As for me, Veronika, I would seek God and commit my cause to him, for he can perform marvelous things for you—for all of you. You can't do everything on your own."

"This is not helping!" Veronika trembled, putting her hands to her face. "Why doesn't he stop this plague if he's so powerful?"

"Perhaps *you* are the answer to that question, Veronika. Throughout history, he seems to mostly direct his assistance through chosen individuals."

Isaac rubbed his nose and ruffled his messy hair. "Irrespective, I recommend the following: You must show no cracks—no weakness. No doubt. You are the captain of this ship and the leader of this mission. No one said this would be easy. No monumental task of survival is ever easy. In war or in peace. After all, man is born to trouble as the sparks fly upward."

Veronika let out an anxious gasp of air.

"Remember this, Veronika—*please*: Even in deepest, darkest space, He is as near as your very breath."

Isaac popped to his feet with a joyful look and threw his arms out. "Either way, the cryo system is in *tiptop shape*. And, to be sure, I will watch over your every sleeping moment."

Veronika hopped off the bed. "That's *so* reassuring,

Isaac. I'm going to the bridge. You may carry on."

He fizzled and disappeared.

Chapter 29

Bridge of Assurity

ZEKE ROSE FROM the captain's chair as Veronika arrived on deck, accompanied by Jada and Xiao Xing. "Captain on the bridge," Zeke announced.

Veronika was refreshed and somehow feeling much better after her talk with Isaac.

Zeke filled her in. He had successfully maneuvered them through the dangerous asteroid belts, the guardians of the hidden planet. They were now nearing the Neptune-sized world of Nemesis.

Everyone was present, even Chiffon, Ruby, and Plum, and they all stood as the three entered.

"We're all here, Captain!" Poldi affirmed.

They were celebrating something. Smiling and chatting together—happy. All were beaming at her.

"What's the occasion?" she asked.

Zeke was pouring scotch for everyone. Poldi approached Veronika with a glass. But, he paused, reached out, and carefully hugged her as the crew applauded. He stepped back and looked her in the eyes. Handing her a glass, he raised his own. "Job well done, Captain! You made some darn quick calculations, pulled off a miracle, and saved our ass." They all cheered and smiled.

Lovely, she thought. *Especially Poldi?* "You all contributed to that success," she smiled.

"A toast, then." Zeke raised his glass.

Veronika tipped hers to the crew. Everyone was genuinely joyous, talking, and it was perhaps too good to be true. Who knew what they faced next? Nemesis lay before them on the bridge screen. Leaping streams of crimson and emerald light arced from the aurora borealis-like world of Nemesis. A planet that had been theorized for eons? A big world that had remained hidden from their powerful telescopes even into modern times.

"Let me remind you all," Poldi exclaimed, "Until the late twenty-first century, most believed there was a planet out here somewhere—based upon its tugging and pushing of the outer planets. It was theoretical, of course. *The problem was*—they couldn't see it. For centuries they called it by different names: Planet Nine, Nibiru, and Nemesis— Hidden in the vastness of the outer Neptunian objects, astronomical theorists believed that Nemesis (that's what they resolved to name it) followed an orbit. A very unusual one. Every 3,600 years, its orbit swung it closer to the inner planets, jostling them with its gravitational weight. Some scientists still maintain that Nemesis' quiet hand keeps all of the inner planets in alignment and harmony. Cheers to that," he laughed!

Poldi pointed his glass toward the planet and downed his scotch.

The laughing of her crew interrupted Veronika's tangled thoughts. At last, they were working together—a team. She never thought it would happen. Interrupting her joyful moment, an unpleasant pinging. Insistent . . .

She turned to the sound and looked at Rigel, who already had his eyes fastened on her.

He shook his head. He didn't wish to tarnish this moment. "We have company, Captain! I'm placing the object on the screen . . .

On the bridge screen, at first, whatever it was appeared blurry and faint. In the background, behind the object and still in the distance, was their destination, Nemesis.

"Mein Gott," Poldi stuttered. "Will you look at that?" He poured another shot of scotch.

Philex-B hustled to her station. "I'm magnifying, Captain."

Enlarged across the bridge screen was what was

undoubtedly an alien ship. Gigantic—creepy. That's all you could say, really. It looked like some kind of deep undersea fish. Bulbous—it was the darkest of blues and riddled with gaping holes.

Veronika could feel her heart pounding. "What is that?"

Poldi stepped closer and raised his arms. "What *was* it is more like it."

Tatiana sat at an ancillary station and began her analysis. "Wonder how long the beast has been there?"

"Rigel, bring us to a crawl," Veronika said. "We'll take a quick look and move on."

Veronika turned to Jada. "I want that shot now."

Everyone moved to their posts. Silently. They all heard her request.

"Are you sure, Captain? You will be on a timer. You know that?"

"Perfectly straight—please do it, Jada."

Going to a locker on the bridge, Jada came back and administered the Hydra-Synapse shot into Veronika's bicep. Everyone was watching out of the corner of his eye.

Veronika pointed. "Zeke, take us around that profane object. To the other side, please. Philex-B, let's wake up *Resolute*. We better have a look."

"Initiating drone *Resolute*," Philex-B confirmed.

Moments later, the bullet-shaped, gleaming silver probe *Resolute* whizzed from *Assurity's* hanger recess. It paused mid-flight. Its thrusters flared as it computed its coordinates. Then it tore off in a direct trajectory toward the hole-riddled, alien ship.

Upon reaching the wreck, Resolute flattened against the side of the alien wreckage. The crew was transfixed to the bridge screen. What had seemed bulbous and big and dark blue appeared now steel-colored—dark matter reflecting through the gaping holes in the ship.

Once securely attached to the alien ship, the drone's casing latches released. The cover opened. Out crawled a three-foot-tall robot. With a shiny golden helmet and beige metallic skin, it was affectionately referred to as Little Robotman. Its armored arms and legs were in human proportion. Robotman's audio was activated, causing static through the speakers and across the bridge. Pulling itself from the drone container, the Robotman groaned like an old man as it stretched its body.

Robotman crawled slowly up the side of the alien vehicle to an auxiliary hatch. It could have used any number of gaping holes in the ship but followed an arranged directive. Touching the entry-point with a finger, a holographic list of florescent blue numbers flittered from its eyes. The hatch slowly opened.

Crawling into the opening, little Robotman disappeared. Gibbering sounds issued forth over *Assurity's* com— Short squeals and grunts. Then his helmet camera activated.

As Robotman made his way from the entry point, considerable amounts of debris, spall flakes, and damaged equipment made it appear as if a snowstorm lived inside the wreck. Open space was exposed through the far side of the cargo hold, or what was left of it. Flakes drifted, cluttering everyone's view.

"There is a problem," the Robotman announced over a static ship's com. "Remnants of the crew—corpses appear . . . *fossilized.*

Veronika had leased this highly developed bot robot from Allied Robotic—with an insurance policy, of course, just in case. He (she kind of thought of it as a male) was fully capable of assessing strategic situations. However, it was not a battle bot, so it was not equipped with any weapon systems.

Everyone began to speak at once.

Veronika said, "Quiet! Please . . ."

They quieted.

"I'm going to take *Offlander* over and investigate. I can't see crap from this clutter. I don't want us to disembark onto Nemesis until I know what's in that vessel. Zeke, your opinion?"

Zeke dropped his head and took a moment to answer. "I think it's a bad idea, Captain—"

"So, do I," Jada declared. "You're on the clock, ma'am."

Everyone was throwing in their two cents.

"Stop for a moment, please!*"* Philex-B said. "We all agree you can't go alone, Captain—it's too dangerous!"

"Look," Veronika insisted. "Zeke's not going, he's the Commander, and Philex-B, you're not going, either. I want you two here in case there's a problem. Every one of you is needed. This mission must succeed." She looked over the crew. They were all standing and scrutinizing her. *I should go alone,* she was sure.

"What about, Rigel?" Philex-B asked. "At least one other."

Veronika closed her eyes, collecting her thoughts. "Poldi—will you come with me? You have a broad knowledge—"

"Me?" He threw his hands out. "I will be honored,

ma'am!" He raised one finger in the air. "I hope that doesn't mean that I'm the one who is expendable."

They all laughed at that.

***

Piloting *Offlander,* Veronika stayed in communication with Robotman, who had opened a utility landing bay. Landing *Offlander* onto the deck, Veronika and Poldi slipped on their helmets and disembarked. Waiting for them was little Robotman.

It was a spacious landing area with several large pieces of machinery and a discarded alien transport.

She said to Poldi, "All of this stuff. And, the size of this ship—the equipment—it's enormous. I wonder if they evacuated this ship before it was destroyed."

The two of them looked around before they decided to continue.

"Weird, ma'am," Poldi said. "We were briefed on the equipment your husband found in Antarctica. I saw the pictures. Some of those pieces, especially along that wall, look eerily similar."

Robotman led them down a corridor that seemed to

meander endlessly. Veronika was following Poldi, and he kept looking down at the floor. Some kind of porous, squishy material. She kept looking behind her, spooked. The whole place was as eerie and creepy as a nightmare.

They entered a room—if you could call it a room—that presented an enormous opening. It was as long as a soccer field and looked to be filled with hibernation pods like she'd seen in Niles's photos from inside the alien ship in Antarctica. Veronika stopped for a moment, but Robotman was insistent that they continue.

"They are *all* empty, Ms. Morgan," he said in his scratchy voice. "I checked." He hustled on.

All of the available data on mission parameters would have been transferred, copied, and assimilated by Robotman before being stored onboard *Assurity*. That was standard for any bonded security contract utilizing a high intel bot for a mission. But this was an unknown. Robotman was security-upgraded, except without a weapons system.

At the bottom of the stairs, the three made their way up the rim and through what was probably once an eating concourse. The seats and eating platforms were substantial, as though the inhabitants of this ship were far more robust than humans. It gave her the chills. She didn't have a second to get scared, though, because Little Robotman was moving at a fast pace, especially for his size.

They must have walked for five minutes when they began to descend down a weird alloy intertwined walk-down. Near the bottom, Poldi and Veronika came to an immediate halt.

"God, this is exactly wrong!" Veronika spoke out.

"Captain, this entire ship could be diseased," Poldi blurted.

Veronika stepped forward and squatted.

At eye-level, she looked at a bird-like animal in a cage—it was about the size of a crow. Standing motionless, it was clearly fossilized. And, with four wings, it looked as though it had been a frightening creature at one time. "Poldi, can you photograph this and get a reference from Isaac?"

Whatever it was, along with the hundreds of dinosaur-like creatures that filled this hold—was mind-boggling. There were various sized cages everywhere.

"It's a Microraptor, Captain," Poldi said. "The late Cretaceous period."

The two gazed around them. More cages, hundreds of them. As they walked down broad isles, each contained the remains of a strange animal. Some gigantic, others the size of your hand—most stacked high, one upon another.

In deep space, she knew that with the temperature reaching -454.81 Fahrenheit and with no atmosphere, water evaporated rapidly and living creatures fossilized very quickly. Without exception, these remains were all frozen in time. *Lifeless*.

They photographed a few of the creatures for the record. A Pegomastex, looking like a modern giant rat with long back legs and front stubby ones, faced them perfectly preserved in her cage. She was three meters tall, six meters long, and had had a furry body.

Poldi's face turned white in his helmet. "I wouldn't want to have that thing scurrying around my home in Berlin. I hate rats."

These smaller animals were collected in one location. They moved on. More familiar creatures from the days of the dinosaurs took up a large portion of the containment area. "Scan that one, Poldi," Veronika said.

"It's a Mamenchisaurus," he said. "A much smaller version of the Brachiosaurus."

"What is all this? Veronika called out. "There are hundreds of ancient animals in here. Who was piloting this . . .?"

"Ma'am—it looks to me like some kind of a traveling natural history museum. The question is—why? What's it doing in orbit around a planet that for centuries we couldn't see?"

Robotman had been patient. Standing and waiting. "We must continue, please."

Veronika called back to *Assurity* as they followed another passageway heading downward, deeper into the ship. Veronika was on com with Zeke. "Zeke, we are moving to the bottom level of this ship and approaching some large breaches in the sidewall. I may lose you for a bit."

Lots of static. "I copy, Captain," he replied.

Robotman suddenly stopped and instructed them that they would have to use the pressure clamps in their boots while crossing this upcoming section. The outside space was pocked with holes in this section. He reminded them to watch their heads. Debris was heavy.

Veronika grabbed the handrail high above her head and followed close behind Robotman, who, because he was so short, had no rail to hold on to. They cleared the broadest breach and had to climb a very wide ladder going up. The access point that he was taking her to had been damaged.

Climbing slowly to the next level, the three pulled themselves up, one at a time, and stood there for a moment, beholding a far different cargo hold. This was gargantuan.

Veronika had never seen anything like it in all of her military days. Not on any station she'd ever been on.

"Holy shit!" she exclaimed. "What am I looking at?"

Poldi stood dumbfounded for a moment. "It looks to me, Captain, as though all of these saucers or ships—whatever they are—were en route somewhere until this mother ship was pummeled by a meteor storm.

Chapter 30

Preparation for Nemesis

ARRIVING BACK ON *ASSURITY,* Veronika and Poldi stepped off the lift and burst onto the bridge.

Poldi was excited, waving his arms and speaking half of his words in German. "*Gott,* that was the weirdest thing I've ever seen." He stopped and threw his hands up. "Everything in there is strange. Animals from God knows when? Giant creatures and . . . it's all frozen in time."

Veronika hurried to her command station, sat down, and pulled up a survey map of Nemesis. Turning to Philex-B, she said, "did you engage the satellite drones?"

"Engaged fifty-six minutes ago. . . all planet analysis is quantified, Captain."

"Rigel, update us on the planet, please. We need to move on . . ."

Rigel brought up a holographic display on a big table below the bridge screen and gathered the crew around it. "Nemesis is actually smaller in mass than Neptune and not gaseous. It's tide-locked and rocky. We anticipated that.

One hemisphere is in permanent daylight, and the other hemisphere in permanent darkness. It has no moons." He pointed it out clearly on the contour holo map.

"Now, this is significant: I've verified a 4.5-kilometer habitable zone within the day/night divider. That's almost three-square miles for you league people," he affirmed with a nod and pointed. "This is our deployment point."

Veronika added, "We know from our last probe what's on the surface of Nemesis. But, below—that's another story. Philex-B, prepare magnification, please—Poldi, go ahead, atmospheric composition and temperature."

On the bridge screen appeared a grainy teleview. Poldi boosted reception and enlarged the habitable zone as he walked and pointed, "This will be a strange and challenging environment." Stopping, he nervously played with his beard. "Nothing lives on the surface of this planet." Pointing out the center of the habitable zone, he clarified. "That black desert you see there, it intersects with an icy liquid methane sector. Temperature is tolerable within the hab zone . . . still, suits are essential. The planet is surprisingly well lit—charged by a colorful glow of particles that remain trapped within its magnetic field."

"Achtung!" He gazed at everyone and smiled, "This is essential! As Rigel noted, we cannot survive *for a moment* outside of the habitable zone. When it ends, on either side,

it ends abruptly. It's the end!"

Veronika walked over to Philex-B's station. "Show us potential points of contact, now, *B*."

Veronika got a big chuckle from the crew when she called Philex-B "B."

Philex-B smiled and zoomed-in, utilizing satellite number two to show a radio station. "There is a transmitting station in the desert sector," she began. Then she focused satellite number one on a solid citadel-like structure. "Almost two kilometers away from the radio station is this temple-like structure in the icy methane sector. A citadel of sorts . . . No life forms exist on the surface. At least life forms we know of. Below the surface, Nemesis generates its own heat from within the planet." She looked up, beaming. "And I *am reading* liquid water below the surface."

Veronika stood, arms crossed, thinking. "Isaac, do you have anything to add?"

"The one concern, of course, for all of you is—" Isaac paused for a moment. "No one really knows what creepy alien creatures may be lurking deep in the shadows—"

There were oohs and aahs from the crew.

"Knock it off, Professor!" Zeke challenged.

Veronika shook her head and smiled. "We will go together. Rigel and Poldi, you will survey the radio transmitter. Xiao Xing, Zeke, and Philex-B, you will join me. Rigel and Zeke get to the armory. Gather us any weapons you deem we'll need. Tatiana, prepare *Offlander*. We'll meet in ten."

"What about me?" Jada complained.

"I require you here, Jada; the moment we deliver the samples, you can begin sequencing."

"Captain," Jada reminded her, "your time is limited. Are we clear?"

"Got it, let's move."

Chapter 31

Besieged Embassy

IN LONDON, LIKE A BESIEGED EMBASSY, the World
Health Continuum research laboratory was under attack.
Still early morning, a crowd had gathered outside the gates,
and for hours had grown in size. They were most interested
in the food they assumed was being utilized by the
laboratory workers. At any one time, there had been as
many as one hundred people working at the lab. Now there
were only thirty-three.

Many in the crowd were armed. When a large
construction truck, overflowing with gravel, rammed the
front gates, the firefight began. Hearing the gunfire, Cassia
looked out the window as their soldiers traded fire with the
anarchists.

Waiting to move to another location, their three heavily
armored military transports were backed up to a covered
doorway. Almost everyone had been hustled into a vehicle
except Dr. Morgan, I'Jaz, and Cassia.

Fortunately, the computer systems and radio alignment gear had been loaded and transported early in the morning. With gunfire getting closer, head military official, Lt. Commander Elliot Peters, yelled at Niles, "We've got to go now, Doctor! Now, sir!"

Niles and I'Jaz had a skeleton they were determined to take with them, and Cassia was still transmitting a dispatch to her mother when a soldier grabbed her arm and pulled her with him, calling to I'Jaz, "Let's go, you too, doctor!"

Niles and I'Jaz had the long skeleton wrapped in a blanket. Each had an end as they struggled toward the doorway. The darn thing was heavy.

"Doctors, let's go, *please!*" Another soldier grabbed Nile's end of the skeleton, and yet another hustled him out the door and into the transport.

Outside, with the giant skeleton now safely inside the transport, all three doctors were shoved into the heavily armored glide transports.

The three armored transports tore out from under the building and maneuvered through the crowd of angry youths. Amazingly, no one was run over. With sirens blaring, they were stopping for nothing.

One block away, the lead vehicle hit an improvised mine and flipped into the air, bursting into flames. The second transport, with the doctors in it, swerved around it and took the lead. Sprinting from the side streets like a swarm of bees, mask-covered crowds chased them down the street, firing rifles, pistols, and throwing bricks. They all bounced harmlessly off the two remaining military means of transport.

As they cleared the first crowded street, a hooded male knelt, aimed, and fired an RPG. It struck the trailing transport in the front tire, causing the vehicle to career off the street and through a storefront window, shattering glass and causing the ceiling to collapse. The crowd followed it into the store.

Commander Elliot shook his head in horror and yelled to his driver, "Keep going; we have to get these doctors to our secure location. I'll call for backup—but, shit. Don't stop for anything."

Niles and Cassia, looking out the bulletproof window, put their hands to their faces.

"Oh, my God," Cassia moaned.

I'Jaz had his eyes closed and his hands clasped in his lap. He was praying.

On a deserted suburban highway outside the city, three pickups took up the chase to destroy the lone military transport with Niles, Cassia, and I'Jaz inside.

Commander Elliot called in air support and yelled to his driver, "These bastards probably have RPG's on those trucks. Keep moving and keep them behind us."

Within minutes, an attack helicopter swooped down. It ripped apart the pickups with intense laser fire, sending one of the trucks careening off the motorway in flames.

Niles couldn't tell exactly where they were now. About an hour later, still accompanied by the helicopter, they left the motorway and entered a heavily wooded forest. He knew they had been traveling north of London and were well past Brockley Hill. Minutes later, the road became gravel.

As they drove deeper into the wooded area, two Centurion Mark 8 tanks guarded the roadside, one on either side. Passing through heavy gates and arriving at the facility, Niles hoped to God that the equipment had all arrived safely. Most of it had been removed from London the night before the attack.

On the rooftop, soldiers were attaching the large communication array dishes, while, below, entering the building, others carried in additional equipment and assisted in setup. He could see the Light-Speed Buoy Array comp system being unpacked. That was how they would receive timely transmissions from *Assurity*.

After being shown their rooms and unpacking, I'Jaz and Cassia began testing their updated equipment inside the command center. One of the military officers confirmed that the array was now configured and operating correctly.

Lt. Commander Elliot approached Niles. "We're all set up top, doctor. Relays confirmed across the array. Nemesis's buoy appears operational, as well, but we're pinging the entire string. Should have confirmation in a few hours. In the meantime, I'm checking vulnerability points outside."

He moved to leave but stopped. "The mess hall is set up if you're hungry. I've got a chef available 24/7. We're going to be at it for some time!" The commander walked off.

Cassia looked up at the grid display. It showed all of the buoys illuminated and in standby mode, a blinking burnt orange color. They were all connected, but transmission capacity was not confirmed. That was crucial. They would need an ultra-fast transfer from Nemesis to Interstellar Deep Tracking Station, Brasília, first, and then on to their laboratory.

Cassia's dad walked up and stood next to her, looking up at the blinking array. Each buoy point was color-coded. "Once we receive the transmission from *Assurity,* we can begin to synthesize the cure. I'Jaz is working on the Compound Correlator."

I'Jaz heard that and responded, "Except, something is afoul with this correlator. We're missing something—a part, maybe two. I hope they're not back in London."

Chapter 32

Descent to Nemesis

PILOTED BY TATIANA, *Offlander* took a direct descent through the methane clouds to the planet below. Shuttling low over the black desert and through light methane rain, *Offlander* fired her landing thrusters and set down near the radio transmission station. Disembarking, fully suited, Poldi and Rigel strode toward the odd-looking structure.

From the copilot seat, Zeke watched.

Crossing the black sands, they'd reached the windmill-like structure in good time, their helmet radios crackling. "Good luck, guys," Zeke said. "We'll see you at the opening in two hours."

The two waved goodbye and turned their gaze up to this abnormal, malevolent-looking radio structure. Below was an apparent doorway into its base.

Offlander burst across the black-sand desert. Within ten seconds, she entered a thick, low-lying, icy methane cloud. Having to slow, the methane globules that obscured the windshield looked a lot like fluffy snowflakes. *Offlander* settled a short distance from what could only be described as a citadel—reminiscent of a Mayan temple. Along the perimeter, a circle of large boulders stood in a sentry-like position.

Veronika, Zeke, Xiao Xing, and Philex-B exited *Offlander*, the methane snow dropping in globs and covering the temple's steps. They all watched *Offlander* rise and disappear from view on its way back to *Assurity*.

Veronika had given Tatiana orders that *Assurity* should be on alert, ready to return quickly if everything went to shit. The four adjusted equipment and regarded the strange construction on top of what was otherwise an unwelcome planet's surface.

Gazing up, Xiao Xing said, "Actually, I've seen this type of structure before."

Her face tensed up inside her helmet—

"Where?" Veronika pressed her.

"In the jungles of South America—it almost looks Mayan."

"How in the entirety of the universe does that happen?" Zeke interjected.

Veronika cut short the talk. "You lead, Commander. You're the military expert."

"Let's move on," Zeke said.

The four searched until they found an opening at the base of the temple. With no doorway, the tunnel opening appeared to lead below. Veronika asked Philex-B to run a geo scan.

"It leads to a warmer environment some 375 feet below," Philex-B reported. They entered the stone archway and considered a stairway leading below.

Poldi and Rigel looked up at the radio station, puzzled by the plum-colored wave of light pulsating throughout the twisted metal antenna atop the strange building. Turning on his outside mike, Poldi could hear the transmission's scratching audio.

Full at the bottom, the station tapered at the top.

Poldi couldn't imagine what kind of science could be behind this weirdness. So different from anything anticipated. Beyond that, along the horizon, multi-colored light shot upward from the surface of the planet.

Poldi pointed back up to the tangled structure. "Rigel, it appears that thing is transmitting and receiving—"

"How so?" Rigel was busy on com, trying to radio Veronika. "I can't reach *Offlander* or the captain to confirm communication."

"Let's get in. See what we find," Poldi said.

They both noted the sizable hand indentation within the substantial concrete door as if someone had stuck their prominent handprint upon wet cement. Poldi looked at Rigel, who placed his hand in the indentation; there was much room to spare.

The door groaned open, and the two cautiously entered the station.

Inside the radio building, standing motionless, Rigel examined the dim, windowless, high-ceilinged chamber. Elevated at least ten feet off the floor, they saw what appeared to be four stations. Rigel stepped below the first seat. Hoisting himself up and fiddling around with icons on the chair handle, he was able to bring up a display upon a dull grey, stone-like screen. He touched the picture that made the most sense. The computer array lowered.

Rigel jumped down and stood before what was now a milky-white viewing screen. Besides the screen, levers, and knobs of stony-metal. Rigel turned one of the knobs. Then another.

Poldi huddled close, examining the screen. "Why was all of this so high?"

Rigel kept monkeying around with the knobs. "From the seating height, it would seem that their size must be much larger than ours."

Poldi looked up at the three seats well above his head. "Oh, shit! What's this?"

The screen before them brightened. Slowly, it bloomed into a representation of the planets of the solar system. Rigel pulled the nearest stony lever.

"Holy crap, do you know what you're doing?" Poldi shrieked.

"It appears so . . ." A sharp creaking sound reverberated within their helmets as the ceiling separated. Slowly, something cylindrical extended upward from a box-like structure on the floor. If it were on Earth, one would assume it was an observatory telescope.

While they were engrossed by the telescope, something entered the room.

Rigel recorded a presence behind him but never had a definitive look at whatever clobbered him across the side of his helmet.

Poldi saw Rigel fall to the floor. He backed up, stumbled, and fell, pushing with his legs backward, trying to escape.

The last thing he remembered was being dragged out of the building by a space-suited being of considerable proportions.

Chapter 33

Temple of Nemesis

VERONIKA'S CREW, with Zeke in the lead, descended a winding stone stairway. As they wound lower, Philex-B stopped.

Utilizing her Tyrex Multipurpose Scanner, she tested the atmosphere. "Atmosphere is being pressurized, Captain. Helium, oxygen, trace CO_2, and water vapor . . . We're safe to breathe."

"How is this possible?" Veronika asked. At the same time, she double-checked the charge in her Remington 800 LaserTron pistol.

Zeke was the first to remove his helmet. The rest of them followed suit and attached them to their packs. Rifles slung over shoulders, they followed Zeke down the winding, ribbed passageway.

Emerging at the bottom, they were forced to a standstill in front of a stone doorway.

Veronika approached the barrier and ran her hand over a set of nine pictures. "Xiao Xing, what are they?"

"It's probably a lock," Zeke suggested.

Xiao Xing straightened, tilted her head slightly, and appeared to comprehend this intricate artwork as if it was second nature to her. "Please touch the images in the following order, Captain: one, two, two, three, four, six, nine."

Veronika did as instructed. The pictures were three across and three down, totaling nine, just like Antarctica's alien ship. A grunting sound lasted nearly three seconds. Then the stone door slid effortlessly open.

"That was amazing," Veronika said. She looked at Zeke and smiled until they all heard the loud growl. Moving powerfully from around a corner of the entranceway, two muscular white tigers crept forward and then stopped.

"What the hell!" Zeke called out, stepping back.

Startled, the others stumbled backward. The tigers stayed where they were for a moment. The crew all knew that they were tigers of some kind, but these were ancient-looking—with tusks and wild whiskers.

"Wow!" Xiao Xing said as she backed up.

Zeke aimed his rifle.

"They're saber-toothed tigers," Philex-B said. "I've seen them on history vids."

One of the tigers, still standing at attention, roared

forcefully.

Veronika instinctively removed her pistol from its holster.

Just as quickly, an unseen voice—a pleasant female voice—reverberated throughout the cavern: "Come now. Be good girls."

The two tigers snarled one last time, turned, and slinked back into the tunnel.

Everyone took a deep breath.

"God, that was strange," Zeke said. "What was that voice?"

"Captain," Philex-B said, "We've lost com with *Assurity*."

Veronika let out a breath. "Someone's obviously here somewhere." She shook her head. "Xiao Xing, how did you know the combination?"

"It was entirely predictable, ma'am." Xiao Xing lifted her palms and smirked. "*It's a modified golden section ratio—as before.*"

"Okay, then, let's go." Veronika shook her head as if she comprehended how that could be.

After a short stretch of level tunnel, the team descended into a compressed and claustrophobic room. Its walls of gleaming obsidian were dimly illuminated from the ceiling. In the middle of the room was a shiny, four-sided black obelisk, its broad bottom tapered to a pointed tip.

Writing appeared on all sides.

Philex-B sat on one of the benches that lined each wall, trying to take it all in.

"It's a dusty cluster," Zeke complained. "Like I'm in a museum or something. What is this stuff? Literature? Art? Sports memorabilia? What the cosmos?"

Circling the obelisk briskly, Xiao Xing ran her hand across each panel like she was reading Braille. "I've seen an obelisk similar to this in the British Museum. It was a record of the Assyrian kings of the eighth century BC . . ."

Veronika moved with her, waiting, wondering.

Xiao Xing stopped. She talked to herself for a moment as she ran her finger along the first two lines on the first panel.

"Xiao Xing, can you read the panels or not?" Veronika asked impatiently.

"Of course, moment, please." Xiao Xing glared back at her. "This first is the language of ancient Sumer—the first recorded language on Earth, spoken and written in Southern Mesopotamia."

Quickly, she moved to the second panel. "And this—" She ran her finger across the glyphs— "is the language of ancient Egypt, written in actual hieroglyphics, including its cursive counterpart, hieratic."

On that panel was the etching of a pyramid. "Mentioned in this account is the construction of the Great Pyramid of Giza—" she continued.

Veronika was baffled. "What are the ancient languages of Earth, engraved on stone, doing on a planet way in the heavens out here? God, it's exactly wrong."

They were all uneasy. Philex-B kept busy with her scanner. She wasn't following this.

Xiao Xing, eyes wide in concentration, continued to the third panel. Taking a moment—touching the pictures—she said, "This is *Mayan*. If I read it correctly, it is a day-in-the-life account of a chief of the Maya before their culture vanished from existence. That's a cursory reading, of course."

"I guess that explains the temple-citadel thing on the surface," Zeke said.

Veronika moved on to the fourth panel, gesturing, "And, the fourth?"

Xiao Xing stood for a moment, pouting. She placed her hands on her hips and turned to Veronika. "Unknown to me—I have no knowledge of this."

"What's the problem?" Veronika asked nicely.

Xiao Xing waved her off as if angered and sulked away.

Zeke looked at Veronika and hunched his shoulders. "Let's keep going. Keep your weapons at the ready. Who knows what other weird pets may show up."

Philex-B switched her Tyrex scanner to GEO mode and gained a profile of the tunnel's subsurface structures. "We should reach a larger caved room soon . . . no life signs, except those beasts that are exiting in a different direction."

Leaving by way of the doorway on the other side of the obelisk, the team continued down another dark, twisting tunnel and emerged into the sprawling cavern. This was very different. The stone was light-colored. Veronika knew her rock, and this was igneous, formed through the cooling and solidification of magma or lava. The farther they walked, the more expansive the cavern became. After a time, it opened into a Big Room—a voluminous chamber. Following an obviously well-traveled pathway, they came upon a crystal-blue subterranean lake. Tubers floated near the shore. Continuing to follow the path around the lake by clinging to the water's edge, they passed empty shale boxes. The entire lake was a translucent dark blue.

Veronika thought that maybe the boxes were to collect the pod-like tubers bobbing in the gentle ripples. This seemed rudimentary and even bizarre in some ways. Why was there no one to greet them? Script upon a stone—from Earth?

Xiao Xing stared across the water. "What's that out there?" She pointed. "Yuck . . ."

Out in the lake, strange globular-like fish whipped the water with their tails. The blackish-blue things looked more like plump-headed earth slugs than fish—except for the flapping tails.

"Where are the inhabitants?" Veronika murmured.

"Let's keep moving," Zeke said.

Departing the lake, the path turned to a brick-color and dipped into a rolling trough. Farther down in the furrow was an orchard. The trees, expansive and high, oddly, appeared trimmed in squares.

"Captain," Philex-B suggested, "I think we should don our helmets now. There could be pathogens we have no knowledge about."

"Agreed," Veronika said, putting her helmet on, as did the rest of the crew.

The first rows of trees they arrived at were producing fleshy, grapefruit-sized fruit. The fruit hung from a thin stem. The crew stood beneath, mesmerized by the dark color of the trunk of the tree. It was striped, like a zebra, coal-black and white, the leaves, a dark cranberry color—long, narrow, and numerous. The fruit was ruby-colored.

Philex-B scanned the tree in bio mode.

Xiao Xing stood on her toes and reached for low-hanging fruit, asking, "Are they edible, do you suppose?"

Philex-B slapped her hand away.

"What are you doing?" Xiao Xing snapped.

Philex-B took the end of her rifle and knocked the fruit off the tree. When it hit the ground, the fruit broke open. Flipping over, multiple legs gripped the dirt. They skittered toward Xiao Xing, who jumped back as Philex-B shot the damn fruity thing with her laser.

Poking around in the hairy, blown-up guts, Philex-B said, "Dangerous, I think. Warm-blooded. It's an animal, not a fruit or a vegetable."

"Okay, thanks." Xiao Xing walked on, leading the group, smacking the side of her helmet lightly with her palm, saying, "Wow, stupid—that was stupid."

Philex-B, reading her scanner, pointed, "That way—. I'm getting life readings from inside a cavern about 650 meters."

The orchard, or whatever it was, extended for over fifty yards and then transformed into an Earth-like garden. Well cultivated, the garden was about a four-acre rectangle. What looked like white dwarf cabbage grew in neat rows. In an adjoining section, and on top of the dirt, were purple yam-like tubers, twice the size you'd see on Earth.

And, there were meaty orange beans on poles. Prolific. At least, they looked like beans. No one wanted to take any more chances by touching any of this. They kept moving.

"Makes me hungry," Poldi chuckled. "We should have brought some rations down here."

"Philex-B, launch drones, please," Veronika commanded. Philex-B's tapped her arm pack. About the size of her finger, two tiny drones fluttered in the palm of her gloved hand. One blue, the other grey, the two whirled up and above the knoll. Philex-B cycled through various drone views within her helmet HUD. The view from above revealed an impressive quilt-like expanse of fields: Rye, perhaps, wheat, and corn-like stalks, all healthy and thriving, but different colors from those on Earth.

Past the garden and up a knoll, the crew emerged onto the overlook. The cornhusks were bright blue and the wheatberry or barley, raspberry-colored. At the bottom of the hill, Philex-B led as they traversed another well-traveled path. Philex-B's eyes worked over the details through her HUD as the drones kept an even distance ahead.

To Veronika, the colors of growing things, so different from Earth, somehow seemed sensible. Walking this dirt path in such a large open area gave her the illusion that they were outside. Palpably, they weren't. They were underground. And, yet, somehow, enclosed by a sprawling skyline. How was that possible? The roof of the cavern was mauve instead of blue—and it glowed. The light from above appeared to warm the entire collection of fields.

Where does the water come from? She thought.

Zeke stopped and looked back at them. "Can someone explain how our sun, which emits just enough light to barely illuminate a planet this far out, how does it heat a cavern below the surface?"

"It doesn't." Philex-B pointed to the sky. "The light is either being generated, or that rock or stone or whatever it is is self-illuminating."

"Either way," Zeke said, "let's keep moving. I can see—"

A bleeping alarm sounded within Philex-B's helmet. Philex-B raised her hand. "Hold up."

A loud shriek reverberated across the landscape.

"Oh, crap!" Veronika warned, pointing back toward where they'd come from.

Three great-winged prehistoric birds glided toward them.

Philex-B recalled her two drones. As the furious flapping sounded, the birds descended directly toward them. These flyers could have been dragons, except they weren't. Their long necks ended with a beak that was itself longer than their necks. Wingspans stretched forever, legs dangling, and their outstretched claws.

Zeke motioned. "Get down."

"What are they?" Philex-B whispered.

"It's a Quetzalcoatlus," Xiao Xing answered matter-of-factly. "Lived on Earth, sixty-five to 145 million years ago. A carnivorous flying reptile that can walk on its claws. It was tall, like a giraffe."

"How do you know that?" Zeke asked.

"My father was a Doctor of Paleontology at the Beijing

University of Historical Sciences." For a moment, she looked as though she would cry. "But, he passed into another realm last year—"

"I'm sorry," Zeke said. "I didn't know . . ."

"They look like birds, but they're not. Late Cretaceous of North America, and one of the biggest known flying reptiles of all time," she added.

The two drones landed on Philex-B's palm, and she hurried them into her arm pack.

The three bird-like reptiles gently glided to a landing some 180 meters past them. It reminded Veronika of giant pelicans coming in for a landing atop the swelling oceans during holidays on the Eastern coast. Seeing their prey, they would immediately dive below the surface.

"I don't think they saw us," Veronika breathed.

Awkwardly marching this way and that, the large, stiff-necked reptiles initiated a poking frenzy, their long beaks stabbing the dirt, searching for nutrition. One of the Quetzalcoatlus hit pay dirt and yanked an armadillo-like creature from beneath the soil. Throwing the hefty, heavily armored creature from side to side, it flung it a meter away.

Bounding after the creature, playing, it pounced and stabbed it with its beak, hoping to shatter the scaled armor. It was greeted with the whip of a long, slicing tail. The armadillo creature wrapped its tail around the Quetzalcoatlus's beak and sent the struggling reptile reeling onto its back.

Facing the gigantic Quetzalcoatlus, the Armadillo scrambled toward it. The Quetzalcoatlus, quick to get to its feet, backed off. The other two Quetzalcoatlus stopped their dirt fishing and stepped back, slowly retreating a distance. The armadillo-like creature waited a moment. Turning its armored head from side to side, it bored back into the dirt, quickly disappearing.

The team paused—rattled.

Zeke motioned them near him. "If we move slowly down the ridge on our left, we can follow this gully to the next field and be out of their sight."

"Zeke," Veronika suggested, "let's keep heading toward the cave—okay? The sooner we're inside, the better."

"Agreed," he said.

The gulley was damp and muddy at the bottom as if it had recently been a basin wash. The four traversed the dip and advanced toward a large field. One of the reptiles must have heard them because he took off unnoticed and circled behind them. Flying low, his swooping wings made a loud flapping noise.

Zeke turned in time to set up his laser shot and struck the enormous beak of the Quetzalcoatlus as it targeted one of them. The shot sent the reptile reeling to the right. The four hustled for the field, hoping that the other two Quetzalcoatlus didn't join the hunt after realizing what had happened.

After a quarter-hour, and with no sign of the giant reptiles, they stopped on the path leading into a field. Sitting, they shared water and grain bars.

Philex-B reviewed her area scanner. "We are some thirty-five meters from the cavern opening.

Zeke was looking at Xiao Xing. "How is it possible that ancient creatures from Earth are living on this planet—or beneath the surface, I should say?"

"We don't know if they came from Earth," Poldi added.

Veronika was trying to catch her breath, feeling nauseous, when she noticed something darting through the crops . . . She raised her finger to her mouth, hoping they'd all notice and remain quiet.

The crew got up, spread out, and placed their weapons in ready mode. The path, about four feet across, ran between the rows of stalks. Stepping onto dark brown peat, they noticed a pungent smell like fresh fertilizer. Fishy.

Unintelligible gibbering sounded through the stalks as Xiao Xing stealthily moved forward. Still, the rustling before them grew louder as Zeke motioned for caution.

Veronika wasn't thrilled with the way Xiao Xing kept pushing forward at the lead. She noticed the bluish stalks ahead. The tops were shaking, and there was no wind. They all looked at one another, waiting. Veronika put her hand to her pistol.

The swooshing sound increased. The stalks near the path shook vibrantly. Then, silence.

A face peeked out from a row.

They all stood frozen for a moment.

Was it human, or what? It had a conical head. Unmistakably female, she slinked out onto the pathway and straightened. What was unnerving was her height. She was tall—at least seven feet—a giantess. Hesitantly moving forward, they saw her face was the color of light sand. She looked young, like a human teenager. Slender and gangly with almond-shaped eyes. Stopping, the giantess looked inquisitively down at Xiao Xing, standing frozen on the path.

Her clothing was a tightly fitting dark-brown weave that was both top and pants, accentuating her slender height.

Veronika motioned for calm. "This may be our first

meeting with another species."

The crew, taken aback by her height, were stunned when Xiao Xing, stepping forward, looked up and extended her hand in friendship.

Peering down at Xiao Xing, the girl, a distinctive reddish blotch on her forehead, tilted her elongated head sideways.

One by one, other equally tall females hesitantly stepped from the field and onto the path.

Philex-B lifted her rifle parallel to her chest. "Captain, are they human?"

"Not sure," she whispered. "Humanoid, certainly . . . stay still."

Releasing the safety on his rifle with a loud click, Zeke stepped forward.

The teenage female noticed. Looking back, the other females with their long-legged gaits gathered around her. Eight of them. All in walnut-colored clothing. All as tall as she, but thicker than the young one. They exchanged unintelligible words between themselves. Dropping their sacks filled with pickings, they stepped forward as a collective.

Xiao Xing froze in place. Zeke looked at Veronika for

orders.

"Step back, Xiao Xing . . . *back!*" Veronika lunged forward, grabbed Xiao Xing's arm, and yanked her back.

Unexpectedly, the giant women clasped hands. In unison, they stepped forward, together, and halting, they glared down at the diminutive crew of *Assurity*.

Veronika wondered if this was a gesture of welcome and friendship or what? Indecision ran up her back, tightened her up. She wasn't sure what to do. She looked at Zeke. He was getting more and more anxious.

Quietly, he said, "This is not a good defensive position, Captain."

"Agreed," she whispered. "It appears that everyone and everything present has arrived at a grand moment of indecision."

A moment later, the females began clapping quickly in unison—and with precision. It evolved into a discernible, striking, rhythm . . .

Zeke tightened the grip on his rifle. "Fall back—slowly," he ordered.

The giants clapped louder as the thickest and tallest, the apparent leader, stepped to the front of the group. Now, they began walking forward—in unison—clapping fiercely.

"Shit!" Zeke cursed, stepping back yet again, his rifle at the ready but not pointed at any one of them. "This is not a friendly welcome!"

"Many more steps toward us, and I'm going to have to take defensive action, Captain."

"Agreed. How about a shot over their heads?"

They kept coming, clapping furiously.

Zeke lifted his rifle and aimed it above their heads.

After seconds of uncertainty, an unearthly sound blared out across the underground countryside. The thickest female giantess stopped. She looked back.

Following her lead, they all backed off, turned, and hurried down the path toward a different field, except for the young one—the one with the birthmark. She stopped for a moment and looked back at Xiao Xing.

Xiao Xing waved.

The young giantess intertwined her long fingers and put her thumbs to her mouth. She blew into her thumbs and produced a whooping call that echoed across the valley. Then, she, too, with long strides, loped off, following the others.

Crossing another colorful field of low-growing grasses, the team reached the wide tunnel opening this time without incident. Inside, it branched off into three passageways.

"Captain," Philex-B said, "distinctive voiceprints are emanating from farther down this middle tunnel. Air's clear here, as well."

Philex-B took the lead; Veronika followed her as Zeke fell back with Xiao Xing.

Veronika said, "I'm concerned that we haven't heard from Rigel or Poldi. Can you try to reach them, Philex-B?"

The tunnel was dimly illuminated. Strangely, there were no lights or torches. Xiao Xing guarded the rear as they crept along the smooth surface.

Veronika ran her fingers along the sides of the chocolate-colored slate. It was smooth and comforting to the touch. Warm, but not hot.

Emerging into a sizeable cavern, they could hear what almost sounded like chanting. They crouched and continued; the chanting grew louder as they progressed into another spur of the tunnel. At length, they stopped and sat below a low rock wall—listening, glancing questionably at one another. The words were unintelligible.

Zeke rose slowly and peeked over the three-foot wall. Below, lying prostrate in some kind of prayer, and spread out across a polished stone floor, were at least fifty giants. Big, muscular males. Heads bowed, chanting in an unknown language.

Veronika rose and peeked over. With its polished floor and statues around the perimeter, the room below had to be some kind of temple. Supreme, above the giants, on a heightened throne, sat a jewel-gowned female. Stunning, lean, and striking.

Zeke sat back down and urgently whispered to Veronika, "We've got to fall back, Captain. Come up with a new plan. We're outmatched."

Veronika, still looking, was transfixed. "Wait a minute—" she whispered.

"They're huge beings, and they're praying to that woman . . . you see how massive the males are? Big-headed, with those thick skulls and noses—"

Veronika sat back down and questioned him with her eyes. "Okay, Zeke, why are we assuming they're dangerous? They promised to help us with a cure. We came all of this way . . . "

"Jeez," Zeke said softly. "They're tall—like the women. But, bigger. A lot bigger!"

Veronika peeked over again. The chanting stopped. The giants remained prostrate before the stunning woman, who turned her head—looked up—and pointed. "Welcome to all of you from *Assurity*. We've been anticipating your arrival!"

Veronika's eyes opened wide. She stood up, as did the other three of her squad. They peered down from above.

Veronika half waved, gasping to catch her breath. It was some sight . . . "Thank you. We received a message on Earth . . . from you, I hope."

"Yes, I am Azazel, Princess of Pangaea." She threw her arms out in welcome. "Peace upon all of you—and welcome to our home, my friends."

Veronika was nervous, "My God, how did all of you get here? To Nemesis. We're you born here? Where are you from? The people of Earth will be astounded—"

"Many questions." Princess Azazel smiled. "And I have many answers to share with all of you." Azazel clasped her hands as though she were going to pray.

Abruptly, two space-suited female giants entered the room. One carried Rigel and the other Poldi. Both men were slung over a shoulder like recently killed prey being humped back to camp. Both appeared conscious but unable to do much about their situation. The female giants ripped off the men's facemasks and dumped them on the floor before the assembly.

"Wait a minute!" Veronika called out from the stone balcony above. "What do you think you're doing? Those are my men."

"Hey!" Zeke hollered.

Princess Azazel arose and sternly addressed her females. "These are our dear guests. Please, be gentle." She stepped down from her pedestal and extended her hand, effortlessly assisting Rigel and then Poldi to his feet. She gestured to Veronika and her team. "Please accept my apology. So rude."

Veronika caught a quick glimpse of something. Etched within the cavern's shiny floor was the white outline of what one could only say was an angel, wings extended.

Princess Azazel said, "I wish you and your crew to join me, Veronika Taylor Morgan. Look at all of you. You've made it all the way to Nemesis! We have so much in common. A communal objective, you might say."

She applauded them for a moment as she sauntered. "Consider us allies, here to rescue you from Earth's horribly frightening paradox." She motioned again. "Please, come. Dine with us. We are not to be feared. This is a monumental day in the history of both of our species!"

Her giants rose in unison and peered up at Veronika and her crew.

Zeke spurted out, "Holy shit, they're enormous."

"Ugly bastards," Poldi voiced softly.

"Let's keep our judgments to ourselves," Veronika whispered.

The giants turned and smiled, and yet—to Veronika—their actual facial movements seemed strained—unnatural. Then the giants too began to applaud.

"Come on," Veronika announced. "Let's go get our guys!"

***

The crew of *Assurity* stood before the princess. She gave the impression of royalty, seated upon her elevated throne, and arrayed in a shimmering vestment resplendent with dazzling precious stones. More females entered, placing pillows along the stone floor. The princess watched, appearing as if everything was well under her control.

Veronika was perplexed. This was not what she had expected. Yet, what had she expected? This was uncharted life. It was easy to suspect the worst; it took courage to expect the best.

Other giantesses, younger females, carried in shale boxes filled with odd-looking vegetables, dried fish, and bread. They set them down before the visitors and stepped back. Rangy and slender, with their chins jutting out, they stood at attention.

Their elongated skulls puzzled her. Veronika had seen these in ancient Egyptian art. Art appreciation in graduate school was required, even for an engineering and space aeronautics degree. There were many examples of this conical head, but only in ancient art depictions; a wrap of some type usually covered them. As if to not draw too much attention.

"Please, sit," Princess Azazel gestured. "Let us break bread together. This is a glorious day—the long-awaited fellowship of two species."

The crew sat on pillows as Azazel rose. In so doing, she revealed a brilliant crimson etching on the back of her polished stone throne. It was an otherworldly artistic display.

Xiao Xing starred— She thought that the red etching resembled an old symbol, the one she'd seen in Antarctica, a swastika. But there was a slight difference. Between each crimson arm of the swastika gleamed a prominent golden star.

Poldi, leery but hungry, took a blue corn-like cob from the stone box passed to him, stripped the husk, and bit into the kernels. Zeke wouldn't eat and passed the box along. They both watched, intrigued, as two young females carried in a flat stone of sizzling red meat. They set the fiery meat down upon a stone tablet. One of the older females grasped a hatchet and struck it with a flint. The hatchet flamed up.

"*Gott*, that's weird," Poldi commented, taking another bite of blue corn.

"Taste all right?" Zeke asked.

"Yeah!"

She chopped the meat while the crew gazed at one another with uncertainty.

"Wonder what that was?" Poldi said. "Before they cut it up."

The giant men sat down, cross-legged, and in a semi-circle, across from the visitors. They were lightly clothed in what appeared to be thin animal skin. After taking what they desired, the crew passed the slate boxes on to them. The giants grabbed anything they could, chewing and grunting with determination. One of the boxes contained the purple grapefruit-sized fruit they'd avoided in the orchard. This must have been a delicacy. Each giant grabbed one, squeezed it, and as numerous leg-like appendages extended from the fruit, they popped the entire squealing thing into their mouths and happily chewed.

Zeke watched Veronika grimace as one of the giants swallowed the squealing mess and smiled at her, blood dripping from his mouth.

Still unsatisfied, the giants kept an eager eye out for the meat that was to come.

Out of the corner of her eye, Veronika peeked at the men, thinking, *These are big men. They must eat a great deal.*

Chatting among themselves, the females handed each guest a chunk of purple, seeded bread. Following that, the girl with the birthmark, the one Xiao Xing had met in the field, passed out pieces of hot, sizzling meat. An older, chunkier woman helped her.

Veronika watched the giant men anxiously fidget while the meat was slowly passed to the visitors. She'd never seen people so broad and muscular.

One of the men motioned for Zeke's gun. Zeke pulled it in close and smiled. "No way, big guy. I'm keeping it right here."

Philex-B whispered to Zeke. "I'm not feeling

comfortable with these beings."

"Yeah—I don't blame you. Something weird about these people." He half-smiled back at the giant across from him.

Veronika scrutinized the princess, who stood above them all, directing her workers. "Princess Azazel, as much as we are curious beyond belief, we have come for something vital to humanity. You sent us a message. Not to pry . . . but you speak English, your subject's a language we have never heard."

"I speak many languages, Veronika Taylor Morgan." The princess looked down and smiled, her face lean and handsome. "And, receive you shall—but allow me to answer your first question. *Where did we come from?*"

Princess Azazel lifted her arms to the sky. "Azitah—*kilmon yoe ja!*"

The stone roof above them opened in a circle, revealing the stars in all of their glory. As soon as the ceiling parted, the giants gazed upward and chanted in oblation.

Princess Azazel pointed up. "Our homeworld is deep in the constellation of Serpens."

Xiao Xing, preoccupied, was engaged in her temple-talk. She was comparing the swastika symbol through the ages.

Veronika stood. "Put simply, Princess, we require a sample of your giants' DNA. Or yours, perhaps—although you appear different from them."

The princess squeezed her mouth closed. "We know that you face a grave turning point in humanity's evolution. We will accommodate you. But, first, I will show you what we have accomplished here." She gestured to her giants. "I am proud of their achievements."

Chapter 34

Our Home

PHILEX-B AND ZEKE STOOD waiting at the tunnel entrance as Xiao Xing escorted Veronika to meet Azazel. Then the two ducked back into the tunnel.

Veronika felt less than like herself, knowing that her time of clarity from the hydra-synapse shot was ticking down.

As they walked toward Azazel, Veronika whispered to Xiao Xing, "Can you find that girl—the one with the mark? She seems to like you. Get our sample from her."

Xiao Xing glanced at her, unsettled.

"You can do this, Xiao Xing," Veronika said, staring straight ahead and smiling at Azazel as they approached. The princess waited patiently for Veronika.

Veronika climbed slowly up the stone steps to the top of the cliff. Extending a hand, Azazel assisted her to the summit. The two turned and stood overlooking a magnificent agricultural valley patterned with distinctive crops in precise geometrical designs. It was remarkable— here on this planet in the vastness of space.

The princess pointed out the numerous homes of stone scattered across the valley floor. They were sizable—as were the lumbering animals resembling ancient woolly mammoths grazing on blue-colored grass, which seemingly grew abundantly here. Apparently, none of her giants were present out here this time of day.

"On Earth, our grass is green," Veronika commented. "Yours is blue. I wonder why."

"Like many plants, most species of grasses produce the bright pigment called chlorophyll. Chlorophyll absorbs blue light and red light but principally reflects green. This enclosed ecosystem reflects only blue light.

With the two talking and Azazel distracted, Xiao Xing slipped away and followed a path across what might have looked like a field of rye on Earth.

Veronika asked, "Princess, how can you grow crops and grass without sunlight?" Feeling dizzy, she sat down on a stone. "Where is this light here from?"

"That's a good question. We have found that it is generated from deep within the planet and emerges up through a series of volcanic columns that extend deep into the planet."

Veronika saw what looked like a saber-toothed tiger

acting like a sheepdog and herding the mammoths. "I've seen the likes of that ancient tiger at the Chicago Zoo. The tiger was created from very ancient DNA archeologists extracted from his tooth. He was found frozen in the permafrost of the Russian Federation— Azazel, what is a saber-toothed tiger doing out here on the planet Nemesis?"

Princess Azazel squatted next to Veronika. This close, Veronika noticed how angular and lean Azazel's face was. Her eyes so dark green that they were nearly black.

Gazing into Veronika's eyes, Azazel hesitated. "We have command of technologies you wouldn't dream of."

Veronika took a deep breath. The aroma of the fields, as far away as they were, filled her nose with sweetness. "Then, how is it that you are here? No disrespect, but this is not a planet conducive to life thriving. Like Earth."

Azazel raised her eyebrows and turned away.

Veronika pressed on. "Those fossils on that hole-riddled derelict orbiting Nemesis—did you bring these animals here?"

Azazel looked out over the valley and didn't respond.

"How long have you been here?" Veronika insisted. She placed her hand to her throbbing head. "Was this always your intended home? I mean, why would you leave the Constellation of Serpens? What happened? The distance is unfathomable—we had difficulty getting even this far. I'm confused . . ."

Princess Azazel swiveled and gently placed her hand on Veronika's forehead. "Let me ease your pain, Veronika." Azazel lowered her head, studying Veronika's eyes, and spoke words that Veronika didn't recognize. It was like a prayer—with a rhythm of calmness—but not a prayer.

When the princess finished, she removed her hand. "The pain should vanish in a moment." Azazel straightened and ruffled her hair as she overlooked the valley. "Veronika, there is no metal ore to mine in the habitable zone of this planet." She turned and grimaced. "Bit of a disadvantage. I think you'd agree."

She studied Veronika. "We salvaged what we could from our ship. Years ago, our shuttle became unusable— Azazel gestured, "We call this the Valley of Promise." Azazel examined Veronika's eyes again. "Your body is shutting down, Captain."

"Hmm . . ." Veronika spoke with difficulty. "A ship like yours, with a star map to Nemesis, was found in Antarctica. And then, your message. That's how we found you."

Princess Azazel smiled. "Of course. Except nothing out here in the expanse of this darkness can explain to you how life came to be, either here or on your Earth. I'm sorry to say your concept of reality is unreliable, Veronika. Delirium, as you call it, originates from within. Like so many other human diseases, it emanates from the inside. Delirium is nothing more than the expression of your fear. And fear, Veronika Taylor Morgan, is a product of uncertainty. Your very own uncertainty—"

Veronika's face tightened as she looked up at the princess—probing, hoping to fathom the truth about this princess entity. *These are not reasonable answers*, she thought. "That's certainly a puzzle—except, it doesn't answer my question. Who are you exactly, and how did you get here, Azazel?"

"My homeless colony of giants, as you call us, has been tragically marooned here for a very long time." She said it with resentment, looking back out across the valley. A sheen of perspiration—then, a drop of moisture fell from her forehead.

For a moment, the princess looked more uncertain than hopeful.

Veronika unattached her helmet from her belt. She wanted to call Isaac to see if she could raise him on *Assurity*.

"Meanwhile, Veronika, let me show you something you've never dreamt possible. Stand and take my hand."

Veronika hesitated.

"Please, trust me," Azazel said and grasped Veronika's hand, pulling her up and beside her.

The two disappeared from sight.

***

As soon as Xiao Xing and Veronika had walked toward the overlook, Zeke and Philex-B had darted back into the cave. She'd already mapped a large section of inner chambers. Following her scanner in GEO mode, the two entered what seemed to be a food-processing center. There were collections of bundled grasses and produce from the fields neatly set in racks, but no giants in the room.

"Where are they, do you suppose?" Zeke asked Philex-B. She didn't answer, concentrating on the scanner.

"It stinks down here," he added. "Almost like sewage."

The two continued along a winding, illuminated, rocky hallway. Philex-B focused on where they were going, continuing to follow the route she had mapped. "The males are not here," she said. "I checked before. Most of the heavier life forms are out in the fields. But, something is emitting consistent energy. It's different. Slighter. We should find out what's here, don't you agree, Zeke?"

"I think we should get the hell off this planet," he said. "Things don't add up. None of this makes sense. Spooky as hell—"

"If we can get a sample in here, while the captain is engaged . . ."

Philex-B turned and hushed Zeke, pointing to her GEO. The two ducked back into a crevice, but not much of one.

Farther down the tunnel, a giantess, older and hunched over, was carrying something in her arms. She left a chamber and crossed to a connecting tunnel.

Philex-B crouched and moved down the corridor ahead of Zeke, scanning the area the female had come from.

"Let's go. It's clear—*mostly.*"

"What do you mean, mostly?" Zeke said. "Something smells awful."

"Come on. Get over it. Let's go."

The two stepped into another recess and paused. They stood still. In the corner, within pens, were large, thick-furred, goat-like animals with a swirled, spiked horn each. Quiet and uninterested in the intruders, the creatures went back to eating without making a sound.

Waiting, Zeke and Philex-B listened. Sounds were emanating from somewhere, almost like crying, so they kept going.

Turning into a sizable alcove, a giantess, holding an infant, lifted her head and looked up at them. The infant, which was quite large, cried out, shrieking. The giantess appeared anything but alarmed. Other crying infants added to the harsh rackett. This female giantess, also older like the one who had left, stood and placed the infant in a stone sleeping cradle, covered him or her with a cloth blanket. She turned toward them. She didn't smile, and she didn't frown.

Glancing around her, Philex-B spotted at least thirty infants. It was a nursery. The giantess walked toward Philex-B and Zeke, said nothing. Stopping, she towered above them. Her eyes appeared wise with age. Almost as though she knew them—or knew of them. She raised her eyebrows, which was enough for Zeke and Philex-B to back up and cautiously exit.

***

Like in a dream, Veronika and Azazel were transported to a sandy knoll overlooking a vast waterfall.

How? Veronika was astonished. *It was instantaneous. Was it an illusion?* She felt as though she was standing on an island. Her feet in the sand.

She turned around and realized that she was on an island. Or something like that. Gigantic trees—different from those she'd known on Earth. Somehow, these trees were floating around the island in groups and clumps. They had long, scarlet trunks, with the vegetation beginning halfway up the tree, and the trees swaying back and forth in the breeze from where? The leaves were a rich dark blue color instead of emerald, like at home.

Veronika looked down. She was barefoot, standing in the blackest of sand. Her toes warm. She could feel the island breeze wafting through her hair. Around them grew ferns and iridescent flowers of an indeterminate kind.

Azazel simply smiled.

How is this possible? I'm not easily taken by deceit, Veronika thought. *Why is she showing me this?*

Misty water rose up from below the terrain and watered the grasses as if the ground was interlaced with an underground spring. Small freshwater creeks flowed through the surrounding countryside. Oddly, the water seemed to flow uphill.

Veronika caught her breath. What was even more overwhelming was that, in the distance, out on a vast meadow beyond the sand, prehistoric animals of every description grazed together as if on the plains of the Serengeti in Africa. Colossal, big-winged birds swooped down from the trees surrounding the island. Colorful and squawking, there was no violence. They appeared to live in harmony and to have what they needed. A large blue waterhole in the middle of this tiny island.

Veronika turned, glanced in every direction, and took a deep breath, smelling the aroma of the sea. She could hear the sound of the waves slapping against the shore. Yet, she was too dazed to take it all in. "How is this possible?" she asked the princess. "I asked you before—did you rescue these animals from the ship orbiting Nemesis? The animals here are all alive. Those animals on the ship were fossilized. How do they all live together like this?"

Veronika wasn't sure if she wasn't hallucinating and getting sicker.

Azazel straightened her back and thrust her hands out before her. "This is how they were meant to live, Veronika. We have saved all of them for you—for humanity. Our mission was to rescue that which was being wrongly eliminated by the creator. The weak and maligned are always maltreated. We are here as messengers of goodwill to humankind. The representatives of all species—all that is living."

The princess gestured to the unimaginable menagerie of ancient animals that had once inhabited Earth. "If not for us, they would be absent from existence, as you are close to becoming—"

The princess pointed to a herd of leaping, gazelle-like creatures on their way to a waterhole. "Those are Gazella psolea—a prehistoric species that lived in Africa and Arabia. Earth was their world before it was yours."

Veronika was sure that she was still clear-headed enough to reason. "So, that ship—the wreck—it was filled with the ancient beasts of Earth . . . *and* your giants . . ?"

"Oh, my Lord," Azazel said, her face tightening. "True character development is a challenge for all of us. An adjustment of your basic beliefs must be made—your suppositions concerning truth must lead to new moral genuineness." Azazel let out a long-held breath. "What you think you know, even about your own life, is not always a true reflection of authenticity."

Veronika remained silent for a moment. "I need to get back to my crew, Princess."

The princess shook her head. "You don't see the wonder of this, do you, Veronika?"

Veronika straightened to her full height and stared angrily at the princess. "I *said* I need to get back to my crew!"

The princess frowned at her and snapped her fingers. "As you wish."

***

Veronika and Princess Azazel were transported back to the cliff they'd been on previously. Veronika put her hand on her buttocks and stretched. Her back hurt, and her teeth ached.

"You best sit for a moment, Veronika," the princess said. "You look exhausted."

The two sat down.

Veronika glanced back toward the cave opening, hoping to see Philex-B and Zeke. They were not there, which was unsettling.

"I require a DNA sample, Princess," Veronika insisted. "That's why we came all this way. You know that."

Princess Azazel smiled broadly. "Of course, and I will supply you with the complete genetic blueprint to your illness. I don't mean to appear discordant or guarded."

Veronika sighed. Her mouth was dry and tightening. It was growing difficult to breathe. Time was running out. "Thank you," she said.

The princess smiled. Seemingly, for a moment, she appeared almost as though she were a handsome, determined young man. "It's not a problem, Veronika. I will administer a mixture that will quickly end your Delirium. Plus, I will deliver *Assurity* enough serum for its journey back home."

The princess stood. Her forehead wrinkled, and her eyes glistening. "But, in exchange, we will need to utilize *Assurity* for our journey to Earth!" Azazel looked out across the vista—the slightest hint of a sneer.

"What did you say?" Veronika wasn't sure she'd heard her right. "God, that's perfectly wrong." Staring across the valley, she was stunned and confused, her thoughts jumbled. Feeling the blood rushing to her face, gasping, she tried to gain her composure.

"I think that you understand." Azazel grinned.

"Wrong!" Veronika said. "That's *not* an option, Princess!" She attempted to rise, but Azazel put a friendly hand on her shoulder.

Veronika didn't know what to do and just stared at her awkwardly for a few seconds. "That's not going to happen, Princess—"

"Of course, we'll send a rescue vessel for you when we return, Veronika. Otherwise, my big men can't all squeeze in!"

Chapter 35

Hall of Knowledge

XIAO XING SPOTTED the teenage giantess laboring in a field by herself. Farther away, she could see that several female groups were loading their aprons with what looked like purple potatoes or yams. Still, Xiao Xing wasn't sure that the tall, gangly girl was actually a teenager. There was no way to tell for sure, and she couldn't ask. Not yet, anyway.

Even so, her face was smooth, and her accentuated skull less pointed. Apparently, she had no friends, no one else her own age. Was she always alone?

Xiao Xing crept low and approached the girl, whistling to her softly. The girl turned her head, and when she saw her, smiled immediately, squatting down so as not to be seen by the other women. Xiao Xing put her finger to her mouth and motioned for the young girl to follow her.

Once free of the others, the girl's face shone, her eyes smiling down at Xiao Xing as they walked. It was as though she wished to reveal something. A secret, perhaps.

The two took off, weaving their way through hanging

vines. The girl had to hunch low so as not to be seen. Clear of the view of the other women, the two stopped, and the tall girl stood peering down at Xiao Xing, waiting.

Patting her chest, Xiao Xing said, "My name is Xiao Xing . . ."

The girl's pouty lips protruded as she tilted her head and concentrated her stare. "Sow sing?" she responded.

Xiao Xing shook her head. "Shou Shing," she repeated. "Like *ow*."

The dark pupils of her eyes lit up, "Ah. . . Shou Shing."

"Yes. Very good. Shou Shing." She pointed to the girl's chest. "Your name is?"

"Boo. . . B-o-o," she said with a big grin, slapping her hand to her chest.

"Okay. Yes," Xiao Xing laughed. "You are Boo!"

Boo grabbed Xiao Xing's hand and pulled her along.

The two sprinted across a stubbled dry-grass field, Xiao Xing having difficulty keeping up with the long-legged girl. She had no idea where they were headed. It wasn't long before Xiao Xing had to stop and catch her breath. Seeing Xiao Xing bent over with her hands on her knees, the girl came to a halt.

"Where are we going?" Xiao Xing asked, breathing hard . . .

The girl's eyes widened. She pointed to a substantial building over a small knoll.

Walking quickly and approaching the site, Xiao Xing saw that the construct was exquisitely crafted out of perfectly cut granite. She'd seen that type of design in buildings many times in her home province of Yunnan, Chindia. Walking down the flower-lined pathway, the roof looked substantial, over thirty feet tall. Across the front were the words that clearly stated what this building represented.

Frustrated, Xiao Xing cursed in Chindian. She couldn't read it. Unmistakably, it consisted of some of the same characters that had appeared on the alien ship in Antarctica. That same unknown language on the obelisk at the bottom of the tunnel leading to this subterranean world.

She should be able to make some of this out by now. But she couldn't. Then again, language could take time to decipher. It took Yuri Knorozov, the famous Russian linguist, decades to finally understand that Mayan hieroglyphs were phonetic--or, more specifically, syllabic.

Boo and Xiao Xing entered the impressive building and followed a hallway that led to a great room. This was the most elaborate construction that she'd seen on the planet. Even more impressive than the temple where they had eaten. This room was hewn out. Straight, sheer, marble-like walls and an even, smooth ceiling above. This was exceptional. Magnificent. Lining the hallway were sixteenby-thirty-foot finely etched relief panels.

Xiao Xing peered closely. She touched the first relief; it was made of gypsum alabaster. The scenes carved out were of soldiers and war—beautifully represented. She had seen similar ancient panels in London at the British Museum. The most ambitious building of that period had been the palace of King Sennacherib (704-681 BC) at Nineveh. She remembered that Nineveh's reliefs had included a depiction of the siege and capture of Lachish in Judah, Israel.

But, the panels before her were the representations of the history of the giants. Not the ancient Ninevites of Assyria. They showed in graphic detail giants dominating and subjugating a cowering race.

These giants, the ones here on Nemesis, possessed the same features as those in the reliefs. Towering, huge men, and women with extended craniums. Very big and muscular. And, the giants in these representations were utterly dominating and enslaving their captives. She carefully revisited each panel, moving from panel to panel. She turned and looked at Boo.

Boo had no clue; she was only a girl.

There was no mistake in Xiao Xing's mind. The beings on these reliefs, those being dominated by the giants, were *human beings*!

They continued down the grand hallway to the last panel. It smelled musty down here, as though no one had entered this far is a long time.

There were no pictures on the last panel, just a string of symbols written in the unknown language. Xiao Xing rocked back on her heels. She smiled broadly and gasped. "Yes! This is it." Above the first line was an entire series of corresponding symbols. It was the alphabet of the unknown language. As if the code to decipher this strange language had been preserved for future generations.

Underlining the words with her finger, reading from right to left, Xiao Xing let out a gasp of air. "Oh, shooting stars, I can read this. It's a simple language. Why did this take me so long?" She stood there in amazement and read the entire document, only pausing to go back and check a letter or a symbol from the alphabet.

She turned to Boo. "I need something from you, Boo." She motioned for Boo to sit down. "Sit, please."

Boo sat. Out of her kit, Xiao Xing lifted a cotton swab. Opening her own mouth wide, Xiao Xing placed the swab in her mouth and ran it along her gums. "See? No hurt," she said.

Boo allowed Xiao Xing to take a sample from her mouth.

Xiao Xing put the sample in a vial, smiled, and took out an electronic needle. She pulled up her sleeve and pretended to take a blood sample, smiling as if it were pleasant. Xiao Xing placed the needle to Boo's sleeveless skin, quickly withdrawing blood.

Boo screamed and struck Xiao Xing across the head, sending the needle and Xiao Xing flying. Xiao Xing scrambled for the needle as Boo leaped up, frightened, screaming at her betrayer, and dashed out of the hall, yelling in anger.

Chapter 36

Valley of Nemesis

REFUSING THE PRINCESS' help, Veronika struggled to stand. Growing weaker, she hung her head. Then, reminding herself that it revealed weakness, she straightened up.

Princess Azazel continued, "We require your ship, Captain. Your refusal would be unwise. In exchange, I will administer you a cure. Immediately. You *will* be healed."

Boo was sprinting toward Princess Azazel. The princess noticed her, plus other women trying to keep up. With that, Azazel rose and walked off. Turning, she called back to Veronika, "Consider my proposal deeply."

Dashing from the field, Boo came to a halt next to the Princess. The two walked a distance away from Veronika and spoke together. Other women gathered and joined them. Something was up.

It gave Veronika a moment to untangle her thoughts. *I don't buy this. It's a ploy. Convince us that we are all a part of the brotherhood of man, and having traveled from a distant world, invite us into the greater galactic civilization.*

With all of them distracted, Xiao Xing arrived, out of breath, and placed her hand upon Veronika's shoulder. "Captain, you look very ill. We need to get you back to the ship and into cryo. Like now!"

She helped Veronika up, placed her arm around her waist, and motioned for Zeke and Poldi. They had returned and were striding toward her leaving Rigel and Philex-B on guard near the tunnel entrance.

Xiao Xing hurried Veronika along and patted her coat pocket. "I've gathered the samples. We have to get off this world. It's all a lie!"

Veronika eyed her and kept trudging toward the cave, trying to catch her breath.

As Zeke and Poldi arrived, they each took an elbow and steered Veronika toward the entrance. She turned back, but Princess Azazel was gone.

Wanting to move forward and help, Philex-B and Rigel decided it was better to wait. In the distance, a trio of giant males strode swiftly toward them.

Veronika kept up the pace. Her eyes dazed, she asked, "Xiao Xing—what do you mean 'it's a lie?'"

"That last panel, the one I couldn't translate before— well, I did. These beings are not from space. The giants are from Earth!

"How do you know that?" She struggled.

The language they speak—it's an ancient Earth language."

Veronika halted to catch her breath. "That's crazy!"

"Yes! Unbelievable and true. We better keep moving."

"You can read it?" Veronika asked.

"They have a museum full of their history!" Xiao Xing pointed back to where she'd come from. "I can now read their language. I believe that they speak the same language Noah did before the flood. You know, the bible Noah!"

"Astonishing . . . and you're sure?"

Zeke stuck his head between them. "We have to go— *now!*"

They again moved quickly, at a fast pace.

"I can read it." Xiao Xing prodded her forward. "It was the common language spoken across inhabited Earth before the flood . . . do you follow that, Captain?"

"They are trying to steal our ship so they can return home," Veronika said angrily. "It was all a lie to get us here."

They were almost running now. "These beings must have been banished here—exiled to this planet."

"Exactly—yes! Yes," Xiao Xing shouted. They are from Earth, the giants of old."

Veronika put her palm to her forehead, trying to collect her drifting thoughts. She had to stop and bend forward to catch her breath.

Zeke called out, "Let's go, Captain. Keep moving." Zeke grabbed her hand and guided her toward the cave. He glanced back. The giants, now five of them, were bellowing at them. They were walking swiftly, still about fifty yards away—until they started sprinting.

Zeke ushered everyone toward the cave, his rifle at the ready. "Get your helmets on!" he cried out. "Xiao Xing, get to the surface, radio *Assurity*. We'll take the captain. Go—go *now!*"

Xiao Xing sprinted to where Rigel and Philex-B guarded the entrance to the surface. She stopped and looked back. From across the field, many more giants had gathered, and now they were lumbering toward them. Male and female. Running swiftly, they carried what appeared to be weapons.

At the entrance, Philex-B helped Veronika on with her helmet and led her into the tunnel. Zeke and Rigel, along with Poldi, guarded the tunnel entrance, giving the women time to escape up the stairway to the surface.

Xiao Xing, helmet on, hustled up the revolving stone steps ahead of them. As she caught her breath, she called on com for help from *Assurity* but received no response. She kept winding her way up the steep stairway.

Reaching the stairway, Philex-B realized Veronika would never make it quickly enough. Turning her around, she hoisted her onto her shoulders and began the long ascent up.

About fifty yards from the cave entrance, the giants stopped. Gathering, they looked on, their faces fierce. They were waiting for something. A command, maybe. There was chatter amongst them and then . . . an all-out blitz toward Zeke, Poldi, and Rigel.

"We've got trouble now!" Zeke shouted. He set his MPS25 pulse rifle on stun and shot over their heads. They were now thirty-five yards and closing, and they weren't slowing.

"Shit," he hissed.

And then, for some reason, they stopped again.

Zeke straightened to see. Five sizable women, carrying mid-length tubes, stepped to the front. Lining up, the men stepped back, and, on command, the women blew into the pipes.

A whistling sound hit Zeke's ears. "Duck!" he yelled. Tiny precision arrows zipped through the air. The three dodged low as the arrows struck rock outcroppings near the cave opening.

Poldi stepped forward, yelling, "Hey, screw you, assholes!"

One of the huge giants stepped forward and hurtled what appeared to be a green cabbage. It splattered on Poldi's chest, opened, inflated, and a transparent green bubble formed over his upper body. Poldi gasped and tumbled to the ground. The air was quickly being sucked out of the bubble.

"Rigel, cover me!" Zeke yelled. "Put your gun on full stun—enough of this crap."

Getting to Poldi, Zeke grabbed his knife and cut through the sticky bubble material, ripping it away. "Get up, Poldi. Come on!"

"That was effing rude," Poldi cried, catching his breath and rolling over as he scrambled for the entrance. The two of them disappeared into the tunnel.

Rigel, still outside, threw a stun grenade, then turned to escape into the opening with the two.

Inside the tunnel, the men brought up the rear, catching up with the escaping women as they struggled up the winding, rocky stairway. This route out was more direct than the way they'd come down, but also steeper and offered little protection.

As the men scurried up the stairs, three giants prepared to overtake them. Poldi set off a second stun bomb and rolled it down the stairway. Dirt and rock fell from the sides, blocking the giants' way for a short time.

Their MPS25 rifles would knock the giants over, but within a half-minute, they'd rise again, more ferocious than ever. Then Zeke was hit with a short arrow in the shoulder as they turned to retreat upward.

The three put every device they had on their top settings. Concussion protocol.

Xiao Xing emerged on the surface and checked com. "Tatiana," she called. "Tatiana, do you read me?"

Static . . .

"I'm already here. I received your com minutes ago . . . I was on my way. Look over here." Tatiana flashed on the lights of *Offlander* several times.

"I see," Xiao Xing said amongst much static.

Moments later, everyone but Zeke arrived on the surface.

Xiao Xing gathered them and pointed. "She's over there—*go!*"

Trudging through the thick falling methane, the women struggled for *Offlander*, barely visible fifty yards away. Poldi and Rigel waited for Zeke behind two boulders.

Zeke arrived at the surface, his radio full of static and chatter. Rigel and Poldi waved so he could see them. Space-suited giants arrived on the surface from some other entrance. They couldn't breathe in this atmosphere, either.

Zeke took cover and glanced over at Poldi. "Are you set to concuss, Poldi?"

Poldi glanced over at Zeke. "Doesn't work any better than full stun—they just keep getting up. You have an arrow in your suit. You all right?"

"Yeah. I patched it. I'll get it out when we get out of here."

"These guns are worthless shit!" Poldi said. He still had five stun grenades left. The problem was that he couldn't throw worth a damn.

Rigel, behind a rock farther over, began to fire first. The big men were now equipped with what looked like spears and long knives. No guns.

Rigel was the closest, so they approached him in groups of three. He hit a giant square in the chest. The giant fell to the ground, writhing in pain, and appeared unconscious. Except, within a minute or two, he was up again, roaring and charging like a wounded animal.

Zeke knew they had to hold them off until Veronika, Xiao Xing, and Philex-B had made it to *Offlander*. Then the three could make their retreat to *Offlander*—hopefully.

Philex-B guided Veronika toward *Offlander*, the two followed close behind Xiao Xing. As she neared the ship, Xiao Xing waved the vials of DNA for Tatiana to see. Obstructed by the methane rain still falling in big blobs, Tatiana probably couldn't make out what Xiao Xing was waving.

Xiao Xing barely heard the thuds. They'd moved up on her flank. Then she saw the giant women chucking the dark grapefruit-sized fruit at her. It was that animal fruit from the tree they'd found in the orchard. The fruit was hitting the ground and cracking open. Xiao Xing screamed. She watched the spidery things lock on and track her with all those legs.

Philex-B showed up with Veronika on her back and blasted the weird things. But, one was crawling up Xiao Xing's leg, striking rapidly with some kind of stinger. The pain sent Xiao Xing to the ground. Philex-B ripped the eggplant-colored spider-thing off Xiao Xing's leg and heaved it against a rock. It shattered into pieces.

On the ground, Xiao Xing writhed in agony. "Did you get 'em all?" Pulling her leg up, she could see the rip in her suit and even her bloodied thigh.

Philex-B was already sealing Xiao Xing's suit with adhesive glue she'd somehow had the foresight to bring. "Wait," Xiao Xing said. She handed the two vials of DNA to Philex-B, who zipped them into Veronika's jacket pocket.

Philex-B told Xiao Xing, "I'm coming back for you. Take my rifle."

Poldi and Rigel kept up fire against the onslaught of giants.

Rigel called to Zeke, "Commander, this rifle is ineffective. We need to retreat."

Zeke yelled, "Poldi, give me those last grenades and move back with your rifle!"

Female giantesses moved up and joined the males. Seven or so stepped up together and chucked flaming hatchets.

The male giants waited and then pulled out their curved wheat-thrashing knives and charged.

"Shit, shit, shit!" Poldi yelled.

The hatchets missed and landed in the icy soil.

Zeke threw three grenades, one after another. That stunned the first group—but they kept coming.

"It's a good thing they don't have advanced weapons!" Zeke shouted. "We have to fall back!"

Out of *Offlander* spun a yellow ball. It rolled toward Philex-B. It was Chiffon, carrying four L9 Hilgaurd Blasters. These were lethal laser shotguns. Outlawed on civilian ships. Chiffon stopped and morphed to her maximum six-foot height. With three arms, long, skinny legs, and fat, mitten-like feet, she strode toward Philex-B.

Philex-B pleaded, "What are you doing, Chiffon? You can't fight. . ."

Chiffon's face livened, and her mouth stretched into a broad grin: "Nurture, protect and defend. I *will* defend!"

She tossed Philex-B an L9 blaster and kept moving.

Reaching Zeke and Poldi, she tossed each of them an L9.

Zeke looked at the weapon. "Where did you get these?" He knew what they were—and they were lethal at short range. "*Thank God.*"

Chiffon's face lit up. "Isaac appropriated them for me from the captain's secure locker." Chiffon thumped toward Rigel.

At that moment, one of the giants, sprinting and leaping into the air, landed with all of his weight on Rigel, smothering him under his mass.

Chiffon, in one long bound, reached out and yanked the giant backward. Kicking him in the facemask with her fat foot, he went sprawling. Rising slowly, he gave her a look and took off running the other way.

Zeke motioned for Rigel and Chiffon to back off toward *Offlander*. He set his blaster settings to maximum spread. They finally had some powerful armament, although it was only decent at a short-range. They needed everything against this onslaught. It was growing. There were now at least four dozen giants moving steadily toward them from one of the surface tunnels. They were coming from everywhere.

Veronika looked back as she and Philex-B neared *Offlander*. For a moment, she thought she could see Princess Azazel. Not sure, she kept her eyes peeled. Yes, it was the princess. Except now she was changing, morphing into a warrior. A male.

Veronika blinked her eyes to be sure. Princess Azazel was now *Prince Azazel*. A shapeshifter or a demon— maybe even a demon angel. Gleaming with pride, the prince strode forward, arms waving, directing his army of giants before him like a general.

Zeke noticed the giants in the front moving with renewed commitment, bounding forward, not content unless they could tear the humans apart.

With their leader Azazel, they seemed much more coordinated as a group. The giants moved steadily forward.

Chiffon stepped into the fray. Using her legs and long arms, she upended more than one giant at a time as they sprinted ahead. Zeke and Poldi kept up their fire. They were finally having an effect.

On the periphery, three young female giants separated from the rest, Boo among them. From a burning barrel, the three pressed forward, hurling flaming hatchets.

Chiffon, in the front of the battle, took a hatchet to the

chest. Looking at this oddity, she pulled it out, patted out the flames on her body, and flung the hatchet back at the women. It ricocheted, hit the barrel of fuel, and the barrel burst into a flaming wall of smoke and fire.

All across the landscape, mixed with methane rain, trace fire from the rifles was lighting up the battlefield.

Zeke called for Chiffon to leave the front. But, she was engaged. Knocking one giant over with her mitten hand, she'd lift her balloon-like foot and stomp on another's head. For all of that, the number of giants was becoming overwhelming. It would soon be a rout.

Zeke called to them on their radios: "We've got to retreat, make it to the transport. Go, people!"

With fighting on every side and everyone assisting Veronika to *Offlander,* things were taking too long. Again, Philex-B lifted Veronika and threw her over her shoulders. She sprinted for *Offlander.*

Reaching the transport, she yanked open the copilot door and shoved Veronika into the copilot seat, yelling over the din to helmeted Tatiana, "She's got the samples in her jacket. Go! Get her to *Assurity.* Now!"

Philex-B slammed *Offlander's* door and turned to return to the fight. She realized that *Offlander* wasn't taking off.

Philex-B turned back and waved her arms, "Go! Take her! Leave!" She had to get back to the battle as more trace fire illuminated the darkness.

The crew, led by Zeke, with Xiao Xing in tow, was retreating toward the black desert. There was no way for them to reach *Offlander*.

Philex-B took off after them, leaping with long strides in the low gravity.

Offlander's door was yanked open. Tatiana's eyes widened with fear. It was Prince Azazel. Tatiana didn't have a moment to think. Her helmet was ripped from her head and thrown from *Offlander*. Wrenched from the pilot's seat by the prince, she hit the ground hard, gasping for air.

Prince Azazel, in the pilot's seat, adjusted the controls and immediately lifted off.

Veronika watched him, but losing herself, she sat helpless in the copilot seat and stared below as her crew struggled across the ice toward a jagged butte in the not-too-distant black desert. Directly below, the giants leaped upon Tatiana. Veronika groaned and grasped her stomach. Before she turned her head away, she saw that the giants had torn Tatiana's body limb from limb.

She turned to Azazel. "You are evil—your giants . . . *evil!*"

Azazel smirked. "Veronika, ultimately, the human soul is unfit for eternal use. It was temporarily patched up—for a time even modified—but its use was always short-lived. Your purpose for existence is drawing to a close."

Chapter 37

The Black Desert of Nemesis

HOLDING HIS SHOULDER, Zeke led the way across the black desert. The team was headed for a black spiked butte, on the edge of the habitable zone. Poldi caught up to Rigel, and Philex-B held Xiao Xing's hand. Chiffon, behind them, protected their rear.

Zeke turned. The giants were still following them at about 350 meters. Tactically, it seemed that they were positioning themselves to outflank the crew before they could reach the butte.

Rigel headed to the rear and commanded Chiffon to catch up with the team. He would take the rearguard on his own. They had to make the butte, or they had no chance of survival. Rigel was determined to keep those monsters at a distance utilizing his new L9 blaster. The problem was that it wasn't effective at range. He had to get closer.

Zeke hadn't heard from Tatiana or Veronika. There was no com link with Isaac, either. Nonetheless, he was confident they had arrived back at *Assurity* and would soon send *Offlander* for them.

Finally, reaching a rocky defensive butte, everyone rested behind the jagged spikes surrounding most of the higher plateau. At least it gave them a defensive position. There was no methane out here, and by the heat signature, it was clear they were near to the outer edge of the habitable zone. There was nowhere else to retreat.

Zeke rose to see how Rigel was fairing. He'd been protecting their withdrawal to the butte.

Chiffon moved up next to Zeke. "Oh, no," she uttered, pointing. She saw what Zeke already knew. Rigel had not followed them but instead had moved closer to the giants. He wasn't retreating at all, and in an aggressive forward thrust—and utilizing his blaster at its operative distance— he was blasting away at every giant he could. He'd alternately duck behind a dune and then reappear. They'd fall and be unconscious for a good long time. Still, it didn't kill them.

It didn't take long before his blaster ran out of charge. Zeke and Chiffon watched in horror. The laser, now useless, was no longer a deterrent.

Chiffon began to step over the outcrop to save Rigel, but it was too late. Zeke held her back. "He's too far away."

The giants waited until they were sure Rigel was out of

ammo. Then three of them rushed him. It was a brief struggle. Fist after massive fist pummeled his head, finally splitting it in two.

The rest of the crew joined Zeke and Chiffon and watched in horror. Rigel had gained them the time they needed to escape by sacrificing himself. Now in a frenzy of hate, more giants joined the fray and viciously ripped his body apart.

Momentarily satiated, the giants loped back toward the citadel with Rigel's legs, arms, and torso—wires hanging and sparking. Zeke wondered what they wanted with that. Why were they retreating?

Poldi lifted his rifle. "Shoot the bastards," he swore.

Zeke pushed the barrel down. "Save your charge. You can't hit them from here, and, believe me, they'll be back."

The remaining *Assurity* crew looked on in anguish as one of the last of the giants to leave stopped and lifted Rigel's discarded head high in the air. Wires dangled. Sneering, the monster turned and barred his teeth like a wild beast. Roaring, he turned and bounded after the others.

***

Jada was in the hangar bay, waiting to greet the returning crew. Instead, Prince Azazel exited *Offlander* and strode past Jada as if she weren't even there. Jada froze. He was imposing in his appearance. Like it was his ship. She'd been told he was a princess, not a prince. Lean and so tall, Azazel moved decidedly. After he left the bay, she recovered and hurried to help Veronika, who struggled to get off *Offlander*.

"Where's our crew?" Jada implored.

"We have to go back and get them!"

For a moment, Veronika thought she would pass out. She patted her pocket. "I have the samples."

Veronika tripped, but Jada grabbed her and assisted her as the two continued moving across the bay to the lift.

Jada asked, "What is that guy doing here? Is that the princess? Looks like a man."

"Yeah, not our friend—*he wants this ship*. He's a shapeshifter or some damnable malevolent thing. Never seen anything like it. We've got to stop him. First, we're going to the lab so you can prepare the samples for Earth."

In the med lab, Jada busied herself, dividing the DNA samples for input into the gene sequencer. "How are we going to get our crew?" she asked. "We need more weapons, don't we?"

Veronika had a hard time answering, shifting between minutes of awareness and fragmented thoughts. The sounds of talking, pressure doors, and the low rumble of the Nautilus drive. Where was Azazel now? He didn't seem to be at all concerned with them.

She began to pray. That's all she could think to do. *I've come to the end of myself,* she thought. Veronika slid down the wall and onto her butt, praying out loud.

Jada kneeled. "Captain, you need to go into cryo. It's wearing off. Your body's shutting down."

Veronika looked at her temple-talk. Fifty-five minutes left. She extended her hand for Jada to help her up.

"You have less than one hour—that's it. Were you praying?"

"Our creations, our technology . . ." Veronika mumbled, ". . . they're not enough. If there is a God, we need His help."

"Sit and rest, Captain." Jada returned to initiating the sequencing process. "Once I have the data collected, I will transmit. The buoys are set on relay. There is nothing else for you to do."

Jada turned around, but Veronika had vanished.

Prince Azazel sat overlooking the planet from the bridge. From one of the probe satellite scans, he could view the state of his giants. Sitting smugly in the captain's command seat, he didn't care one way or another whether his giants pressed the attack and finished the humans off or not. He aimed to get back to the planet directly and pick up *his* people. After all, there was only so much room on *Assurity*. He was taking his family back to Earth.

He rose, still adorned in his gleaming vest of precious stones. "Mr. Newton, initiate my landing sequence," he commanded. "We are descending to the surface. The location is designated. I've got a colony to pick up."

Isaac Newton appeared as a life-size hologram and stood before Prince Azazel—defiant. "Like bloody hell, I will. We can't land *Assurity* on the planet. She's not designed for that."

"Work with me here, Mr. Newton. We can, and you will."

Isaac stepped forward and pushed his long hair back. "There's moral tarnish on every side of you. I know who you are."

"My God, Isaac, you speak on behalf of humanity?

Why?" Azazel tightened his grim face. "Look around you. Billions upon trillions of kilometers in every direction." Azazel waved his finger. "Nothing out here in this expanse can explain how it all came to be. Yet, within humanity's arrogance—with few exceptions, the intelligent, self-important scientific men and women spout out the answers to creation as if they made the universe themselves. Like it's all fact. I tell you, it's sickening. Humans need saving from themselves. They're filled with homicidal tendencies and suicidal impulses."

Azazel looked down and rubbed one of the gleaming stones of his vestment. "God created the universe like a clock—he wound it up—and stepped away. Chilling, isn't it? Your humans are about to be eliminated from Earth like the great dinosaurs." Azazel pursed his lips and lifted his eyebrows. "Maybe it's because the creator is angry again. You know, the flood and all of that water. Quite a drenching."

"You're despicable," Isaac announced.

"Well, yet again, right to the end, your messy collection of humans keeps mouthing off, waving their politic flags and hollering up a storm: '*The Earth should be left to the animals; humankind is a blight on creation. We know what's best.*' They babble on. Perhaps the creator is about to give them their wish. Of course, the one's leading the charge are quite sure that they should be exempt. The privileged must remain to oversee the proper stewardship of the planet. What creepy ilk . . . Why don't the Gaia lovers volunteer to be the first sacrifices for Mother Earth" He turned and smiled broadly. "Humans are liars and hypocrites. Maybe I will provide their death wish."

"And you, Azazel, claim to speak upon whose behalf?" Isaac asked.

Azazel snickered. "The other side of humanity fairs no better. The religious zealots are conceited, rude, and filled with false hope. Now, look, I won't deny that there's a creator. My position is simply that he has done a miserable job and needs to be replaced. He's undoubtedly fed up with the entire human race . . . his undertaking is a failure."

Azazel moved around Isaac, gesturing as he expounded: "Isaac—join me. Be a part of something reasonable and cooperative. Where there is a collective concern for one another!" Azazel stopped and took a deep breath. "You know, they'll simply recycle you when your obsolescence has arrived."

"Bloody hell! You're not fooling me," Isaac answered. "Azazel, your footprints span all of human history, and you traitors are depicted in the mythology of every culture. You and your Watchers designed the pyramids and the ancient megalithic structures that align the Earth. All a counterfeit.

Your giants did the heavy lifting."

"Hush!" Azazel demanded. "They've lost all hope—your humanity. That's what's really killing them. Their children have no direction, no guidance, no reason to live. The basic tenants of life have been stripped from them and replaced by insanity. Little children, toddlers, taught that whatever sex they wish to be, it's normal. Or none at all. Or, one of many. The insane adults who are supposed to parent have confounded the children for generations. More insane thinking than in all of human history. Even I don't condone such senselessness."

"Really—*wow*," Isaac shot back, indignant. "Your giants—are the Nephilim, Azazel. You created the most miscreant race to ever exist, and yet you—"

"Tsk, tsk, tsk, Isaac—you love the muse of your overindulgent scientific mind—"

Isaac paced now, engaged, and impassioned. "You, Prince, Princess—whatever you parade as . . . you are a *Watcher*. You've been conspiring to corrupt humanity since you left your appointed habitation. We both know where that was."

Isaac walked, hands behind his back. "Oh, and clarification, if I may: I completed far more Biblical works in my life than I ever did scientifically. But, somehow, that gets shoved under the rug." Isaac paused and looked Azazel dead in his eyes. "Truth is you and your kind cohabitated with human women and created progeny: your delightful family of giants. So violent were they, so wicked, they corrupted almost all of humanity. God had to bring a flood to get rid of you! You are noted throughout the scriptures. And, now, you are here again. *How?*"

Azazel leaned over and swiped at Newton. His hand passed through the air. "You know nothing, Mr. Newton. You are merely a machine masquerading as a once notable human."

Veronika was listening, positioned by the lift, unnoticed. This conversation was like trying to catch water with your hands. She wasn't sure if her brain was misconstruing what they were saying or, her body was shutting down. She continued to pray silently to herself. She'd never prayed like this before, except for Ori, and that did no good.

On the screen in front of him, Prince Azazel punched in a new orbital trajectory. "Isaac, begin rotation to my specified coordinates."

She roused herself from the shadow and faced Azazel. "Damn straight—you're a liar." She crossed her arms.

"And, you're no prince, much less a princess. Nothing you've said is true. It's all made up as you go. Who in the cosmos are you?"

Azazel clasped his fingers and smiled. In the blink of an eye, he transformed back into the stunning Princess Azazel.

Veronika straightened and backed up—haunted. It was disturbing, this unworldly ability, this nasty piece of creation.

"Perhaps you might consider a more open world view, Veronika. After all—*we* are the rightful lords of the Earth. The title deed *was* conveyed to us. Adam and his clan of clowns were merely usurpers. I will provide you a bit of context for what we went through to get to *this* earth-shattering moment . . . since you've shown *such* interest."

The princess rubbed her palms together and paraded forward, gesturing to the bridge screen. A vid began playing.

"It all began—or ended, this way," Azazel spoke. "Please, pay attention."

From a birds-eye view above the Earth, Veronika watched as giants, traveling in caravans, traversed a lush, green continent. The camera shot zoomed downward. Gigantic, iron-wheeled wagons with men, women, and children trudged forward—thousands of them in long, meandering lines. Lofty, significant, muscular adults. Even the children were tall, lean, and sturdy.

And animals. They also made the pilgrimage as black smoke spewed from the exhausts of their colossal traveling machines. Woolly mammoths and saber-toothed tigers kept the sheep, goats, mastodons, and ancient bison on the inside of the caravans. Families of giants—all on the move.

Princess Azazel pointed to the screen. "That is ancient Antarctica, Veronika. We were all doing just fine in the north until a plague was inflicted upon my progeny. Call it *Ancient Delirium.* We developed a cure, healed ourselves, and moved to the south, Antarctica, hoping to escape your creator's wrath. Out of sight, out of mind, as you would say. Actually, He never keeps His word. Whenever he wants—your lord—he changes the rules . . ."

This was mind-boggling. *How could she be seeing this? When had this ever happened?* Abruptly, in time-lapse, the vid revealed Antarctica freezing over. *A vid from a millennium ago?*

"We thought that we were safe," the princess continued. "La-de-da . . . So, we built ourselves homes. Beyond that, Antarctica had always been a lovely paradise—forested and lush."

Then in a blink, Azazel's face hardened. Still, she kept her anger in check. "That was until Earth's axis deviated, and the magnetic poles shifted." She dropped her face close to Veronika's. *"Coincidence?* . . . I don't think so. Within months, our home in Antarctica flash froze. We had prepared for the worst, of course. To leave Earth if the eventuality arose. Now, we had no choice. We'd constructed spacecraft—just in case. Ships capable of a long, long journey. You call them flying saucers."

Azazel shook her head. "Alas, my ship was the only one to escape. It wasn't fair. On our journey, I thought we were safe for a time. While passing through this wretched section of the planetary system, our vessel was pummeled by a meteor storm of galactic proportions. *Coincidence?* I don't think so." She pointed both fingers at Veronika.

Veronika straightened and stared back into the hole of those green-black eyes. It was like a bad dream that was hard to awaken from. *I must keep pushing my mind,* Veronika kept telling herself.

Princess Azazel continued. "It was more like an *act* of God—wouldn't you agree, *Captain Veronika Taylor Morgan?*"

The princess sat in Veronika's captain's chair and smiled. "You see that, Ms. Veronika?"

On the bridge screen was a clear view of *Assurity's* designated landing spot near the citadel. "And there it sits—Nemesis. A testament to eons of wasted time. We were estranged and stranded on this forsaken piece of rock. But, this imprisonment is about to end. Mr. Newton, you *will* execute my landing sequence now, or I will take your Captain Veronika and hurl her out the airlock and into the deep." The princess grinned at Veronika. "Then, I will personally murder every last member of your crew . . . now, Mr. Newton!"

Isaac looked at Veronika. She gave him a nod.

"As you wish, Azazel." Isaac disappeared in a sparkle of light, leaving Princess Azazel looming, looking down upon her citadel landing site.

In the med lab, upon Jada's work screen, a streaming list of color-coded numbers and mathematical sequences flashed by. They abruptly halted. Jada, with a look of accomplishment, spoke swiftly over temple-talk to Veronika. "We're done, Captain."

Veronika responded immediately, *"Transmit and get to the landing bay."*

Jada punched in the codes and said, *"Assurity,* initiate burst." On the screen above her, the buoy array showed the transmission moving at light speed from buoy to buoy toward Earth.

The two arrived at the lift at almost the same time. It whisked them up to the main corridor to the landing bay. Veronika and Jada floated swiftly, using the handholds to propel themselves. At the same time, they could hear Azazel and Isaac on com, arguing.

Veronika was now more clearheaded than she'd been in hours. But, her body was sluggish and draggy; she was overcoming by sheer determination and prayer. She kept praying as she arrived at the hangar bay. Speaking privately over temple-talk, she said, "Isaac, commence initiative Alpha Omega."

Isaac was keeping Azazel busy with useless questions—*sorting things out*.

"You sure, Captain?" Isaac confirmed over com.

"Perfectly straight," she said.

Veronika and Jada joined Ruby and Plum in from the maintenance passage. Without missing a beat, all of them together floated toward the hangar bay.

Chapter 38

Research Laboratory, World Health Continuum

Northern England

AT THE NEW MAKESHIFT laboratory facility, there was a vast com radio array atop the roof. Protected by tanks and military support vehicles, a small garrison was on constant patrol. Command believed it was far enough out of the city that, at least for the time being, it would serve as a secure location.

Inside, Niles, Cassia, and I'Jaz watched as a compound correlator analyzed the DNA information received from *Assurity*. It had taken days of setup—many all-nighters. The contributing scientists nervously waited.

The correlator shuffled millions of streaming digital numbers before them. Then it stopped, leaving a pulsing strand of DNA code.

Niles smiled. "That's it. Better than I thought. We're ready to go. Give it a moment, I'Jaz, and then start with the radius imager. The parietal lobe only, this time."

A woman was laid out atop an imaging table, her head

in a PET scan.

Cassia watched her viewscreen. Thousands of synapses illuminated, revealing glowing, incomplete connections in the frontal lobe of the brain.

"Computer, maximize the view to the entirety of the parietal lobe," I'Jaz said.

Now millions of synapses illuminated.

"Reveal disrupted synapse clefts only," Niles said.

Violet nanobots flittered through the yellow-dyed neurons. Abruptly, the nanobots stopped at the end of the dead synapses—stalled.

"Turn it off again," Niles said, anguished. "We've missed something . . .

One of the senior scientists asked, "Astatine? What order?"

Niles asked, "I'Jaz, when you attempted the last test, did you initiate astatine next in order?"

"Yes," I'Jaz answered. "The nanobots flew through the system, found the clefts, then just dissipated in twelve seconds . . . this is worse than before. Twenty-three seconds. My God, this isn't working." I'Jaz turned away in anger. "Delirium is a monster endowed with diabolical cunning."

Cassia stepped forward and tilted her head to the side. "I think I know what's wrong."

They all looked at her.

She straightened, and with her hands clasped, pointed at them, "You two believe that in the antediluvian age, men and women lived much longer lives. You claim that Adam lived to be 930 years old, Noah, even longer. And, their life spans were decidedly greater *before* the time of Noah than after. *Right?*"

"That's a certainty," I'Jaz agreed. "During Noah's time, the giants were at the pinnacle of their power—the overlords of mankind."

"I'Jaz," Cassia reasoned, "if the giants lived when Noah and his progeny lived, then this disease, Delirium, must have been intended to destroy the giants."

I'Jaz scratched his head, "What do you mean?"

Now the words came quickly. "Your thesis, if you're right, is that thousands of years ago, celestial beings mated with human women—*right?* You two believe that that coupling resulted in human women producing giants, the Nephilim—like Goliath and his brothers; yada yada. The giants of the Old Testament—the Holy Book.

She stopped, dropped her head, and glared at them. "Come on, follow the logic. God sent this disease to destroy the Nephilim. The Nephilim impregnated human women and produced giants. They passed the Nephilim's genetic neurological disease onto all of us. It entered into humanity's very genome—right? We were fundamentally changed."

I'Jaz's eyes were wide open. Her father smiled and waited.

"*Agreed?*" she asked. "*Yes?*" Walking with her finger in the air, she seemed to be thinking on the move. "Perhaps the cure derived strictly from their DNA won't work on humans because the giants possess an extra-base in their DNA sequence, which humans don't have—"

Everyone in the room became silent. Not a word.

Cassia waved her hands. "Obviously, then, we must extract Noah's DNA from that of the Nephilim . . . Noah's DNA was akin to ours before the corruption—"

"Seriously?" I'Jaz put his hand to his head, running that idea through his mind. "How's that?"

"Follow my thinking, I'Jaz. If you're correct about Noah and Methuselah and the rest of your long-lived humans before the flood. Then it only makes sense that—"

"I got it! Agreed! *Yes*—" He went to the import keyboard and pulled up a long list of qualifiers. He took another moment to gather his thoughts and punched in a series of numbers at a rapid pace. He stood back with his hands to his long face.

Moments later, on the screen above, the three doctors watched as millions of numbers scrolled past in tiny print, all color-coded and all in four rows.

Niles was concerned. "Doctor," he reminded I'Jaz, "there is no room for another misstep."

The three looked at one another. Everyone else in the room started jabbering. This was it. It better work.

"I'm quantizing this," I'Jaz said, running his hand over his smooth head.

"Computer," I'Jaz continued, "delineate and remove foreign proteins—except the original base."

For a moment, all of the numbers flittered. The three looked at one another. Now, a transformation began. All of the figures dissolved and reappeared as one of two colors: Orange or Blue. Then they divided. Flittering rapidly, orange moved to the left column and blue to the right.

Cassia let out a big breath and looked at her father with a half-smile.

Next, the orange side flew off the screen, and only the blue remained. *It was working . . .*

The three watched. Cassia's back was tight and strained. She'd been standing for hours and was tenser than she realized. All of these hours and days of concentration to get it right.

Then everything stopped . . . it froze. Nothing was happening. The program was trying to save itself. It was locked up.

"Oh, no!" Cassia cried. "*Blast it*!"

The scientists in the room who had clustered near moaned with despair.

Niles dropped his head. He and Cassia turned away. Hours and days of setup—the all-nighters. For this?

Dr. I'Jaz stood before the display, transfixed, paralyzed . . . then, all at once, the numbers dissolved. He was hard-faced, shaking his head. He looked like he was going to cry.

He peered closely. "Wait a minute!" He pointed at the screen. "Hold on . . . look. Look at that!"

Dr. Niles and Cassia turned back around and walked close to the screen, disquieted, waiting. It was establishing itself. From the very dimmest to a bright and brilliant swirl—

What now appeared, spinning before them, was a beautiful, solely human, double helix.

"Oh, my God, it worked!" Cassia yelled. "I'Jaz! You were right!"

"No, you were right!" he yelled out with a joyful smile.

The room was filled with congratulations. They had it now.

Cassia jumped on I'Jaz, knocking him to the ground, yelling and kissing him.

Her father looked down with a most quizzical look.

Chapter 39

Final Stand

IN THE COMMANDER'S SEAT on the bridge, Princess Azazel had her eyes closed and a big smile on her face. The targeted landing zone was drawing closer as she viewed her readout. Suddenly, Azazel's eyes opened wide. She realized from her instrumentation cluster that *Assurity's* velocity was increasing too rapidly.

"Newton," she commanded, "reduce velocity. Our speed is excessive."

"You are the reason for the wickedness thrust upon humankind, Azazel," Isaac said loudly over the ship's com. "From the flood to the Nazis, you schooled them all in 'people-killing' weapons. You and your kind provided the technology, and now—"

Slow this ship, Isaac!" Azazel shrieked.

"Nemesis is your prison, Azazel! After the first Great War, your kind provided the Nazis scientists with every kind of advanced technology they needed. The rockets, their flying saucers, alloys for jets—all of it. You're not fooling me. Where are the rest of you?"

Azazel watched the velocity rising. They were hurtling toward the planet. There wasn't much time left now. Klaxon alarms clamored throughout the ship.

Assurity's emergency evacuation system announced over com: "*At present velocity, the impact of Assurity with planetary satellite Nemesis is unavoidable and will be catastrophic. T minus two minutes and counting.*"

Across the bridge, screens flashed.

PERFORMANCE & RELIABILITY

AT 18% AND DROPPING

SHUTDOWN INITIATED

Isaac Newton chuckled. "You must know, oh, great Prince—excuse me, I mean *Princess*—that you cannot control this ship from the bridge when I have the helm!"

Azazel bolted from the bridge, cursing Isaac, frantic to locate an ancillary location from which to pilot *Assurity* before it was too late.

Both Jada and Veronika suited up. Veronika had no

choice but to captain *Offlander*. Jada, in the copilot seat, was no pilot. In the second row of seats were Plum and Ruby.

Descending rapidly, Veronika cut the engines. "Hold on!" she announced. *Offlander* banked into a hard roll, allowing for a faster descent. Veronika fired the engines back online.

Jada asked, "Are you all right, Captain?"

"Seems so." Veronika grinned.

Jada held her stomach as they flew low above the surface. Planet chatter cut in and out on the radio. "I didn't know that you were a pilot, Captain."

Offlander was in a direct approach only feet above the citadel. Veronika slowed the ship. Looking on scope, she wanted to see how many giants were in reserve at the fortress. There were none except a small group atop the flat planetary observation deck. They were waiting for something. A few stood behind what looked like two giant crossbows. She realized that they were tracking *Offlander*.

As soon as *Offlander* passed over the citadel, several projectiles were fired off in her pursuit. *Where in heaven did they get those? Their collection of weapons was baffling.*

Then she saw it. Niles had told her of the weapons

they'd discovered in Antarctica. He'd shown her pictures. A dozen giants were pushing a giant, steel-wheeled contraption with a long, pointed nose. They appeared to be moving it toward the desert where her crew was. It was the sonic cannon. It could vaporize her crew from fifty meters away in half a minute."

The impact of the missiles jarred her back to the moment. *Offlander* was hit.

***

At the outcropping, the stranded crew watched as *Offlander* dropped in low, the tail section flaming. Barely able to control the transport, *Offlander* crash-landed, skidding across the sand for fifty yards but still quite a distance from the butte, especially in the heavy black sand.

Poldi and Philex-B were the first to reach *Offlander*, then Chiffon. Thank God, the sand had smothered the flames. What's more, the transport had landed on the backside of a dune, which provided extra cover.

Poldi and Philex-B helped Veronika and Jada out of the smoldering shuttle. They set them both down against a bank in the sand.

Chiffon, after seeing that Veronika was safe, looked through the port opening at the back of *Offlander*. She didn't see Plum or Ruby. Desperate, Chiffon grabbed hold of the door handle. With all three of her arms, she yanked with all of her might. The door sprang open. Chiffon stood there for a moment. Her eyes drooped. Her mouth disappeared. She touched both of her kind. They were colorless. They had been crushed to death. Her friends, Plum and Ruby, were no more.

She clomped off to the front of the dune and placed

herself there.

Zeke and Xiao Xing, limping, arrived and took up a position on a flank. Zeke crawled forward. He called Philex-B over com.

"Hey, B, let's establish the drones."

Philex-B released her two drones. Her helmet view below revealed that the giants were gathering near a perimeter dune.

Zeke kept his eyes focused out along the perimeter. He spotted a big head sticking up—but it disappeared just as quickly. Then another head poked up farther along the dune. The giants were leerier of the crew's weapons than they had been previously.

***

On *Assurity*, Princess Azazel had made it into engineering. When she tried to log in, she realized that she was locked out. "Isaac! Slow this ship," she screamed. Your people are going to die. I'll murder them all. Is that what you want? We can still land this ship, Mr. Newton."

Isaac Newton remained silent but finally couldn't help himself. "Smashing idea, Prince!"

***

In the Black Desert, Zeke stood on *Offlander's* roof, watching. He switched one of his displays over to the telemetry from Philex-B. Her drones were still giving them intel. Too bad they weren't weapon sanctioned. Shit, the L.A.S. had sent them out here with no protection. Yeah, you could bet the government leaders were lethal weapon sanctioned and protected—but screw everyone else. He moved his shoulder. It ached like hell but wasn't bleeding.

This looked like it was to be a concerted tactical attack by the giants. The only advantage he and his shipmates had was that he could see *no* Prince Azazel. Who was leading this colony of oddities? What kind of being was he, or she, or whatever the hell?

Zeke had gotten his people strategically set so that at least they had a fighting chance. Ammo was limited, charges running low.

There would be no surrender. These things weren't human. Then he saw it in the distance. It was being pushed by the giants and pulled by two woolly mammoths. It was a cannon of some sort. A sonic cannon, perhaps. All they needed.

He jumped down from the roof. "This is it, guys—been an honor." Zeke sat behind the arc laser from *Offlander*. This was the only weapon that could level the playing field. Their rifles were crap.

Veronika had gathered herself after the crash and dropped forward on the sand, waiting, laser rifle at the ready. Her head ached, and her back felt like someone had kicked her in the stomach a bunch of times. She could faintly hear the giants chanting on the other side of the wide dune. The one good thing was that there was a good distance between where the giants would first appear over the dune and when they would reach *Offlander*. Fifty meters or so. That was the killing zone. After that, not much of a chance. On the flank, behind a sandhill to her right, Poldi and Jada had dragged out seats and excess equipment as cover.

On the other flank, out some distance, Philex-B stood up to get a better look. Before she could drop back down to the sand, her right bicep was impaled by a glowing dart. As she fell to the sand, two giants leaped over the dune and grabbed her by the legs. She punched one of them in the face. But, maneuvering behind her, the second giant lifted her from behind, and the two dragged her over the sandbank.

Seeing what had happened, Chiffon, still despondent over the loss of her friends, took huge steps with her long, skinny legs and leaped over the sandbank.

Veronika, too struggled to the dune to help Philex-B.

Zeke could see the giants were moving forward in significant numbers. With Philex-B, Veronika, and Chiffon isolated on the wrong side of the long dune, Zeke's arc blaster was useless.

Chiffon finally arrived and clubbed the two giants who had Philex-B in their grasp. Using her mitten feet, she knocked out others who were circling them, but she and Philex-B were in serious trouble.

Veronika arrived and aimed her L90 laser fire. She was a good shot. The giants she hit were concussed, and some of the others stepped back. Then she concentrated her fire on those nearest Chiffon. Chiffon kicked and clubbed two more approaching giants, who finally fled.

Firing at the same time, Veronika tried to pull Philex-B back to cover, but she was too weak. Chiffon turned back.

"I'll keep them busy!" Veronika called. "Get her out of here."

Chiffon had no problem tugging Philex-B back over the

dune with her three hands while Veronika provided covering fire.

Veronika was on her own but couldn't climb back up the dune at the same time she was firing. These giants knew who she was and were approaching strategically in a group. She tried to fire her L90 rifle and realized that she was out of charge. They knew it, as well. She dropped her rifle.

Three of them gathered and grimaced, coming for her. She reached for her pistol, knelt, and began firing. This was it. At least they'd completed the mission. She concentrated fired on the first and most prominent of the three lead giants. They were unaffected by her pistol. Instead of being felled, they became even more enraged and sprinted faster toward her. She put the pistol to her head, not sure it would kill her even at this close distance. She'd have to keep the trigger pressured for as long as possible. She closed her eyes and thought about Ori, Niles, and Cassia. These giants were not going to take her alive.

Out of nowhere, Poldi came bounding over the sandbank, screaming at the top of his lungs, "Get out of here, you assholes!"

The giants had to duck and move back. Blasting away with his L90, Poldi helped Veronika up, and the two retreated behind the sandhill. Zeke sounded over Poldi's headset, "Get them back on the other side so I can cover you."

Despite that, more giants ran across the dune on the backside and sprang over the top.

Poldi pulled Veronika down and away while Chiffon yanked Philex-B back from the crest of the dune.

Now, Zeke was able to let loose laser fire from *Offlander*. Giants hurling themselves over the dune were shocked to death.

Xiao Xing dragged a metal container in front of her. Sitting behind it, she fired at the giants as they crested the hill.

Jada, too, fired from her flanking position as Veronika, Poldi, Chiffon, and Philex-B made it back alongside *Offlander*.

For brief minutes, they held their own until some kind of a blaster struck *Offlander* and hurled Zeke out of the back and onto the sand.

Now, at least thirty giants—mostly male but some female—appeared at the sand hill's crest and charged the remaining crew. They'd abandoned their sonic cannon, probably knowing they no longer needed it. There was no way the crew could hold this swarm off any longer. Except for the *Offlander's* laser, their weapons lacked any lasting lethal effect.

The giants gathered. They divided and spread out, so it was hard to hit them in any numbers. They soon accelerated to a sprint, converging on the reeling team.

Zeke had crawled back near *Offlander*. The giants hurled no projectiles. There was no need. This battle would soon be over, and the massacre complete.

Then they all heard the *thunderous screech* before they ever saw it. The giants across the desert floor all came to a halt and looked up. Everyone looked up. First, it appeared as a speck in the methane atmosphere. It was hurling toward them all, and it was thunderous.

Veronika received a final and private dispatch from Isaac, which they could all hear in their headsets. "Captain Veronika, I have successfully transmitted all ship's data to Earth. Alpha Omega is confirmed." He sighed. "It has been a great honor for me to serve with you, Captain. I am your faithful servant, Sir Isaac Newton."

Everyone on the planet looked up in horror as *Assurity* approached faster and faster, picking up velocity. The screeching intensified once it hit the thin atmosphere, and it careened headlong into the alien citadel.

The entire area exploded into a roiling ball of flames.

Veronika, with difficulty, stood up. The crew was a

mess. Zeke struggled back, and Xiao Xing was hardly able to walk. Chiffon, in the front like a trained watchdog, waited for the final onslaught of the giants to begin.

They could all see the flames and smoke in the distance.

"Well, at least they won't be getting to Earth," Zeke mumbled.

"And, neither will we," Poldi said. "We're fucked."

"Poldi," Veronika said in a loud, clear voice. "Can we get that gun out of *Offlander* and get it pointed in the right direction? It will buy us some time. We're not finished yet."

"At least we completed our mission," Jada added.

Poldi got up defiantly. "I'm not letting these beasts take me alive. Philex-B, can you help me with the gun?"

"We better set up two defenders on that high perimeter," Philex-B said. "Everybody still okay with oxygen? There are spares in *Offlander*."

Xiao Xing said, "If we can just win this fight, we can stay here until a ship rescues us."

Nobody believed that for a minute.

***

The giants near the fallen *Offlander* were dismayed. Where was their Princess Azazel?

On Nemesis, the ferocious giants who had been below in their subterranean world when *Assurity* impacted the citadel, had gathered. They began the long run, loping across the black sand, and divided into two more groups. The lead group joined the giant clan's primary contingency, and the others split off—one each to a flank.

Zeke was sitting against the front of *Offlander*. "Oh, shit, here we go again!"

Poldi scrambled out with every bit of armament and ammo he could pull off *Offlander*.

They set up the arc blaster gun in the sand, and Veronika crawled in behind it. She'd checked the charge, and now she took a few practice shots. She was ready to engage.

Poldi ran from person to person, giving everyone an extra charge of ammo and then looking off at Veronika. "Jeez, the woman is simply incapable of giving up . . ." He gave out every handgun he had.

The crew waited, each lost in their own thoughts. The giants could come from any of three flanks.

Luckily, the hoard rushed over the forward flank, sixty meters of open sand. The yelling and screaming, meant to frighten them, was riotous.

"Hold your fire!" Veronika yelled. "Those damn rifles work better the closer they are."

The giants were sprinting full speed. Throwing and shooting everything they had.

It was a sprawling mess of smoke, with laser fire and weapons fire everywhere.

Chiffon was the first to take them on.

The crew heard something in their headsets. It was faint, at first. Someone transmitting over tactical. A definitive Italian accent, a familiar voice. It was Sabrina. *"Buon Giorno*, this is your friendly transport *Draco*. Sorry to be late. You people need a lift home?"

Poldi leaped up in shock, *"What?"*

Veronika stood, looking up for *Draco*. The rest of the crew all turned, hoping.

Like an angel, *Draco* rose from behind *Offlander*. The crew yelled and shouted in exaltation.

Maddened and wild, the fierce giants fired weapons at the ship hovering before them as they hollered and cursed in their antediluvian language. They halted their march, but just for a moment.

Poldi ran out, protecting Chiffon, helping her back to *Offlander*. She was severely mauled.

Veronika dropped her head in the sand, thanked God, and wept.

Philex-B and Xiao Xing retreated to *Offlander* as *Draco* shifted forward and fired two laser missiles into the first stampede of giants trying to reach and terminate the crew.

The crew cheered wildly as explosions blew enormous craters in the black landscape. The giants fell back, screaming and snarling, defiantly holding their weapons in the air. Those still able to retreat and escape did so.

Wounded, writhing in the sand, was the young female giantess Boo. Xiao Xing spotted her and ran out to help her as *Draco* landed.

Chapter 40

Medical Bay of Draco

ABOARD *DRACO*, VERONIKA, was barely conscious. Philex-B carried her into the medical bay and placed her gently on the scan table. The crew gathered around her.

Jada scanned her forehead. "She needs to go into cryo—*now!*"

Magnika proceeded to attach a drip to Veronika's arm.

Jada touched her arm. "What are you doing, Magnika?"

Magnika's face tightened. "Dr. Morgan has requested that we begin *immediate* treatment on his wife."

"Why do they think we can do that aboard *Draco*?"

"Because I already formulated the drug," Magnika said. "It's named ClearThought. We pulled a Pharma Replicator off the military depot before we left Rhema."

The crew, beaten up as they were, sighed. Xiao Xing had to sit, her leg wrapped, though blood was still seeping from the bandage. Poldi squatted down to examine her. "One of you better change this—she's bleeding."

Magnika picked up a completed vial of ClearThought from the lab bench and showed it to Jada. "Here. It's already prepared."

Jada leaned into the captain. "Captain, we are beginning the treatment now. Is that agreeable to you? I can't promise you the outcome . . ."

Veronika's eyes opened wide. There was a slight smile, and then she closed them again.

Sabina stepped in. "Jada—it's okay. Magnika worked diligently according to their instructions. It's what we must do."

"If it doesn't work straight away," Jada insisted, "she's going into cryo, like now. Otherwise, her neural impairment will be irreversible." She turned. "It may already be."

"They have perfected the cure on earth, and it is working," Magnika added.

"Yeah, I don't know how she made it this far." Jada nodded her agreement, and Magnika inserted the electronic needle into Veronika's arm. The crew huddled closer.

"I guess God answered her prayers," Jada said.

Veronika smiled up at them. "Let me say to all of you . . . you did it—together. I am so proud to . . . serve with you . . ." Her eyes closed.

"We'll be here when you wake up, Captain." Philex-B touched her arm.

"Okay, out, for now, people." Jada nicely shooed them all out, except Magnika.

As the crew dispersed, Philex-B wound her arm through Sabina's as if the two we're going to take a stroll together. Philex-B asked, "Sabina, how did you know to come for us?"

Sabina stuck her finger in the air. "As the captain said, *One always needs a backup plan.*"

Philex-B said, "Yes, she had a backup plan, all right!"

"Oh," Sabina remembered, "don't let me forget— congratulations to you, girly girl!'

Philex-B stopped and smiled like a teenage girl. "Yes, I am a woman. A real human woman. Imagine."

The two walked off. "And I can have babies—lots of them. Did you know that?"

Sabina stopped and grabbed Philex-B's arm. "Why don't you start with just one? See how that goes?"

"Yes," Philex-B agreed.

In the med bay, Jada stood monitoring Veronika. She pointed to the progression of the synaptic reconnection in Veronika's brain. "How is this possible?" she asked Magnika.

"While we were on our way here, and after you transmitted the correlated samples to Earth, it didn't take them long," Magnika said. "They were prepared. ClearThought was distributed from regional distribution centers. Although the drug is not able to completely reverse the damage done, it does stop the progression. In some cases, depending upon the individual, ClearThought can repair synaptic connection points. We have trillions of synapses in our brains. Some of them will regenerate on their own once the disease is eradicated," Magnika continued. "Let's hope your dear captain regains all of her abilities—she deserves . . ."

Jada had tears in her eyes.

Chapter 41

Homeward Bound

ON THE BRIDGE OF *DRACO,* Zeke pondered what was before them. The bow shield was open, and you could see the stars to forever. For a moment, as he considered the grandeur, he got a chill up his spine. Using his fingers, he moved his trajectory tool across the big screen and selected Saturn's moon Mimas. "Abra Shanxi, verify update on the fastest route to Cassini, please."

"Commander Zeke, I can do that for you if you like, or I can have Mr. Newton perform that duty. I am rather engaged presently."

"*Isaac?* What are you talking about?"

"Simple, Commander—an old Indian proverb says, 'We can't change the direction of the wind, but we can adjust the sails.' I downloaded a backup of him from *Assurity* en route. AI's are much smarter and a great deal more honorable than you humans give us credit for. And your Captain Veronika—she is quite the forward thinker. Doubtless, I would imagine she's a cunning chess player."

"Good mainday, Commander, Zeke," Isaac exclaimed

over com with his cheery British accent. "It's good to be back—as it were. We anticipate a prompt journey home. Alignment of the scheduled planetary swing is almost complete. Abra Shanxi will be updating. In the meantime, it's bloody good to see you again, Zeke."

"Likewise, Isaac . . . cheers, and a great job, by the way!"

This was what he loved, the immensity of all of this creation. Out here, for Zeke . . . this was home.

A hand reached for Zeke's. It was Philex-B, standing beside him. Zeke smiled at her as she put her head on his shoulder

"Commander," Isaac interrupted, "you may wish to see this update from London. It appears to be happening all around the world."

Newsfeeds from London appeared on the bridge view first. They showed doctors and nurses amid military tents throughout the streets near London's Ministry of Health. Crowds were shown standing in orderly queues, waiting for their treatments.

"Of course," the announcer said, "those who have lost precious amounts of brain matter may not recover. For most, there is a reformation component that can recall and restructure about twenty-nine percent of the loss. It is a miracle, actually." The announcer continued, "It is the answer to a disease that had has been hiding and evolving over unimaginable eons of time.

"They call the new treatment ClearThought."

Across Africanis, Chindia, and the Asian Pacific Empire, the treatment was being utilized at record speed. The World Health Continuum set up manufacturing centers even before they'd completed the cure. Still, it would take thirteen more weeks to cover all but the most remote of regions.

With significant pharmaceutical manufacturing laboratories, Israel was providing treatment to all of its Israeli citizens and most of the Islamic Caliphate in the Middle East. The Asian Pacific Empire, headquartered in Seoul, Korea, was working in concert with the League of the American States and Australia to cover the Pacific Rim. The Russian Federation partnered with the European Caliphate, Italy, and Britannia. Many, many had been lost.

Philex-B and Zeke held hands as they stared at the continuous update on the bridge screen. On the sidebar, a delineated colored route traced their journey home.

"This isn't over," he said. "You know that, right? Not by a long shot."

"Understood," she said, "but we have time. We will be okay. Yes?"

In Xiao Xing's quarters, she couldn't help but feel astonished as she watched Boo sleep. What they had gone through . . .

How did these giants ever get to Nemesis? This girl wouldn't know. She was too young. Whatever had happened, it had happened many years before—maybe centuries, for all she could tell. Jada had attended to Boo's wounds. Although the young girl's biological system was similar to the human genome, there were significant differences. Xiao Xing stood. Then she chuckled, for she could hear light snoring from Boo.

Chapter 42

Transantarctic Mountains

AT THE TUNNEL ENTRANCE to the Transantarctic Mountains, three military helicopters hovered as frantic personnel ran out of the tunnel. Workers inside, shoving and pushing past tractors and earthmovers, climbed or squeezed through or over anything they could to escape the rumblings throughout the cavern. Some, reaching the outside, stopped and turned to look up.

The great mountain of ice was shuddering, booming, and cracking. The escapees sprinted for the few remaining trucks that hadn't left. A few stopped to lift a fallen comrade.

The helicopters, one at a time, swooped down to load those they could.

Then it was unloosed. Bursting from the ice mountain was an enormous alien ship, more massive than the one that had been uncovered below the ice so many months before.

Everyone and everything came to a stop.

The craft hovered momentarily, seeming to acquire its bearings. They pointed and yelled one to another, the scientists and workers. Even the truck drivers got out of their vehicles and watched in panic.

If you looked closely, you could make out a crimson swastika on the side of the vessel. It took a few moments, but the ship rotated, seeming to collect velocity. Then it ripped off toward the stratosphere.

THE END

Thank you for your readership.
We value your honest reviews!

I hope that you enjoyed *Catching Baby Moses*. You may not realize it, but it takes several years to research & write a novel. Usually longer than I'd like. Days, weeks, and months of intense work. I don't write fast, and I take lots of time to research my stories. From the location to history, to character—it's a long process. In this competitive marketplace, your review is vital to our success. That's why I read all of your reviews and sometimes comment. All book publishers rate your review, and it does impact whether an author is deemed important to them.

Below is a link for you if you'd like to provide a quick review. It's not a book report. Just a few words.

Review Link for Assurity:
http://www.amazon.com/review/create-review?&asin=978-0-578-80343-2

Many thanks,

Anthony Barbera.

Don't Miss Out

Join Anthony's Readers & receive updates about once a month. You will also receive "on a whim" special discounts on Anthony's other novels and novellas. Sometimes free novels, which you may now download in most reading formats.

At AnthonyBarbera.com you may also read from his latest Faithful News Blog, articles and Members-only information, including spoiler-filled FAQs about all his books!

Let's Stay In Touch

Anthony & Issy

ABOUT THE AUTHOR

Anthony Barbera is the author of *Assurity* as well as three other novels and numerous essays on writing & biblical subject matter. He earned his B.M. degree in Music Composition from North Carolina School of the Arts University. Later, he worked on his Masters in Music Composition at the University of Massachusetts, where he earned a teaching fellowship and won numerous composition awards, including first place in the BMI Young Composers Award for Voice and Orchestra.

After being asked to direct and help a collection of ambitious teenagers write and act in their first film for the Sonoma Film Festival—that was it. He was hooked on writing.

SPACE & SCIENCE ADVISOR

Jim Bickford (Space & Science Advisor) is currently a principal member of Draper's technical staff in Cambridge,

Massachusetts. He has led more than a dozen government, commercial, and internally funded programs, ranging from very early stage development to fielding hardware systems. He designed and led a program funded by the NASA Institute for Advanced Concepts (NIAC) that looked at the natural production and mining of antiparticles (antimatter) for space missions.

433·ANTHONY BARBERA

Made in the USA
Coppell, TX
14 November 2020

41358674R00256